William Andrews

North Country Poets

Poems and Biographies of Natives or Residents of Northumberland...

William Andrews

North Country Poets
Poems and Biographies of Natives or Residents of Northumberland...

ISBN/EAN: 9783744771917

Printed in Europe, USA, Canada, Australia, Japan

Cover: Foto ©Raphael Reischuk / pixelio.de

More available books at **www.hansebooks.com**

North Country Poets

Poems and Biographies

Of Natives or Residents of Northumberland,
Cumberland, Westmoreland, Durham,
Lancashire and Yorkshire.

Edited by

WILLIAM ANDREWS, F.R.H.S.

(President of the Hull Literary Club,)

Author of "Historic Yorkshire," "Historic Romance,"
"Modern Yorkshire Poets," etc., etc.

(MODERN SECTION)

✻   ✻

LONDON:
SIMPKIN, MARSHALL & CO.
MANCHESTER: ABEL HEYWOOD & SON.
HULL:
A. BROWN & SONS, AND J. R. TUTIN.
—
1889.

PREFACE.

The kindly reception by the public and the press of the first volume of this work has encouraged me to continue my labours.

I am grateful for the valuable assistance I have received from the contributors of the biographies here presented, and for permission from the owners of many copyright poems to reproduce the same.

Several authors have been good enough to contribute original poetry.

Mr. J. R. Tutin, of Hull, has kindly compiled my index.

A third volume is now being prepared for early publication.

WILLIAM ANDREWS.

Hull Literary Club,
   1st October, 1880.

CONTRIBUTORS OF SKETCHES.

ANDREWS, WILLIAM, 1, 53, 59, 76, 172, 216.
ASHTON, W. A., 92.
BARLOW, E. HELEN, 146.
BARON, JOS., 202.
BRISCOE, J. POTTER, 119.
BROCKIE, WILLIAM, 98.
G., 153.
HALEY, ALICE, 25.
HARTMANN, F. C., 28.
HUDSON, WILLIAM, 6.
J. B. S. 109.
JOHNSON, R. W., 34.
LANCASTER, GEORGE, 79.
LEWIN, WALTER, 128.
LISTER, THOMAS SPENCER, 206.
MC.DOWALL, WILLIAM, 211.
MINTON, E. E., 160.
PARTINGTON, E. E. E., 101.
PEACOCK, C., 219.
PRESTON, J. E., 178.
QUAIL, JESSE, 71, 223.
RICHES, EDWARD H., 42.
ROSS, FREDERICK, 186.
SHAW, J. G., 167.
TAYLOR, R. V., 14, 190.
TOMLINSON, W. W., 47, 141.
TROTTER, JAMES, 87.
TUTIN, J. R., 125.
WALKER, JOHN, 199.
WALLER, JOHN ROWELL, 66, 83.
WALLIS, ROBERT, 114.
WATSON, AARON, 21.
WILDRIDGE, T. TINDALL, 193.
W. D., 104.
WOOD, JOHN, 134.

NORTH COUNTRY POETS.

Mrs. Laura A. Whitworth.

AMONGST the sweet singers of the North of England Mrs. Laura A. Whitworth is entitled to a leading place. Although still young, she has for many years been before the public and won golden opinions from all sorts and conditions of men. Her poetry bears evidence of being the outcome of a deeply religious nature, and she appears at her best when dealing with the soul's aspirations, and the delight of mankind in God's wonderful creations. She has not ignored the joys and sorrows of humanity, but depicts them with truth and much feeling, as one of whom it may be said "a deep distress has humanised her soul."

She is the eldest daughter of the Rev. Richard Dudding, and was born at Manchester in 1851. From her childhood she wrote what she called poetry on every scrap of paper that she could find. She carried in her pocket a little book to jot down the poetical thoughts which passed through her mind. At the age of five years her first verse on record was written down by her mother, and at eight, poems were printed on cards for her friends, and shortly afterwards a tiny volume called "Forget-me-not," was produced, and a few years later a book of hymns.

She was educated at St. Mary's Hall, Brighton, a school for clergymen's daughters. At school she gained great distinction for her musical attainments, and has since published not a few musical compositions which have been favourably received. The organ is her favourite instrument. Music rivals her love for poetry.

The first fifteen years of her life were passed at Bennington Rectory, near Boston, Lincolnshire, where her father was the Curate. He is now Vicar of Saleby, near Alford, in the same county.

In 1875, she married Mr. Edwin Whitworth, an inventor and engineer. They first resided at Manchester, next at Ripon, then at Sleaford, and have their abode now at Nottingham. Her chief literary work was done at Sleaford, but she has left some pleasing memorials in poetry of her home at "the fair city" of Ripon. Two of her volumes of poems were published during her residence at Sleaford, and these established her reputation. The critics found much in the books to praise, and the reading public gave them a cordial welcome. The first appeared in 1882 under the title of "Thought Waves," and the second in 1884, entitled "Glimpses 'Beyond the Veil,'" and it is from these books that our selections are made.

Mrs. Whitworth has contributed numerous stories to the English and American magazines and journals.

WILLIAM ANDREWS.

A

THE DESERTED MANSION.

Its chambers are deserted now,
  No sound of voices from within;
No happy children romp about
  With all their merry din.
      The echoes sound through empty halls,
      As the grey dusk of evening falls.

Deserted is the white rose bower,
  No fluttering robe flits down the walk;
Neglected hangs each lovely flower,
  All dead and drooping from its stalk.
      Rank weeds are trailing all about.
      'Tis dark within, and drear without.

Red lichens cling about the walls,
  The solemn rooks flit over-head,
Waking the echoes as they go.
  It seems as though the place were dead.
      So mournful is the slow decay,
      When signs of life have passed away.

At nightfall shadows haunt its glades,
  Which give the place an evil name;
The people cross themselves and pass,
  Low muttering of its ghostly fame.
      And none dare pass within its gate,
      For fear of some dark awesome fate.

Yet once fair women graced its rooms,
  Love whispers sounded in its bowers;
Proud courtly forms of young and old,
  Passed in and out amongst the flowers.
      While sights and sounds of life were there,
      To make the picture passing fair.

A LITTLE GRAVE.

Only a little grassy mound, no headstone marks the spot,
But primrose pink, and primrose pale, and blue forget-me-not.
And yet how much of love lies here, all hidden from the sight
Of her whose arms are empty now through all the dreary night.
Who toiling through the sorrowing days in poverty and pain,
Yet missing that one winsome face would wish it here again ;
Tho' others climb about her knee, and play around the door,
One entereth not their play to share, and entereth never more.
Yes, dearer now than all the rest, seems that one angel child,
Whose little soul is safe in heaven by sin all undefiled.
Enshrine his memory in your heart like some sweet holy thing,
But go no more with heavy grief—yea, cease thy sorrowing.
You would not wish those wings were soiled, so spotless now
    and fair,
Or live to see that angel face all clouded with despair :
For God knows best what flowers to cull for bloom in Paradise,
So cherish those He leaves thee still, and own His ways are
    wise.

A SUNNY PICTURE.

We stood amidst the golden corn.
All bright and smiling was the morn,
The reapers, singing, passed us by,
And not a cloudlet flecked the sky.

Love flooded o'er our lives with light.
Our hearts had ne'er known sorrow's blight :
If sorrow in the world might be,
We knew it not, and what cared we ?

We knew what love and summer meant.
" The winter of our discontent "
Seemed yet so very far away,
Grim Time might never bring the day.

So kissing 'midst the golden corn,
Our hearts were one that summer morn,
When Hope and Sunshine seemed to say :
True love can *never* pass away.

ST. BOTOLPH'S BELLS.

[BOSTON].

Oh ! sweet St. Botolph's bells,
Again your chiming swells
     In floods of music on the still night air ;
Of many a bygone year it tells,
     And many a home scene fair.
Within their sound I dwelt long years ago—
Their distant music set my heart aglow,
     When listening to its chime,
We watched the Old Year dying solemnly and slow,
     In that dear bygone time.
Our childish hearts untouched by grief or care,
We had no sorrow for the passing year,
     And heard no sadness in the bell's sweet sound ;
Flung wide the casement to the keen night air ;
     Thus we a New Year's presence gladly found,
Whilst all the neighbouring bells with clash and clang,
To greet the infant Year wild pæans rang.
     Then we in gentle sleep
     Its early hours would keep.
Ah ! now we greet the sound through mists of tears
And half-forgotten memories of past years—
     So wake to weep.

BY THE OCEAN.

I heard the voices of children
     Float in thro' the open door,
As they played beyond in the meadow,
     That stretched to the sea-girt shore.

Voices and rippling laughter,
  With the sea's soft murmur wrought
A spell o'er my weary spirit,
  That happier memories brought.
    Play on, O happy children,
      By the murmuring mystic sea ;
    Life is a deep, vast ocean,
      But its depths are not for thee.

What tho' thy sand-built palace
  Is swept away by the tide,
Build them still higher and higher,
  With castle and keep beside.
We too have built our castles
  On the shifting sands of time,
But the waves of life o'erswept them
  In the days of our youth and prime.
    Play on, O happy children, &c.

CRADLE SONG.

Sleep, baby, sleep,
Soft pillow'd is that little head,
And mother watches by thy bed ;
Sleep, baby, sleep.

Smile, baby, smile,
Angels are whispering in thine ear
Sweet soothing words of heavenly cheer ;
Smile, baby, smile.

Weep, baby, weep,
Thy father tossing on the sea,
This moment may in danger be ;
Weep, baby, weep.

Rest, baby, rest,
Enshrin'd within thy mother's arms,
Safe from the world and all alarms ;
Rest, baby, rest.

John Holland.

JOHN HOLLAND was an active literary man and a volumi-
nous author. His first book was published in 1820, and his
last in 1870; and for a much longer period he was a frequent
contributor to newspapers and periodicals. His separate
publications comprise biography and history, topography
and local antiquities, botany and other branches of
science, industries and manufactures, theology and belles-
lettres. We have not space for a complete list of the
volumes published by him, but must be content to name his poetical works.
Of these the principal are " Sheffield Park " (1820), " The Methodist "
(1820), " The Cottage of Pella, and other Poems " (1821), " The Village of
Eyam " (1821), " The Hopes of Matrimony " (1822), " Flowers from Sheffield Park " (1827), " The Pleasures of Sight " (1829), " Tyne Banks "
(1832), " Handley Church " (1845), " The Great Exhibition " (1851), " Diurnal
Sonnets " (1851), " A Poet's Congratulation in Verse " (presented to James
Montgomery on his 80th birthday, 1851), and " The Bazaar, or Money and
the Church " (1861).

In " The Tour of the Don " (1837), " Memoirs of the Rose " (1824, re-
published in 1840 under the title of " The Queen of Flowers), " Evenings
with the Poets by Moonlight " (1867), and other prose works, there are
inserted some original poems.

The volumes named are far from containing all Mr. Holland's verses.
" Annuals," magazines, and newspapers were enriched with his effusions ;
and much fugitive verse was circulated by him on leaflets. He also wrote
hymns for Sunday School anniversaries and similar occasions. It is to be
regretted that his poems have not yet been collected and published.

Mr. Holland was a warm friend and a generous benefactor according
to his means. He lived in the fear of God and did his work under a deep
sense of duty. He considered himself a member of the Church of England,
but regularly worshipped with the Wesleyan Methodists. Some of his
friendships were very happy. He was for many years the close companion
of James Montgomery, memoirs of whose useful life he eventually published. Mr. Holland was never married, but many of his poems were
addressed to ladies. He was a man of great tenderness of feeling. When he
was touched by something pathetic the natural result was a poem, and in very
many cases the poem was a sonnet. He was distinguished as a writer of
sonnets. Few if any poets have written more in that form. As a son-
netteer he was publicly complimented by Montgomery. If he had written
less in respect of quantity, and had revised with greater rigour, his labours
would have been less pleasant, but his works might have become more
widely known. But he was not guided by considerations of popular favour.

He read extensively, and was very helpful as a referee. One who knew him well has said of him, " He could always tell what no one else could tell, and his stores of information were placed freely at the disposal of all." Another has said truly that he " was a large part of the complex idea Sheffield." He had intense local sympathies, and much of his work related to Nottinghamshire, Derbyshire, and Yorkshire (Sheffield particularly). Accordingly, his biography, published by Messrs. Longmans & Co. in 1874, has been described as "a supplementary history of Sheffield." But he had no lack of versatility.

Mr. Holland was a Christian. In the Report of the Sheffield Literary and Philosophical Society, published after his death, it was said that " his devotion to literature was only surpassed by the rare excellence of his heart and his many Christian virtues. In his daily calling, in society, and in his literary capacity, he ' adorned the doctrine of God our Saviour.' "

William Hudson.

THE RAINBOW.

The evening was glorious, and light, through the trees,
Played the sunshine, the raindrops, the birds, and the breeze ;
The landscape outstretching in loveliness lay
On the lap of the year, in the beauty of May.

For the Queen of the Spring, as she passed down the vale,
Left her robe on the trees and her breath on the gale ;
And the smile of her promise gave joy to the hours,
While rank in her footsteps sprang herbage and flowers.

The skies, like a banner in sunset unrolled,
O'er the west threw their splendours of azure and gold ;
But one cloud, at distance, rose dense, and increased
Till its margin of black touched the zenith and east.

We gazed on the scenes, while around us they glowed,
When a vision of beauty appeared on the cloud ;
'Twas not like the sun, as at mid-day we view,
Nor the moon, that rolls nightly through starlight and blue.

Like a spirit, it came in the van of the storm ;
And the eye and the heart hailed its beautiful form ;
For it looked not severe, like an angel of wrath ;
And its garment of brightness illumed its dark path.

In the hues of its grandeur sublimely it stood
O'er the river, the village, the fields, and the wood ;
And river, fields, village, and woodland grew bright,
As conscious they felt and afforded delight.

'Twas the *Bow of Omnipotence*, bent in His hand
Whose grasp at creation the universe spanned ;
'Twas the presence of God in a symbol sublime,
His vow from the flood to the exit of time.

Not dreadful, as when in the whirlwind He pleads,
When storms are His chariot, and lightnings His steeds ;
The black clouds His banners of vengeance unfurled,
And thunder, His voice to a guilt-stricken world ;

In the breath of His presence when thousands expire,
And seas boil with fury, and rocks burn with fire,
When the sword and the plague-spot with death strew the plain,
And vultures and wolves are the graves of the slain :—

Not *such* was that Rainbow, that beautiful one !
Whose arch was refraction, its keystone the sun ;
A pavilion it seemed which the Deity graced ;
And Justice and Mercy met there and embraced.

A while, and it sweetly bent over the gloom,
Like love o'er a death-couch, or hope o'er the tomb
Then left the dark scene, whence it slowly retired,
As love had just vanished, or hope had expired.

I gazed not alone on that source of my song ;
To all who beheld it these verses belong ;
Its presence to all was the path of the Lord ;
Each full heart expanded, grew warm, and adored.

Like a visit, the converse of friends, and a day,
That Bow from my sight passed for ever away ;
Like that visit, that converse, that day on my heart,
That bow from remembrance can never depart.

'Tis a picture in memory, distinctly defined
With the strong and unperishing colours of mind,
A part of my being, beyond my control,
Beheld on that cloud, and transcribed on my soul.

TO A PRIMROSE.

(On finding one in a solitary walk).

Meek little flower, retired and shy,
I will not pluck thee; no, not I;
And though no other poet's eye
  E'er gaze on thee,
Thy smile may tempt some passer by
  Less kind than me.

No, pretty floweret, blossom still;
Expand thy moon-beam-tinctured frill;
Adorn and scent this little hill:
  Thy vernal day,
Ere the first linnet wakes his trill,
  May pass away.

Why should I pluck thee? Soon enough
Perhaps some heifer's trampling hoof,
Without regret, without reproof,
  May break thee down.
Such crushing stroke, untimely rough,
  May be mine own.

Yet thou shalt live when I am dead;
And when the grass springs o'er my head,
Perhaps my grave's cold hallowed bed
  Shall bear a flower,
Like that which once its sweetness shed
  On life's warm hour.

O, could I tinge thee with my name,
And sweet, O sweet, the poet's claim
Inscribe, without a blush of shame,
    On mossy seat,
Perennial then would spring my name,
    With primrose sweet!

Affection then might mark thy peep;
There Morning's dewy eye would weep;
And Spring's young sunbeams love to sleep
    Upon thy breast.
Her earliest court would Flora keep
    Beneath thy crest.

The village maiden, wandering there,
Would cull thee, braid thee with her hair,
Or place thee on her bosom fair,
    With guileless art.
The poet's flower her breast would share,
    Himself her heart.

Yet vain this anxious wish for fame;
The poet's dear but envied claim
May never bless my humble name;
    And should it not,
I'd still pursue the poet's aim,
    Then be forgot.

Then modest floweret, fade and die.
A humble Spring flower too am I;
Yet, as the early smiling sky
    Warms thee to birth,
Be thou to friendship's partial eye
    My star on earth.

NATIVE SCENERY.

Born where the Sheaf and Don unite their streams,
Near that old town, far-famed Brigantium's pride,
Sheffield, for arts and industry renowned,
My eyes, first opening, there beheld the light.
My very cradle was a scene outspread
Of panoramic splendour.   Summits blue
Defined the fair perspective to the west ;
East, on the horizon Laughton's lofty spire
Attracts the eye ; or, farther still, like a dim speck
Seen in the flush of morn, proud Lincoln Minster ;
The wooded hill of Beauchief to the south ;
While northward, in luxuriant charms runs out
The vale of Don, by shaggy Wharncliffe bound—
The far-famed region of the dragon's den.
O charming spot of my nativity !
Where all things, from my first-remembered glance
Conspiring, tended to pervade my soul
With landscape beauty and poetic dreams !
    True, there are mountains by Jehovah's hand
Piled more sublimely high than yonder hills ;
And there are woods and forests nobler far
Than yon sweet amplitude of scattered trees,
Or yonder scatter'd clumps ; and there are vales
Of more capacious sweep than those I see,
And in their bosoms lakes surpassing much
Those neighbouring dams ; and there are rivers, too,
More deep, more wide, and more magnificent,
Rolling their ampler volumes to the sea.
But say, thou travell'd artist, say, my friend,
Where is the spot afar, or where at home,
In earth's wide circuit or in Britain's isle,
That in sweet combinations doth surpass
This chaste and charming landscape ! Oh, I feel
These scenes inspiring to my partial pen !

So when the limner with a filial heart
Paints a dear mother's portrait, love may yield
Unwitting, undesign'd, some better line,
Some graces to the contour, yea, some tints
Which the cold critic judgment scarce may hope
In the beloved original to find.

SUMMER EVENING.

Oh, what a glorious harvest-field of thought
Is a rich Summer's evening.   'Tis the time
When friendship's golden grain, if fully ripe,
Should aye be reaped, and bundled up, and housed.
Evening is friendship's friend.   It hath a charm
To tranquillise, to sweeten, and draw out
That converse mutual and reciprocal,
Which, passing from the lip into the ear,
Doth make true hearts in friendship truer still.
O Summer evening, thou art dear to me,
As ever thou hast been !   A boy, I loved
To ramble and to mark thy various vest,
As gorgeous, when in sunset beauty dipped,
Or in that grey sobriety of shade
Which twilight gives, or when 'twas spread
With here and there a star.   I loved in youth
Thee, O sweet Summer evening.   Golden dreams
Oft haunted me alone ; but neither gold,
Nor gems, nor aught else precious deemed of wealth
Had ever power to tempt me from thy charms.
And now in manhood, though the flying years
Have borne my youth away, still have they left
Me all the exquisite delights of youth,
Yea, left me much of boyhood's young romance
In loving thee, O Summer evening sweet !

SOLITUDE.

The man who, when with toil or care distraught,
  Or when at ease in body or in mind,
  In self-communion can no joyance find,
Hath not in Wisdom's school been fully taught:
To dive in silence for rich pearls of thought,
  Deep in the waveless ocean of the soul,
  Is to enjoy, beyond the world's control,
A bliss in tumult often vainly sought:
Thus, in my chamber, or the flowery field,
  When with me human form or voice is none,
  I feel nor sad, nor dull, nor all alone;
For still the intellectual part doth yield
To its own powers companionship; the while
O'er all my inner being spreads contentment's smile.

THE SWALLOW.

Bird of strange instinct and untiring wing,
  Thou art as welcome as the smile of May,
  Herald and earnest of that gentler sway
Which nature wields o'er every living thing,
What time stern winter to the genial spring
  Resigns our changeful year. The sloe's white bloom,
  And daisies springing from their grassy tomb,
At thy return their flowery welcome bring.
Come, rest thee from thy long, mysterious flight;
  Come; and, ere yet the beech unfolds its leaves,
  Build up thy plaster nest beneath the eaves;
And if thy summer song but half-aright
I may interpret, it will doubtless be
Of trust in Providence, a lesson read to me.

John Ryley Robinson, LL.D.

OHN RYLEY ROBINSON was born at Dewsbury, on the 5th day of September, 1829, and is the son of Mr. Joshua Robinson, a popular local preacher among the Wesleyan Methodists. This Joshua Robinson married a daughter of John Ryley, who for twenty-six years was the master of the Blue Coat School at Leeds ; who also wrote a brief "History of Leeds," and is spoken of by Taylor, in his "Leeds Worthies," as having "enriched almost every periodical publication in mathematics for nearly half a century, and was also justly admired for his problems and demonstrations, possessing a soundness of judgment and a quickness of perception in mathematical knowledge which deservedly ranked him as one of its first professors."

The subject of our sketch was partially educated under a noted teacher, George Elam, of Birstal, near Leeds, a man whose abilities endeared him to many business men in the West Riding, who were proud of the honour of having been under his tuition. To this day Dr. Robinson has made his home in Dewsbury, where he is a member of the Town Council, Chairman of the Gas and Water Committee, a Director of the Grammar School, and also a noted literary and antiquarian student, as well as a celebrated poet. Though he has commendably cultivated his poetical powers, he has by no means been indifferent to other studies, not being one of those who imagine that poetry and the exact sciences are diametrically opposite, and that a poet must of necessity be an impracticable person, if not an idle dreamer. At school he had distinguished himself by an ardent devotion to languages, especially the ancient Greek, and the arts and sciences have always had charms for him. He has had the honour of being elected Fellow of the Royal Geographical Society (in 1865), and subsequently of the Society of Antiquaries of Scotland, the Royal Society of Northern Antiquaries, Copenhagen, a member of the Geological Society of Edinburgh, the Royal Asiatic Society, the German Oriental Society, the Asiatic Society of Paris, and several others of a similar nature. In 1868 the Senate of Tusculum College, at Greenville, in Tennessee, conferred on him the degree of LL.D., the diploma being signed by the President of the United States, along with the Senate of the College.

To an extended knowledge of the beauties of his native land, and especially of his own county, he has added an intimate acquaintance with the sunny climes of the south of Europe, the winter *habitat* of our summer birds of passage. On visiting Italy in 1867, he wrote several pretty fragments, which have since appeared in Mr. Wm. Smith's "Trip to Rome," and other publications. Still, with all the charms of Italy brightening the remembrance of his visit, he is able to express his feelings in favour of the country of his birth. "Steer, father, straight to me," has, with others, been set to music, by Mr. J. Waring, of Heckmondwike, which do credit both to the West Riding poet and the West Riding musician. A host of similar smaller poems by Dr. Robinson have been printed by Messrs. Campbell & Tudhope, of Glasgow, as illuminated leaflets, and published in cheap packets, which will be acceptable to Christian philanthropists and Sunday School teachers. We believe they have had, as they deserve, a large circulation. Several of the tracts of the Weekly and other Societies are from his pen, such as "John Asquith, the pious shoemaker," and "The Evil of the Love of Gold," &c. His larger poems are chiefly on Scriptural subjects, as "The Messiah" (now in the second edition), "Joseph," "The Deluge," "Esther," "Daniel," &c., several of which have appeared in the *Methodist Quarterly*, to which he was a regular contributor. Others have appeared in numerous publications besides those mentioned in this sketch, as well as in the various newspapers throughout the country.

Dr. Robinson has been Vice-Chairman of the Dewsbury School Board for about nine years; President of the Dewsbury Naturalists' Society from its commencement until quite recently; Wesleyan Circuit Steward for several years; and for over twenty years has had a Sunday Bible Class, which contained at one time nearly one hundred members; and is also President of the Chemists' Association, numbering over thirty members.

Though still residing at his native Dewsbury, he has rambled through most of the United Kingdom, France, Italy, and Switzerland, climbing Alpine summits in the Mont Blanc range with the same vigour that had taken him to the top of Snowdon, and other mountains of his native land. His "Reminiscences of a Visit to Switzerland and Northern Italy" appeared in Yorkshire, Nottingham, and London papers, and others appeared in the *Argonaut*, &c. His latest printed poems are "Esther" and "The Deluge," which first appeared in the *Methodist Quarterly*, and afterwards in a separate form. He has also several other poems on "David," "Moses," "Joseph," "Daniel," "Samson," and "Ruth," ready for the press; and he is the author of a number of North of England tractates, including "Yorkshire Worthies," "Howley Hall," "Halifax Gibbet," and the battles of "Towton," "Marston Moor," and "Adwalton Moor," &c.

Dr. Robinson is a writer of whom Yorkshire has no cause to be ashamed, and an earnest worker for many a good object. He has also published hundreds of short poems, mostly of a religious character, or with a moral attached, which ought to be re-published in book form, *pro bono publico.*

R. V. TAYLOR, B.A.

KIRKSTALL ABBEY.

Behold these hallowed walls ; these ruined towers :
The moss-grown cells, where monks in days of yore,
Studied and prayed, and wept. Where abbots proud
Planned their ambitious schemes ; and, hiding deep

Their secret thoughts, went forth to those who lay
Just on the verge of death, and, holding up .
Before their glazing eyes, the holy cross,
Drew such a picture of their past career :
Indulgence in the vanities of earth,
Neglect of God, and of the church, with all
The crimes, the open sins, which in the time
Of the stern warrior's manhood, they nor dared
To speak or hint at.   And, despite of all
The cloak of their religion, threatened him
With endless misery, in torments dire,
Unless he made atonement for the past ;
By leaving to the Church his vast estates.
    How did thy roofs re-echo to the sound   ⸰
Of the Te Deum, when thy Abbot came
Rejoicing, and victorious in his suit,
And told the anxious monks, how at the feet
Of the old Earl, Hugh Bigot, he had knelt,
Beseeching him, with tears and earnest prayers,
With protestations of his innocence ;
Imploring mercy, till the Earl, o'ercome
By his well-feigned humility, restored
The Bernoldswick estates, from which the monks
Had been by law ejected ; and the King,
The second Henry, witnessed and confirmed
The charter.   Short-lived triumph : for erelong
The Abbot Alexander died, and he
Who came from Fountains, Hageth, struggled hard,
But all in vain, to grapple with thy foes.
Of no avail his costly gifts, although
With chalice of pure gold, and holy text
Of the four gospels, with the greatest care
Engrossed by scribes, he sought to gain the King.
'Twas fruitless all.   Disheartened and distrest
At thy decaying fortunes, he resigned,
And left thee to thy fate.   Then Lambert came,

Who, with high hand, regardless of the hate
Of all beneath him, from their homes expelled
The cottagers; but, as the timid worm
Will turn again when trod upon, they rose,
Burned down his grange, with all that it contained,
And slew the three lay brothers he had placed
In charge of it. He died, and passed away.
Then came Turgesius, gloomy and devout.
No secret license now; no revellings;
No feasting on rich dainties, with choice wines;
No lovely damsels at confessional,
Breathing their secret hopes into the ears
Of young, unmarried, and licentious monks.
Austere, and clad in sackcloth; tasting not
Wine or strong drink; barefooted, for the space
Of nine long years he practiced abstinence,
Resigned,—and died, and went—we hope to heaven.
    Then came a change in thy affairs, for he
Who followed him was Heylas, and, by means
Of Industry, and Prudence, once again
Fair fortune smiled on thee. For centuries
Thy fame and thy prosperity increased.
Endowments rich thy abbots gained from those
Whose deathbeds they attended; and thy monks
Lived on the choicest dainties, till the time
Of retribution came, and he whom they
Pompously called "Defender of the Faith"
Decreed thy dissolution, and the fate
Which, soon or late, o'ertakes all human things,
Attended thee. The sharp, corroding tooth
Of Time hath eaten deep into thy stones;
Thy lofty towers, which pointed to the skies,
The fierce, wild, wintry winds, the frequent storms
Of centuries have wasted. Massive walls,
Which seemed to mock decay, defying time
Itself to work their ruin, yield beneath

A meaner foe ; pierced by the tender shoots
Of ivy, which, enlarging as they grow,
Feed on the mouldering dust which years have made,
And vanquish the firm, strong-built masonry
Which in their infancy a lodging gave.
Above seven hundred years have passed away
Since thou wert founded ; and the noble lord
Who owned these lands, and vast estates beside,
Soon passed away.   His honour and renown
Well-nigh forgotten where his will was law,
His word command, which none dare disobey.
His body mingled with its kindred dust.
And thou, by thy admirers almost deemed
Imperishable, hasteth to thy fall.

    May we this lesson learn from thy decay :
That, though the solid rocks in sunder cleave,
And earth's most firmly built foundations fail,
Yea, all beneath the skies shalt pass away ;
There is a changeless mansion for the just,
Eternal in the Heavens ; and he who lives
A blameless, holy life on earth, shall dwell
In happiness and joy unspeakable,
Enthroned at God's right hand for evermore.

GORDALE.

Mid scenes like this how sinks the human mind
When man, and all his deeds, we contemplate.
Dwarf'd by the giant force around display'd,
We shrink into ourselves, and own that all
Which we had thought worthy our boast, was nought
Compared with nature's powers when thus set free.
Here, far from earthly things, and busy scenes
Of toil, and bustling, anxious, worldly care,
We see ourselves more as we ought, and own
That, trusting in our strength, we are but weak

And feeble mortals ; void of all the fond
And proud pretence of power which some have claim'd ;
Yet, claiming, show in that their folly too.
'Tis in His strength alone that we are great :
His strength, who form'd the world, the sun, the moon,
And myriad stars which gem th' ethereal sky,—
Each one the centre of a system ; each
A sun itself to other worlds like ours.
Yet, though His might, all powerful to control
The universe itself, did first create,
And now sustains, upholds, and governs all :
Sees nought beneath His care. The smallest germ
Of vegetation springs, grows, ripens still
At His command. The meanest worm that crawls,
Shares the same Providence which feeds the great,
And noble animals that shake the ground ;
When their huge figures tread the forest path.
The smallest particles of moss, which here
With loveliest green relieve the solitude,
Are known to Him, for He directs their growth.
And shall we then, the noblest of His works,
Forget that He hath made us ? and that He
Hath promised by Himself,—the greatest, best
Security that we can wish to have,—
He will be ours, our God ; if we but serve,
And worship Him sincerely, and obey
His every law, and His commands perform ?
Oh ! may we then, with heartfelt gratitude
For all His mercies, give to Him ourselves,
All that we have and are, and live to Him
So long as our earth's pilgrimage endures :
That, when the end shall come,—the end of all
Life's troubles, griefs, and cares ;—Death may but be
The portal to that blest inheritance,
Which He hath promised in the realms above,
He will prepare for His own chosen ones.

FLAMBOROUGH LIGHTHOUSE.

Brightly from the beacon streaming,
　Comes a light across the sea,
Through the darkness ever gleaming,
　Warning sailors constantly,
Lest they here might find their graves,
Underneath the treacherous waves.

Light of mercy! still shine brightly,
　Guiding vessels on their way;
May thy rays direct them nightly,
　Safe into the welcome bay:
From all fear of danger free,
Riding in security.

Emblem of that glorious beacon,
　Guiding with its heavenly ray,
O'er the darkness of life's ocean,
　Pilgrims on their homeward way:
Rocks of sin and sorrow past,
To their blessed home at last.

Robert Spence Watson, LL.D.

SHOULD like to write the life of Robert Spence Watson at such length as would be quite out of proportion to a work of this kind. His poems are the least part of his achievement. They were written chiefly for the delight of his family, and mainly on the subject of his travels. Only in one instance has he appealed to the wider public through the medium of verse, this being with a group of songs entitled "The Children's Christmas," written to the music of Myles Birket Foster, the son of his distinguished cousin, Birket Foster, the artist and illustrator. Robert Spence Watson, born in 1837, educated at the Friends' School, York, and University College, London, is a man of exceptional activities, both of body and mind. He is a member of the Alpine Club, and he has written an admirable little monograph on "Cœdmon," the first English poet; he is one of the leading English politicians out of Parliament, and he has travelled in Morocco; he is a solicitor in successful practice, and is deeply instructed in ancient and modern art; he was the first Christian to enter the sacred city of Wazan, and he was condemned to death by the French during the Franco-German war. In Newcastle, of which he is a native, Mr. Watson is much the foremost man in the Liberal party, and he might long ago have been in Parliament if the honour were not one which he is resolute in declining. A member of the Society of Friends, he went out to France, as one of the Commissioners of that body, to distribute relief to the starving peasantry during the war. He has written "A Visit to Wazan," published by Macmillan; "The Villages around Metz," an account of his relief experiences; the aforementioned book on "Cœdmon;" numerous pamphlets on art and political subjects; two volumes of poems for private circulation; and a paper on "Wordsworth's Relations to Science," in the recently published transactions of the Wordsworth Society. Mr. Watson's remarkable and winning powers of oratory have made him known throughout all England, and during a recent period of political excitement he probably addressed more meetings, in widely separated places, than any other politician of the day.

AARON WATSON.

PYGMALION AND GALATEA.

She was not woman! No—too doubting wife:
With the rude rock thou watched my daily strife
Till painfully it took its perfect form:
Then the Gods breathed on it and gave it life.

Yet 'twas *my* work that lived and breathed and moved ;
My work, by thee so watched and praised and loved :
How could I fail to love her when she grew
A thing of beauty, by the Gods approved.

I watched the sunbeams toying with her hair
As the light zephyr tossed it here and there,
And kissed it in an ecstasy of love :
Gods never made a creature half so fair.

She trod as though upon the necks of men !
The flowers kissed her glancing feet, and then
Rose sweeter, brighter, happier, than before—
Longing to feel that proud foot-fall again.

But when I gazed into those tranquil eyes
Beaming with new-born consciousness' surprise,
As when the sun, awakening the world,
In floods of self-created glory lies,—

Each simple movement seemed a world of grace,
Fresh pictures shone forth with each change of place,
And best loved poems grew weak words beside
That which I read writ in that perfect face.

Soul-wak'ning song breathed in her slightest word,
Her softest tones the heart's recesses stirred ;
Surrounding silence truly told her power,
And men grew noble when that voice they heard.

No more they hear it : never, never, more !
The image stands as perfect as before ;
The marvelling crowd still cry " the marble lives ; "
I know, alas ! the glory that is o'er.

LOVE ONLY LIVES.

Ah love, if love had willed that I should ne'er
　　Hear the soft music of thy gentle voice,
Or press the silken rapture of thy hair ;
　　Willed that thy presence, wherein all rejoice,
Thy life, which is to mine a fount of gladness,
Had been to me unknown,—thought near akin to madness :

Could the earth then have seemed to me so fair,
　　The summer moon still smile, the planets roll,
The wee birds sing, the flowers perfume the air,
　　Spring gaily bound from winter's stern control ?
Would not all joys to me be cold and dumb,
Untaught by her from whom their truest beauties come ?

Love whilst love lives, for even love must die ;
　　The tenderest flower first fades 'neath winter's breath :
Love whilst we may ; our love shall one day lie
　　Withered, yet sacred,—in the grasp of death.
Weep not because night ever follows day :
Love's light alone may shine when all things else decay.

SPRING.

Sweetest time of all the year,
When the gentle Spring awakes,
And, with scarcely opened eyes,
Quietly and softly lies,
Lest by moving the spell breaks :
When the sun-light warmly falls,
Out across the moorland brown,
In the weary smoke-dried town,
Gladdening the dull brick walls
With its magic making.

Winter lieth on her bier
To be buried 'neath fresh roses :
Soon the violets appear :
Every day fresh joy discloses ;
Every day some bud comes peeping,
Every day some flower quits sleeping,
Every day some stranger bird
In the busy woods is heard ;
Darkness sooner flies away,
Heaven's light holds longer sway.

Hearts beat gladly when they feel
The sweet influence of renewing :
Modest lilies ring a peal
Soft and low as lover's sueing,
And the brooklet gaily dances ;
Gentle days bring gentle fancies.
Leaflets clad the naked branch,
And wee flowerets once more launch
Fragrance into dewy air,
Sweetness seemeth everywhere ;
Whilst from forth her boundless treasure
Bringeth Spring, in bounteous measure,
Nights of calm and tender beauty,
Days of undefined pleasure,
When the earth in quiet lies
Smiling at the smiling skies.
Joy exists without alloy ;
Life itself is full of joy ;
And the world is full of beauty ;
Happiness becometh duty.

John William Inchbold.

OHN WILLIAM INCHBOLD, the author of "Annus Amoris," a volume of sonnets, and other poems, better known to the world of art as a most refined and poetical landscape painter, was born at Leeds, but at a very early period in his career left Yorkshire to take up his abode in London. His father, Mr. Thomas Inchbold, publisher, of Leeds, was one of the first to introduce the art of lithography, both as an art and a trade; and doubtless this fact had much influence in his son's choice of a profession. Of Mr. Inchbold's fame as an artist, it is not for us to speak here, saving that this fame is inseparably linked with the poetical inspirations to which reference is now made, for each single poem may be regarded as the expression, only in a different mode, of one of those exquisite pictures on canvas drawn by this master. "Annus Amoris" was the only volume published by Mr. Inchbold, and is the expression in song of his ardent worship of Nature in her loveliest, no less than in her sternest, aspects. The book was received with marked pleasure by all true lovers of poetry, and was most favorably reviewed by the leading journals. *The Spectator* speaks thus : " The book is full of graceful imagery and of suggestive thought, and the poems are marked throughout by delicacy of feeling, beauty of expression, and an entire freedom from the conventional diction so dear to the poetaster; " and the *Athenæum* declared "the compositions to be remarkable for the manner in which outward phenomena are made the mouthpieces of inward thoughts and moods."

Mr. Inchbold's death, which took place January 23rd, 1888, was deeply lamented by a large number of distinguished friends and admirers, among some of the most intimate of whom may be mentioned Mr. John Dennis, Mr. Coventry Patmore, Dr. Russell Reynolds, and Mr. Geo. Howard (now Earl of Carlisle), with whom he stayed at Castle Howard some months before his death.

We think it is not inappropriate here to quote briefly from an exquisite poem to the memory of Mr. Inchbold by Algernon Charles Swinburne, a friend of early years, which appeared in the *Athenæum*, and was afterwards quoted in other journals, as a " Poet's tribute to a Painter."

For if, beyond the shadow and the sleep,
A place there be for souls without a stain,
Where peace is perfect, and delight more deep
Than seas or skies that change and shine again,
There none of all unsullied souls that live,
May hold a surer station: none may lend
More light to hope's or memory's lamp, nor give
More joy than thine to those that called thee friend.

And we conclude this notice with the following beautiful and most pathetic lines, by one of his closest and dearest friends, Mr. John Dennis, which appeared in the *Spectator*:

> Bleak is the wind, and all the woods are bare,
> No rift of blue gladdens the wintry sky,
> But nature mourns her lover with a sigh,
> Hiding beneath her snow-white veil her care;
> Ah! well he wooed her when her face was fair
> In the warm summer, 'midst his Yorkshire hills;
> And dear to him the music of her rills,
> And dear the stillness of the moorland air.
> O loyal painter! steadfast to thy vow,
> Scorner of men who make art merchandise!
> O loyal friend! weak though these words be now,
> Sweet are the memories that bedim my eyes;
> Farewell! God's love has called thee to thy rest!
> Bless'd art the pure in heart, and thou art blest."

ALICE HALEY.

ART.

Mysterious force, as beautiful as strange,
And pure with beauty and with mystery;
Queen of the world in wide extent of range,
Through every motion of the sky and sea,
And the sweet mother of all joy, our Earth
Whether in moment of her snowy rest,
Or autumn eve, or summer noon, or birth
Of spring time o'er an Alpine mountain's crest,
To touch thy robe is life, but to receive
Thy touch of fiery lip, then pierce with eye
Made clear and strong, and afterwards to weave
With all our heart, fair forms that cannot die:—
This bliss supreme being ours, thine own free gift,
Makes life one joy and dull time keen and swift.

STRATFORD-ON-AVON.

Just as of old sweet Avon winds its way,
Embracing yellow corn and meadow-land,
The harvest moon makes night a sweeter day,
Just as of old on Shakespeare's brow and hand,

The willows droop upon the river's breast,
The silvern swan is in its loveliest dream,
An image beautiful of twofold rest ;—
O mellow sky, and moon, and stars, and stream !
All Nature's spirit, free as song of bird !
Send now sweet Love upon the fruitful earth,
And let the exulting song far off be heard
Of Love's wide melody and purest mirth,
Until the gentle conquest be complete,
And Death, and Sorrow are in full retreat.

ONE DEAD.

Is it deep sleep, or is it rather death ?
Rest anyhow it is, and sweet is rest :—
No more the doubtful blessing of the breath,
Our God hath said that silence is the best ;
And thou art silent as the pale, round moon,
And near thee is our birth's great mystery :—
Alas, we know not thou wouldst go so soon !
We cannot tell where sky is lost in sea,
But only find life's bark to come and go,
By wondrous nature's hidden force impelled,—
Then melts the wake in sea, and none shall know
For certain which the course the vessel held ;—
The lessening ship by us no more is seen,
And sea and sky are just as they have been.

Allison Hughes.

LICE HALEY, who writes under the *nom de plume* of "Allison Hughes," is a native of Leeds. From early childhood she displayed a predisposition to poetry and poetic expression, which may be attributed to the fact that from both parents she inherited a literary taste. Her father, in the leisure permitted him during a busy life, devoted much of it to the composition and adaptation of sacred music, most of which had far more than a local crculation ; and at the present time a published collection of his work is still admired and cherished by those fortunate enough to possess copies. On the other side, her maternal grandfather, Mr. Thomas Inchbold, was a well-known publisher in Leeds, and was at one time proprietor of the *Leeds Intelligencer*, now incorporated with the *Yorkshire Post*, to which he was a regular contributor. But what perhaps had the greatest influence in guiding and directing the literary predilections of Miss Haley, was the advantage she possessed of frequent association and correspondence with her distinguished uncle, Mr. John William Inchbold, the well-known artist and poet, whose untimely death last year the art and literary world, generally, deplored. Mr. Inchbold, as a friend of Tennyson, Ruskin, Rossetti, Swinburne, and others, would be apt to imbue his young disciple's mind with some of the impressions which he himself, no doubt, had received by association with such poetical luminaries. At any rate, her poetic nature began to find expression at an early age, as when still in her teens she composed many of the pieces which compose the bulk of her first volume of poems, published by Henry S. King & Co., London, entitled " Penelope, and other poems," now out of print. When published, it was received with the greatest favour in literary circles. Most of the London, and the principal provincial reviewers, considered it worthy of special and extended notice. One critic compares her to Mrs. Barrett Browning, Christina Rossetti, and Jean Ingelow, contending that she possesses in a degree something of the distinctive graces of each. Another says of her verse that " if it moves stiffly it is because the substance is rich and carefully wrought." Another, referring to some word-painting in the poem entitled " Penelope," says :—" Here is a picture of sunset of which the Laureate might be proud." Many more references of an equally eulogistic character might be cited. It is said that much of her work is composed in a mournful key. This may perhaps arise from the comparatively secluded surroundings of her early life ; but of late years Miss Haley has resided a good deal abroad, and the vivacity and continuous changes of foreign life have no doubt imparted to her more cheerful views of life, which find expression in her newly-published book, " Reed Music " (Kegan, Paul, Trench & Co.). Miss Haley has been a contributor to *Good Words, Glasgow Weekly Citizen,* &c., and has received the eulogies of such authorities as the late Principal Tulloch and Professor John Stuart Blackie. The three pieces published here will give a fair idea of her quality and style.

F. C. HARTMANN.

JOYS OF LIFE.

Just to lie at early morning,
  Half asleep and half awake,
When the first faint flush of dawning
  In the East begins to break.
Just to muse in mute quiescence,
  Beauteous visions hovering nigh,
Subtle in their evanescence
  As the changeful Eastern sky.

Such are joys God gives when giving
  Man to breathe of mortal breath—
Joys too brief, since round the living
  Floats the mystery of Death !

Just to climb steep upland passes
  Scarce to mortal footsteps known,
Just to roam through dewy grasses
  By scent-laden breezes blown,
Just to catch a fading glimmer
  Of the sunset waning West,
Just to watch white moonbeams shimmer
  Coldly fair on Ocean's breast.

Such are joys God gives when giving
  Man to breathe of mortal breath—
Joys too brief, since round the living
  Floats the mystery of Death !

Just to mingle with the flowing,
  Surging, heaving human sea,
With the heart's blood fiercely glowing,
  Just to mingle and *to be.*
Just to feel the warm pulsation
  Of that life whose weakest aim
Ne'er shall know annihilation,
  Ever dull or fair shall flame.

Such are joys God gives when giving
　Man to breathe of mortal breath—
Joys too brief, since round the living
　Floats the mystery of Death !

Just to mark dear eyes gleam brighter,
　Lit by fire from eyes as dear,
Just to know light hearts grow lighter
　When some form beloved draws near,
Just to clasp some bright form visioned
　Far off once on Fancy's shore,
Just to catch a smile, safe prisoned
　In the breast for evermore.

Such are joys God gives when giving
　Man to breathe of mortal breath—
Joys too brief, since round the living
　Floats the mystery of Death !

Just to labour 'mid the yearning
　Myriad souls of brother-kind,
Striving oft to ease some burning
　Grief, or soothe some restless mind.
Just to laugh that happy laughter—
　Sunlike, rippling round life's pain ;
Just to sing, forgetting after
　Silence shall ensue again !

Such are joys God gives when giving
　Man to breathe of mortal breath—
Joys too brief, since round the living
　Floats the mystery of Death !

Just to track with dauntless daring
　Lonely heights of fair renown,
Just to tread earth's low vales wearing
　Hope's imperishable crown.

Just to wander through life's mazes,
  Led by gentle unseen Friend,
In whose hand bright love-torch blazes,
  That shall guide unto the end.

Such are joys God gives when giving
  Man to breathe of mortal breath—
Joys too brief, since round the living
  Floats the mystery of Death !

Such are mortal joys and fleeting,
  Shed like blossoms round our feet,
Transient as the rainbow's greeting,—
  If as transient, still as sweet.

Such are joys which men receiving
  Hail with thankful heart and breath,
Since for ever round the living
  Floats the mystery of Death !

THE GRANDMOTHER.

Through the wide-open door the westering sun
Streamed in warm splendour ; in the casement set
Red summer roses and sweet mignonette.
Beside her wheel the old grandmother spun
Her flaxen thread against the day was done,
And seemed in smiling reverie to forget
Long vanished years of fevered toil and fret—
Time led more gently toward life's boundary stone.

The little children played around her chair,
Their laughter made light music in her dreams.
Each passing neighbour gave "good night."   Faint gleams
Of gold within the west heavens lingered fair.
"Grandmother, wake ! the evening meal is spread !"
"Hush, children dear ! she banquets with the dead !"

SILENCES!

The silences that float
Between two kindred souls aflame with love :
Those brief, sweet seasons, when that life is drowned
In magic quiet, and far, far remote,
Dim, shadowy, and strange, the vast world seems !
When fancy idly folds her lightsome wing,
When speech swoons on the rippling breeze and dies,
And even thought is lulled and lost in dreams,
By drowsy, hushful stillness circled round.   .   .   .

The silences that lie
Between our souls and the belovèd dead :
Those regions of ineffable despair,
Those shrouded depths unseen by mortal eye,
Those dreary wastes of empty nothingness,
Which border the abode of spirits fled.—
What though we stretch into the vacant air
Mute hands that plead for one sweet whispered word
To dissipate the dread infinitude
Of silence that for ever is unstirred ?
No sound e'er steals across the motionless
Abyss of separation which doth brood
Between the voiceful living and the voiceless lost ! . . .

The silences that fall
Within that secret chamber of the soul,
When mystic strains steal from heaven's viewless shore,
And mingle with life's tumult, until all
About our hearts great waves of music roll,
And earthly discords weary us no more
For a brief season, but forgotten sleep.
Then comes a sudden hush, the refrain dies—
And, as of old the Temple's child did hark,
In wond'ring awe, for speech to fill the deep
And sudden void between him and the dark
Unrestful world that stole, so hearken we,
And toward the Infinite dumbly passionate cries
Our waiting soul,—but answer none—none—none—
Save silence !   This the deathless voice of God.

John Harbottle.

HE surroundings of the modern man of business are ill-fitted to inspire the spirit of poetry. The bustle and din of city life, the eddy and whirl of the times, the engrossing cares of business, the relentless competition and the callousness of the commercial *régime* all tend to dull those finer sensibilities and crush those softer emotions which are the very fountain of the poet's inspiration. The business man to-day must be practical whether he will or no. In his high-pressure life there is no time to nurse impressions; in his pre-occupied mind there is no room for sentiment. He is a struggling swimmer down the stream of time; not a musing wayfarer on its banks. Others may stop to note the beauties by the way; he must act.

But if the environment of the business man of to-day is not of the kind to produce poets, there are, nevertheless, those who have so far freed themselves from it as to aspire to poetry. Despite the influences which militate against it, there are in the ranks of our commercial men those who have wooed and won the muse. One who has done so very successfully is Mr. John Harbottle, of Newcastle-on-Tyne. Living and working in no more congenial environment than is afforded by a business life on Newcastle Quayside, he is at heart a singer, and never tires of tuning his lyre in praise of his native hills and streams.

John Harbottle was born in Newcastle, in 1851, and is the eldest son of Mr. Thomas Harbottle, an old and respected tradesman of that city. The rhyming faculty which ultimately developed into genuine verse, betrayed itself early in youth, and numbers of fragments and acrostics which he produced while still in his teens, served to indicate the bent of his mind. But it is to another and stronger characteristic that we owe the numerous songs and poems which have made the cognomen of " Streams of the North " familiar to many in Newcastle. The mere faculty for rhyming does not make a poet, and poetry is not the product of fireside ease in a cosy parlour. There must be communion with nature, or the song that rejoices in field and flower, in the music of the murmuring stream, in " the brightness of morning," and the "red of the gloaming" will never be written. An enthusiastic angler, he has for twenty-five years, from boyhood to manhood, and from manhood to middle age, plied his rod in the streams of his native Borderland with a devotion that only a fisher knows. Wandering by the banks of the lovely Coquet, or amid the wilder scenes of the Tyne and Reed he has learned to note their charms and sing their praises in joyous measure. His songs have the freshness of the mountain breeze; their music is of the waters. They are now bright and gleesome as the dancing of the brook in the morning sun, or now softly pathetic as the low murmuring of the placid river. Almost their one theme is the sport he loves to praise. But though his songs have one theme they are not lacking in variety. The associations and reflections called up by each are distinct and different, and their metrical treatment is as diversified. He handles the stately heroic couplet, and the ranting rollicking measure of "Cappy's the dog," with equal facility. Some of his best productions are little pastorals, written in the Northumbrian dialect, of which he is a complete master, but his more humorous poems are penned in the broad Doric of the Newcastle keelman, which he uses with a facility thoroughly racy of the soil. These latter, however, written mainly for the Northumberland Angling Club, of which Mr. Harbottle is an active member, will not appeal to the general reader on account of their personal allusions and purely local character, and they are not therefore included in this selection. Some of his poems of a more general character have from time to time appeared in the Newcastle papers, and when the *Northern Weekly Leader*, a few months ago, offered a prize for the best poem on the Tyne, " Streams of the North " competed and won the first prize. This poem is by far his most comprehensive effort. It is dignified in style, chaste in expression, and tenderly pathetic in sentiment, recounting the history and industrial achievements of a great river with honest sympathy and poetic insight. The " Dawn of Morning " is a little poem which for beauty of conception and delicacy of touch is unsurpassed by anything he has written. This together with the poem on " The Tyne," just mentioned, will serve to illustrate his serious side. Of his fishing songs it is difficult to make a representative selection in the limited space at disposal in this volume, but there are two which could not be overlooked without loss to the reader. These are " A song to the Coquet," and " The Angler's Courtship." The first of these sings the praises of his favourite stream with the tenderness of a lover. Indeed, there is about it a keen appreciation of the charms of that lovely river which recalls the poems of Roxby and Doubleday. " The Angler's Courtship " is in a more humorous vein. It is remarkable for the completeness of its allegory, and the aptitude and point with which the comparisons between the lover and the fisher are worked out. It requires an angler to thoroughly appreciate this poem.

These are but specimens from some thirty similar songs of almost equal merit, which "Streams of the North " has penned as the result of brief fishing excursions. They of course appeal most strongly to anglers ; but there is in them an inborn love of Nature, a bright and lively fancy, and a vein of moral reflection, which make them true poems. They are essentially the product of the soil, and it may yet be found that since the days of Roxby and Doubleday, no lay poet has sung so well the natural beauties of our North Country fishing haunts.

R. W. Johnson.

THE TYNE.

" I know not where to seek, even in this busy country, a spot or district in which we perceive so extraordinary and multifarious a combination of the

various great branches of mining, manufacturing, trading and shipbuilding
industry, and I greatly doubt whether the like can be shewn, not only within the limits of this land but upon the whole surface of the globe."—*Extract
from speech of Right Hon. W. E. Gladstone, M.P., on his visit to Newcastle-on
Tyne,* 1862.

Drear is the heart, no pleasant past recalls,
No ivy tendrils clinging round its walls :
No bright green spot, no sunlight on its sea,
No memory's land where it may wander free.
And sad my own, if e'er the image fade
Of those fair scenes wherein my childhood played,
Where all the joys of life have found their birth,
And spread their wings around a Tyneside hearth.
Home of all Northern hearts my Muse's shrine ;
Once loved, still loved, the dear old banks of Tyne.
Hail, glorious stream ! thy shore is hallowed ground,
Where'er thy sturdy Northern sons are found,
For through the heart of each Northumbrian son,
Throughout all time thy gentle streams shall run.
I've wandered all thy beauties near and far,
From moss-girt cradle to the harbour bar ;
What hours were mine spent by thy Northern stream,
By heather blooms, where lonely lapwings scream,
O'er Belling's crest, wild Wannie's heaving fells,
By Kielder's moors and lone romantic dells,
Where thy young life, fed by thy creeping rills,
Wakes all to mirth amidst thy sleeping hills.
Down rocky vales thy crystal cascades pour—
The boisterous stream of boyhood's happy hour,
Here by thy pebbled shore, with hope-lit eye,
Bent the old rod and led the mimic fly—
O'er linn and pool, and from thy waters cold
Oft dragged the gleaming salmon from his hold.
On, rolling on ! no backward thought is thine ;
No slogan cry—no feud of " auld lang syne ; "
No clash of steel disturbs thy peaceful way,
Unstained thy tide by reiver's bloody fray.

On, rolling on ! by many a cairn and mound,
Marked by the fireside tale as haunted ground.
Beneath the shade of moss gray tower and keep,
The rugged heroes of the Border sleep.
On, rolling on ! no time to sleep or dream,
Thy panting heart yearns for the parent stream,
Where thy sweet sister South, the gentler one,
Bids kind farewell to moorland, bleak and lone,
To Alston's hills and all her verdant plains,
Where dwell Tyne's rosy maids and sturdy swains,
Until at last, all youthful wanderings done,
*North blends with South their beating hearts in one.
Deeper thy currents now by Hexham town
†And Wilfred's sacred pile of old renown.
Here in the past the fires of conflict burned,
When every eye in England on thee turned ;
The mouldering tower on Dilston's ancient walls
The days of Edward and King Charles recalls.
When princely blood o'er all the margin shed
‡Proclaimed the White Rose victor o'er the Red !
Here friendship's hand signed truce 'twixt Tyne and Tweed,
And hushed the feuds that made our noblest bleed.
Historic stream ! on thy green banks a home
Once found the conquering sons of ancient Rome.

*The river Tyne is formed by the junction of North and South Tyne, a little westward of the ancient town of Hexham.

†The Bishopric of Hexham, founded in 674, by Wilfred, Archbishop of York.   Hexham Abbey said to have been the fifth stone church erected in England.

‡Battle of Hexham, fought May, 1464.   Defeat of the Lancastrians by the Yorkists, between Dukesfield and the Linnels, on the south side of the Devil's water.   The year book, Edward IV. states about the Feast of Pentecost the Lancastrian Lords " took their King Henry with all their power of people and took their field in Hexhamshire, in a place called Linells, on the Water Devylle, against the Lord of Montague, brother of Lord Warwick, who joined battle with them and had the victory of the enemies aforesaid ; and there Lord Somerset was taken and his head cut off."   In the Arundel MSS., the executions at Hexham are recorded as follows :—" 15th May, beheaded at Hexham, the Duke of Somerset, Edmund Fitzhugh, Knight, Bradshaw, Walter Hunt, Black Jack, or Jaques, &c." *History of Newcastle, 14th and 15th century, by Richard Welford.*

We trace their mighty works by time revered ;
From sea to sea their mighty barriers reared.*
Here in the shrine of many a lovely vale
Bold Aidan taught the Gospel's gentle tale ;
Here noble Bede, the learned, wise, and good,
Shed o'er the land the truth's pure vital flood.
The voice of ages bids us ne'er forget
The days of Norman and Plantagenet,
Nor when thy plains were trod by Danish horde,
Who dipped in Saxon blood the wasting sword.
Through Time's dark shadows we the struggles trace,
Of all that made our sturdy Northern race.
These fevered, fierce, and fitful days now o'er
Leave not a trace of sadness on thy shore.
What rustic scenes here meet the wanderer's eye,
Those bright green fields of patient husbandry !
The clustered flocks o'er all thy plains are seen,
The gay flower bank and pine wood's darker green.
These pictures past, now thy broad bosom wears
The darkening hues of all thy future cares.
Thy sunny hours of youth and play are done,
Now life's stern duties with thee are begun.
On by the Northern city rolling still,
Deep are the channels now thy waters fill ;
Where yonder spire rears high its head sublime,†
And Norman keep defies the waves of Time ;‡
Where all those thronging fabrics rise to view,
Might of the old and triumphs of the new.

Hail, stream of progress ! Now thy furnace fires
Glow like the zeal that Northern hearts inspires.
Hark to the hammer's clang, the rushing steam ;
See whirling wheels and lamps electric gleam,

*The Roman Wall, eighty miles in length from sea to sea, built in the year 120 by Hadrian.
†The spire of St. Nicholas Cathedral, one of the finest in England.
‡Keep of the old castle of the days of William Rufus.

Tall tapering masts, from towering chimneys pour
Dark breath of toil in all her busy hour.
Here grim King Labour sits on high enthroned,
His regal sway by all his subjects owned.
Tyne's grimy sons to honest toil inured,
Strong hearts, strong minds, by honest toil matured.
Here Armstrong's genius is bequeathed to fame,
His glorious lot to guard his country's name.
Here float those ships like belted knights of yore,
Old England speaks where'er his cannons roar.
Where'er the rushing engine thunders on,
There rides the soul of mighty Stephenson !
And 'twixt thy shores high in the murky air,
His wondrous skill hath hung a pathway there.*
Far down below in womb of Mother Earth
Our hardy miners pour Tyne's treasures forth,
Heroes in labour 'midst their deadly toil,
Rugged in speech and racy of the soil.
Mark well the ships, those racers of the sea !
That speak their builders' glorious energy.
The noble docks, and estuary wide,
Where laden fleets steam safely o'er the tide ;
Those mighty piers that mark the untiring will,
The stable monuments of intrepid skill,
O'er all thy banks, art, science both combine ;
While o'er their works the beams of genius shine.
Honour to thee old Tyne, still proudly roll,
The gentle nurse of many a noble soul,
Strong sons of freedom, whose undying names
Shall rouse our own to great and noble aims
The first to strike in freedom's glorious cause,
And shield the weak from stern oppression's laws.
Hail, glorious Tyne ! thy banks, thy woods, thy streams,
Thy toil-stained tide with inspiration teems ;
Theme of historian, poet, and of sage,
A glorious epic thou in every age.

*The renowned High Level Bridge, built by George Stephenson.

Hail, gentle Tyne! the birthplace of the free,
Strong are the links that bind our hearts to thee.
Where'er, in distant climes, thy sons may roam,
Kind are the thoughts that turn to thee, their home;
And when their lamp of life but dimly burns,
Still to thy shores their lingering vision turns.
In life's last hours give them a Tyneside friend,
The light of heaven, then welcome is the end.

THE COQUET.

The wind blaws saftly frae the west, the dew hings on the lea.
The spreckled lark aboon my head sings a' his sangs to me;
The glint o' Coquet's lovely charms, my heart can ne'er withstand,
Sae with my trusty rod ance mair I'll try my eager hand.

The morning cloud is lifting fast, aboon wild Cheviot's brow,
The bleater's plaint is sounding sweet frae ilka grassy knowe;
The thrush upon the hawthorn spray pours forth his sweetest strain,
The joys that burst frae Nature's breast but waken a' my ain.

I'll wander then by Coquet's brink adoon her flow'ry vale,
And freedom breathe, my native air, the scented heather gale;
And lightly fling my " heckle flee " across the foaming gleam,
Where mony a bonnie dimpled trout lies waiting in the stream.

The music o' thy waters clear an angler's heart shall fill,
Thy crystal deep shall hide for me a store o' pleasures still;
And glorious memories linger round e'en as thy mosses cling,
Nae ither stream in east or west the same sweet sangs can sing.

Tho' little leisure is my lot and mony cares oppress,
If parted often frae thy side I love thee nane the less;
And when life's slender line shall break, this blessing I shall crave,
To hear the murmur o' thy stream and sleep beside thy wave.

THE DAWN OF MORNING.

Upon a couch of dreams the morning lay,
And gently slept the dewy hours away,
While nature meekly lingered by her bower
With patient longing for the waking hour.
Till weary of her vigil, nature said,
Come, angel sunbeam, wake my sleeping maid.
Soft breathes my love, the perfumed eglantine,
While pearly dewdrops in her tresses shine.
My love is fair—but, oh! I long to see—
Her bright eyes radiant, beaming upon me.
Come, bid her wake, nor twilight hour prolong,
The world doth patient wait her matin song.
As from the flower the bee the honey sips,
The sunbeam softly stole and kissed her lips,
The lingering dews of sleep kissed from her eyes
And whispered, oh so softly—"love arise."
Thus woke the rosy morn in golden light,
And cast aside the mantle of the night.
Hark! now afar o'er mountain hill and dale,
A thousand notes wing on the scented gale.
Earth lives again—list to the city's din,
Where some to pleasure wake and some to sin.
The ponderous wheel of life now slow revolves,
To bear our hopes or crush our heart's resolves.

THE FISHER'S COURTSHIP.

Sae blithe owre the hills when the spring breezes blaw,
Gans the keen fisher lad ti the courtin' awa,
An' where yon green valley dips doon ti the West
Is the love o' his leal heart, the stream he loves best.
What virtues aye shine in her waters sae clear;
For the stream is the maid that the fisher holds dear.

Her sweet modest features wi smiles still await
Her warm hearted lover be he early or late ;
While her pure heaving bosom wi beauty doth shine,
As coyly she waits for the kiss o' the line.
What glances o' love frae her fountains she flings,
An' aye as they wander what love sangs she sings ;
Or whispers sae saft in the shades o' the dell,
Where the birds a' a tale fu' o' tenderness tell.
An' aye she will gie him affection's best seal,
In the bright glitterin' treasures that lie in his creel.
Like the fish oft' the heart is ensnared wi the silk,
Fine dressin' an' feathers an' things o' that ilk,
Tho' the barbs o' the Cupid hae caused grief and pain ;
"Bide a wee," like the troot, "he gans at it again !"
An' the times he's been "hookit" he still will forget,
Till at last he is ta'en in the mesh o' love's net !
There's a link o' fine hair he'd fain use in the art—
Tho' t'will scarce haud a troot, it may bind fast a heart ;
An' love's sceptre, the rod, that he aye loves to bend,
Has a re(a)el ring an' splice that won't break at the end !
Oh ! little ye think o' the pleasures that beam,
When a fisher gans courtin' awa to the stream !

Rev. Arthur Vine Hall.

N these hurrying days we are apt to suppose that there is not a tendency amongst us to give a welcome to the delights of "imagination" and "feeling" when meeting them in the form of what is commonly called poetry. Imagination and feeling are, nevertheless, most necessary and constant factors of our daily life, though not generally recognised as such. It is doubtless a fact though that people as a rule, who say that they do not care for poetry, and cannot be induced to read it, have never rightly considered what poetry really is.

A little thought would soon convince such that poetry is a something which, though not recognised by them, is nevertheless, greatly enjoyed by them. The idea of poetry to some is but a hazy notion of a kind of tedious metrical expression of sentiments which, to appreciate with relish, should be written in what they would ignorantly describe as prose. They fail to see that the poetic germ exists whatever the setting may be. If, however, poetry be regarded in its generic and larger sense, it should be plain to us that it is in reality the expression of imaginative truth in any form, provided that form be suggestive and symbolic. And it is in this sense that there is poetry in painting, sculpture and architecture,—in fact, all nature is poetical because the Divine Maker of all things has so clothed it with forms which are expressive of a vast and various suggestiveness. The man or woman failing to recognise as such the poetry existing in the world around, can admire the snow-capped mountain, can be moved by the rippling music of the lake's shore at sunset, can listen with rapture to the forest, and so forth, though all the time quite oblivious of the fact that it is the poetry of these things which makes for delight. They could exclaim, with the poet before us,

> O thou ever restless ocean,
> How I love the mad commotion,
> Love the thunder and the glee
> Of thy waves so wild and free,

and yet scarcely recognise that their own emotion was of the very essence of poetry.

In the volume of poems published this year by Simpkin, Marshall and Co., there is much which has fallen from the pen of Mr. Vine Hall which cannot fail to greatly charm one. There is much thought expressed by him with natural taste and exactness of suitable metre, which carries one away from the sordid and the every day. One cannot but feel glad that so much rich thought has been transferred from manuscript into type. Mr. Hall has had the advantage of travel, and his sundry sojourns in Switzerland and an extended tour in Egypt and Palestine, have greatly influenced much that he has written. Mr. Hall is fully alive to the fact that one of the most powerful instruments of vice, and the most fatal of all its poisoned weapons, is the abuse of words by which good and bad feeling are blended together, and deformity concealed by an apparent alliance to some proximate virtue. One of the evils of refinement is to give harsh deeds soft names. but to the attuned mind of Mr. Hall, covetousness is not frugality, flattery is not good breeding, prodigality and dissipation are not liberality and high spirit. There is much in Mr. Hall's writing which peeps out suddenly and forcibly with a charm and surprise which is truly appetising. He is evidently fully alive to the sterling fact that the best of poetry is ever in alliance with uncorrupted Christianity, that with the degeneracy of the one of necessity comes the decline of the other, —that it is to Christianity we owe the fullest inspirations of the celestial spirit of poetry. There is an originality too of no mean order in Mr. Hall's poems, ever bubbling to the surface, and there is a grace and finish pervading all that he has penned with so much freshness and vitality.

A tantalizing obscurity, too difficult for the ordinary apprehension, in which so many poets license themselves to indulge, is entirely absent in Mr. Hall's writing; in rhythmical music, irresistibly pleasant even to the most unattuned ear, come here bounding upon our senses, beautiful sentiment and dazzling flashes of sublime thought. In reading Mr. Hall's poems, one recognises to the full that metre acts as a powerful auxiliary to the senses, that he has well suited his metres to the soul of the poems,—in the same sense that the painter puts in the sky which is appropriate to the movement or repose of the picture beneath it.

Mr. Vine Hall is the son of the Rev. Arthur Hall, and nephew to the Rev. Newman Hall, LL.B. He was born at Luddenden Foot, Yorkshire, in the year 1862. He entered Cheshunt College in 1883, where he took the Arts and Theological courses; and in 1887 was elected to the pastorate of the South Cliff Congregational Church, Scarborough, as the successor to the Rev. R. Balgarnie. The volume of poems from which we give a few short extracts is dedicated by permission to Dr. George Macdonald. In the three verses selected from the poem entitled "To an Eagle," there will be perceived a fine illustration of the union of sound and sense. There is an example of musical verse in "After the Wreck," which we also append. In "On a Picture" will be seen pathos, a description of natural scenery in the poem "Mont Blanc," and a specimen of imagination from "Night."

EDWARD H. RICHES, LL.D., F.R.A.S.

From "TO AN EAGLE."

What though thou seem'st but a speck in the blue,
Sweeping still up as if hast'ning to woo
The Goddess of Fire from her home in the sun,
Careless of where the round earth may have spun!

All is but seeming! thou never can'st rise
Half of the distance that Fantasy flies—
Glancing not back till from planets afar,
Earth glimmers faint as the tiniest star.

Eying the sun as thou whirlest along,
But pouring no greeting of rapturous song;
Plumage of gold in the westering glow,
Thoughts all the time with some carcase below.

AFTER THE WRECK.

We took her away,
Far from that bleak northern bay;
Away to where the scented air
Might be a sweet narcotic to despair.
  But still she said that evermore
  She heard the roar
  Of waves upon a rock-bound shore;
  For ever—evermore.

  In cities antique,
Gemmed with palaces, to seek
Release from spell which was her knell,
We wander,—then mid Alpine châlets dwell.
  But still she said that evermore
  She heard the roar
  Of waves upon a rock-bound shore;
  For ever—evermore.

  One morn, snowy, wild,
Came a hunter with a child—
Found closely pressed to frozen breast;
That babe looked up, and smiling, was caressed.
  But still she said that evermore
  She heard the roar
  Of waves upon a rock-bound shore;
  Though fainter than before.

The lonelier one,
That day forward was her son ;
As after shower up looks the flower,
Her drooping spirit lifted from that hour.
And she would say : " Now nevermore
I hear the roar
Of waves upon a rock bound shore ;
Never—O nevermore."

From " NIGHT."

O loveliness sublime !
Weird, awful Goddess of the Raven Locks !
Thy streaming tresses by hushed winds upborne ;
The dazzling darkness of those glorious eyes,
The spell-bound twilight lingers to behold ;
That peerless brow the constellations crown ;
Her right hand holds a magic wand,—it waves !
The nations sink in sweet unconsciousness ;
And from her left—by starry chains suspended—
The pearl-set silver casket of the moon,
O'erflows with splendour pale.

ON A PICTURE.

He loved her as they love who early throw
The arms of manhood's strength and tenderness
Around a gentle wife ; while soft caress,
And thousand little things would daily show
Her love was such as hearts must feel to know.
And yet a quarrel came ! They part with less
Of farewell love, but, in their proud distress,
Conscious how soon forgiving tears will flow.

And thus they meet! Within this darkened room,
    He kneels beside a pale and lifeless form,
And round his head her long dark tresses lie!
Ah, did we pause to think how soon the bloom
    May quit the lips we love, would April storm
Chase for an hour the sunshine from the sky?

MONT BLANC.

Dread monarch! mountain king! well may we gaze
    In silent awe, as thy vast snow-fields lie
    Serene against the blue immensity;
Or, as resplendent in the level blaze
Of setting sun; or when through pearly haze
    The Moon beholds thee with a loving eye,
    Glad that her silvery beams, beneath the sky,
Can rest on purity; as she arrays
Thy head with crystal coronets of light,
    Awful e'en then thou art!—but how much more
When from thy frozen caves at dead of night,
    With shriek unearthly, and with deafening roar,
Th' imprisoned Spirit of the Storm breaks free,
And tempest, lightning, whirlwind circle thee!

Canon Dixon.

"HERE is," wrote the late D. G. Rossetti in a letter to Mr. Hall Caine, "an admirable but totally unknown living poet named Dixon. . . . If I live I mean to write something about him in some quarter when I can. His finest passages are as fine as any living man can do." This poet whose volumes Rossetti valued so highly was born in London in 1833. His father was the Rev. James Dixon, for many years one of the most eminent preachers in the Wesleyan Methodist Connexion, remarkable no less for the beauty and force of his personal character than for the brilliancy of his intellectual powers. His mother was the daughter of the Rev. Richard Watson — another great preacher and theologian in the same community. Receiving the ground-work of his education at King Edward's School, young Dixon afterwards proceeded to Pembroke College, Oxford. In 1856, while yet an undergraduate, he started in conjunction with Mr. Burne Jones and Mr. William Morris, *The Oxford and Cambridge Magazine*, to which Rossetti contributed some of his finest poems. He took his degree of B.A. in 1857, and M.A. in 1860. Ordained in 1858, he commenced his career in the Church of England as curate of St. Mary-the-Less, Lambeth. In 1863 he was appointed second master in the High School, Carlisle, and in 1874 he was made Hon. Canon of Carlisle Cathedral. He accepted the vicarage of Hayton in 1875, and that of Warkworth in 1883. His various literary works were published in the following order, viz :—"Christ's Company, and other Poems," 1861 ; " Historical Odes," 1863 ; " Essay on the Maintenance of the Church of England as an Established Church, being the essay which obtained the second of the prizes offered by Sir H. Peek ; " Life of James Dixon, D.D., Wesleyan Minister," 1874 ; History of the Church of England from the Abolition of the Roman Jurisdiction," Vol. I., 1877 ; Vol. II., 1880 ; Vol. III., 1885 ; " Mano : a Poetical History," 1883 ; Odes and Eclogues," 1884 ; " Lyrical Poems," 1886. As a prose-writer Canon Dixon's reputation is firmly established by his important work on the history of the Church of England—a learned and deeply interesting account of the Reformation from the Anglican stand-point. Whether recording the events that led up to the suppression of monasteries, or discussing the principles underlying the great religious movement of the 16th century, his style is always clear and vigorous, attaining in the weightier passages an appropriate elevation and distinction. His portraitures of the leading statesmen and ecclesiastics of the Tudor period manifest a singularly penetrative insight into character. This power is especially displayed in the sympathetic analysis that he gives of the character of his father in the last chapter of his life of that great preacher. Among the poets of the 19th century, Canon Dixon's position is unique. There is little trace in his work of the modern spirit. The religious sentiment of his poem, " The Holy Mother at the Cross," like that of Newman's "Pilgrim Queen," or Lanier's "Ballad of Trees and the Master," is purely mediæval. The effect of the quaint symbolism and archaic diction is somewhat bizarre, though not inartistic. In his presentment of religious ideas through the medium of sensuous images he resembles George Herbert, with whom he might sing :—

> When first my lines of heavenly joys made mention,
> Such was their lustre, they did so excel,
> That I sought out quaint words, and trim invention ;
> My thoughts began to burnish, sprout and swell,
> Curling with metaphors a plain intention,
> Decking the sense, as if it were to sell.

His longest and most ambitious poem is "Mano," a poetical history of a very picturesque period—the close of the 10th century, when Christendom believed that the end of the world was at hand. The story of the adventures of Mano—a Norman knight sent from Italy by Count Thurold to bring succours from home—as told by an old monk named Fergant, is written in the manner of a chronicle, and abounds in striking incidents. The metre adopted is the ' Terza Rima,' which is hardly suited to the genius of English poetry, and even in Canon Dixon's hands proves but a refractory instrument. Though the excessive use of obsolete words—many of them not worth reviving—is undoubtedly a blemish, yet we gladly pass over it in admiration of so much real poetry ot the highest order of excellence that Canon Dixon has given us.

W. W. Tomlinson.

IOANNA.

[From "Mano," pp. 174-5.]

Fair was Ioanna ever, I avise :
But I have heard of certain that e'en now
Her day of fairest beauty seemed to rise,
    When sorrow and long love had made her brow
Tenderly radiant, as the hanging skies
When the south wind moves every wingèd bough :
    Such o'er the changing wood the May cloud flies,
Soft, bright, and light, was she : one lovely fold,
That seemed to gather to grave thought her eyes,
    Of bygone sorrow and old anguish told,
One sweet contraction, delicate and fine :
But youth to bear love's burden still is bold :—
    Her looks were strong ('tis age that has to pine)
Her eyes were quick, and lightsome as of yore,

Her rounded cheeks as perfect as their line :
　　Her step was like the deer on ferny floor,
Her figure tall, and like a balanced tower,
Which from his place seems stepping evermore,
　　So wondrously 'tis fashioned through art's power.—
She had those years which bring perfectness,
And stood full blown, like to the lily's flower.

Ah ! now consider well in her fair dress
This lily of earth's field, her lovely head
Who rears amid the waste, companionless :
　　Wide open stands her heart : no secret dread
Bids her enfold her petals, like the rose,
Over her golden bosom undismayed.

Oh, undefended thus to friends or foes,
Shall she endure, then, in her perfect state,
Until she ripen to a timely close,
　　By the kind season carried to her date ;
Or must she tremble on her lofty stem
At the rough hand of sudden working Fate,
　　Scattering to the winds her diadem,
Brushing the tender gold-bloom from her heart ;
And die in her full hour, a perfect gem,
In whose fair essence all sweet things have part ?

HUMANITY.

There is a soul above the soul of each,
　　A mightier soul, which yet to each belongs :
There is a sound made of all human speech,
　　And numerous as the concourse of all songs :
And in that soul lives each, in each that soul,
　　Though all the ages are its lifetime vast ;
Each soul that dies, in its most sacred whole
　　Receiveth life that shall for ever last.

And thus for ever with a wider span
  Humanity o'erarches Time and Death ;
Man can elect the universal man,
  And live in life that ends not with his breath :
And gather glory that increases still,
Till Time his glass with Death's last dust shall fill.

THE HOLY MOTHER AT THE CROSS.

Of Mary's pains may now learn whose will,
  When she stood underneath the groaning tree,
Round which the true Vine clung : three hours the mill
  Of hours rolled round ; she saw in visions three
The shadows walking underneath the sun,
  And these seemed all so very faint to be,
That she could scarcely tell how each begun,
  And went its way, minuting each degree
That it existed on the dial stone :
  For drop by drop in wine unfalteringly,
Not stroke by stroke in blood, the three hours gone
  She seemed to see.

Three hours she stood beneath the cross ; it seemed
  To be a wondrous dial stone ; for while
Upon the two long arms the sunbeams teemed,
  So was the head-piece like a centre stile ;
Like to the dial where the judges sat
  Upon the grades, and the king crowned the pile,
In Zion town, that most miraculous plat
  On which the shadow backward did defile :
And now towards the third hour the sun enorme
  Dressed up all shadow to a bickering smile
I' the heat, and in its midst the form of form
  Lay like an isle.

Because that time so heavily beat and slow
   That fancy in each beat was come and gone;
Because that light went singing to and fro,
   A blissful song in every beam that shone;
Because that on the flesh a little tongue
   Instantly played, and spake in lurid tone;
Because that saintly shapes with harp and gong
   Told the three hours, whose telling made them one;
Half hid, involved in alternating beams,
   Half mute, they held the plectrum to the zone:
Therefore, as God her senses shield, it seems
   A dial stone.

Three hours she stood beside the cross; it seemed
   A splendid flower; for red dews on the edge
Stood dropping; petals doubly four she deemed
   Shot out like steel knives from the central wedge,
Which quadranted their perfect circle so
   As if four anthers should a vast flower hedge
Into four parts; and in its bosom, lo,
   The form lay, as the seed-heart holding pledge
Of future flowers; yea, in the midst was borne
   The head low drooped upon the swollen ledge
Of the torn breast; there was the ring of thorn;
   This flower was fledge.

Because her woe stood all about her now,
   No longer like a stream as ran the hour;
Because her cleft heart parted into two,
   No more a mill-wheel spinning to time's power;
Because all motion seemed to be suspense;
   Because one ray did other rays devour;
Because the sum of things rose o'er her sense,
   She standing 'neath its dome as in a bower;
Because from one thing all things seemed to spume,
   As from one mouth the fountain's hollow shower;
Therefore it seemed His and her own heart's bloom,
   A splendid flower.

Now it was finished; shrivelled were the leaves
   Of that pain-flower, and wasted all its bloom,
She felt what she had felt then ; as receives,
   When heaven is capable, the cloudy fume
The edge of the white garment of the moon,
   So felt she that she had received that doom :
And as an outer circle spins in tune,
   Born of the inner on the sky's wide room,
Thinner and wider, that doom's memories,
   Broken and thin and wild, began to come
As soon as this : St. John unwrapt his eyes,
   And led her home.

George Cotterell.

EORGE COTTERELL is a new-comer in the North of England. He removed to York from London in the autumn of 1887, to take the editorship of the *York Daily Herald.* Born in 1839, at Walsall, in Staffordshire, he adopted the profession of the law, and for some years practised as a solicitor, but yielding to the strong bent of his mind he eventually exchanged the law for literature. His first published compositions—consisting chiefly of poems on classical subjects—appeared in *Once a Week,* in the flourishing days of that periodical. At a later period Mr. Cotterell became an active contributor to the literary journals and the daily press, as well as to the magazines. A volume of poems by him was printed for private circulation in 1870. He is the author of a satire in verse, called "The Banquet," published anonymously by Messrs. W. Blackwood and Sons, in 1884, and a second edition of which appeared a few months later. A volume of Mr. Cotterell's miscellaneous poems is shortly to be published, under the title of "Yesterdays and To-Day." Professor Dowden says of Mr. Cotterell's poems :—" They seem to me to be remarkably free from the vice of being manufactured poetry. They seem rather the overflow of true feeling through an imagination that can interpret the feeling. And the general impression they leave is that of a many-sided nature, in which external beauty and humanity, public events, and private joys and sorrows find a place."

WILLIAM ANDREWS.

ENGLAND AND GREECE.

I.

Queen, O Queen of the Sea !
Mighty by hearts that are steadfast and ships that are
    strong,
England ! O hater of wrong !
This thing that thou doest is all unworthy of thee :
Never hath England fettered the brave and the free ;
Never till Egypt groaned, and her people uprose,
Did fleet of thine, that had scattered thy proudest foes,

Strike at the weak and crush them—never till then !
Penance be thine, O mother of nations and men,
Shame for that tyrannous thing thou didst amiss,
But let not thy penance be this.

II.

What name stands fairest by thine ?
What fount hath fed thee with wisdom and made thee bold—
What name but Greece?　And did her lore divine
Give thee no higher courage than to spurn
The lessons thou didst learn ?
Great England, nurtured by that Greece of old,
Is it, then, nought to thee
That Moslem banners wave in Thessaly ?
That vales made lovelier by Apollo's face,
And hills that were the high gods' dwelling-place,
That these are Greek no more, and glad no more,
But from Olympus to the Ionian Sea
Are darkened by disaster and made sore
By tyranny and by treachery?
Nay, for though glory of arms endure but a day,
And the glory of pride be quenched, and of beauty cease,
Her gods and her greatness are glories that pass not away—
Immortal Greece !

III.

Out of the depths she cried to thee, then,
When the hordes of the Crescent were drawn afar
For the Moslem's war,
And thine heart went out to her once again ;
Thy pledges were fair, thy words were brave,
And cheered by these she strove no more with fate,
But waited, nothing loth to wait,
Certain that thou at last wouldst help and save.

IV.

At last ! and there did come at last a time
When thou couldst help her, when a word from thee

Had made her all that she had hoped to be ;
Not the proud mistress of her olden prime,
The Greece of Marathon and Thermopylæ;
But once again a country, once again
The ruler of her lands from sea to sea,
The mother of one people brave and free,
The Greece of Byron's dream and Shelley's strain.

V.

That time hath been ; 'tis gone ; thou lett'st it go.
Now, rashly prodigal of thy ships of war,
With bigger cannon than carried Trafalgar,
Thou settest thyself again to overthrow
A helpless city, a land that looked to thee,
A little loyal land that claims its own.
Beware ! beware ! for the record shall all be known ;
Thou wert great, so great, how great ! in the ages gone—
Let the sons of thy sons deem thee great in the ages to be !

IN THE TWILIGHT.

Far off ? Not far away
    Lies that fair land ;
Shut from the curious gaze by day,
    Hidden, but close at hand :—
Let us seek it who may.

Lie by me and hold me, sweet,
    Clasp arms and sink ;
There needs no weariness of the feet,
    Neither to toil nor think ;
Almost the pulse may cease to beat.

Eyes made dim, and breathing low,
    Hand locked in hand,
Goodly the visions that come and go,
    Glimpses of that land,
Fairer than the eyes can know.

Is it not a land like ours ?
    Nay, much more fair ;
Sweeter flowers than earthly flowers
    Shed their fragrance there,
Fade not with the passing hours.

Soft are all the airs that blow,
    Breathing of love ;
Dreamily soft the vales below,
    The skies above,
And all the murmuring streams that flow.

No sorrow is there, no sin,
    Nor any snare ;
And death cannot enter in,
    That comes with care,
But rest that is sweet to win.

Hunger, nor thirst, nor tears,
    Age, nor its fruit ;
But youth grown younger with years,
    And living at root
With love that lives and endears.

There are daughters of beauty, the host
    Of nymphs of old time,
All the loves of the poets who boast
    Of their loves in their rhyme—
Loves won, and the sadder loves lost.

Fair, passionless creatures of thought,
    Most fair, most calm ;
The joy of whose beauty has brought
    To the soul its own balm ;
Not desire that cometh to nought.

There are dreams that were dreamed long ago,
    Unrealized still ;
Though the things that the dreamers foreknow
    The years shall fulfil,
The fleet years and slow.

Dreams, memories, hopes that were bright,
    And hearts that are young;
All the stars and the glories of night,
    All the glories of song;
In that dear land of delight.

Wilt thou seek that land then, sweet?
    Yea, love, with thee ;
Fleet, as thy soul's wings are fleet,
    Shall our passage be :
Soft, on wings of noiseless beat.

Bid my wings with thine expand ;
    So may we glide
Into the stillness of that land,
    Lovingly side by side,
Hopefully hand in hand.

A CHILD'S THOUGHT.

I lie awake in my bed,
    When you think I am fast asleep,
With the coverlet over my head,
    But a fold through which I may peep ;
And I peep sometimes as I lie,
    And out through the window I see
A little twinkling star in the sky,
    Winking and peeping at me.

A star, if you call it a star,
   For it seems no more than a spark,
And I cannot think that it shines so far
   Through all the air and the dark;
But if it be what you say,
   Then would I had wings to fly—
Perhaps I could go and come in a day
   The nearest way through the sky.

And what if I never came back?
   Well, Heaven, you say, is up there,
And the nights down here are dreary and black,
   While the stars are white and fair:
And here there are tasks to be done,
   And endless lessons to learn—
But you sometimes would miss me for one,
   And I think I should want to return.

Alfred Lishman.

LFRED LISHMAN is a native of Leeds, and was born June 28th, 1854. His father, Mr. Matthew Lishman, was a notable man, and in his earlier manhood followed the same trade as Hugh Miller, the famous man of letters and science, namely that of a stonemason. Mr. Lishman had a thirst for learning, and gained an unusually competent knowledge of classics and mathematics. His scholarlike tastes and attainments caused him to give up the work of the artisan and enter into the scholastic profession. In his new calling he was successful, and for the last seventeen years of his life occupied the position of head master of the Fockerby Grammar School. His wife was a Miss Walker, a member of a well-known yeoman family of Wharfedale. He enjoyed the close friendship of some well-known men, and amongst the number the Rev. Robert Collyer, "the poet preacher of America." Mr. Matthew Lishman died on June 7th, 1885.

Alfred Lishman received his earlier education under his father, and was intended for the university, but eventually his plans were changed, and at the age of sixteen he proceeded to Middlesboro'-on-Tees, as a teacher and student in an educational establishment conducted by a learned gentleman named W. Grieve, LL.D., of Trinity College, Dublin. Here he made excellent progress and passed the Senior Local Examination at the Durham University, gaining the title of Literate of Durham University. He next entered the York Training College for Teachers, and had a successful career, closing with obtaining a certificate of the First Division. From his boyhood he has had a great love for literature, and from his earliest years has enjoyed the pleasures of authorcraft. At college he conducted the "College Magazine," and has since contributed to many publications, including the well conducted columns of the *Leeds Mercury Weekly Supplement.* It is in the latter journal that his best work has appeared, and one of his poems in it was largely quoted and much admired by competent critics, namely, "Ye Labourers of England," which we reproduce. His published poems are by no means numerous, but all the work of a true poet, and much above the verses that usually fill the Poets' Corner of the newspaper press and the pages of popular periodicals. We are confident that he will win a high place in the ranks of the leading poets of the North Country.

Mr. Lishman has held three schools under Government, and on the death of his father he succeeded him as head Master of the Fockerby Grammar School. In addition to his duties as a teacher he fills the important offices of Clerk to the Drainage Commission, and of two School Boards of his district.

His amusements are chiefly literary in their character, consisting of writing and studying the works of the master minds of his own and other lands which are to be found on the shelves of his library.

Mr. Lishman, shortly after finishing his training at college, married the daughter of the late Mr. W. H. Monkman, solicitor, of York.

WILLIAM ANDREWS.

GLENCOE.

With eye undimmed and stalwart form
MacIan breasts the raging storm,
    An aged chieftain he.
The wintry blast with might and main
Essays to stay his course in vain,
Clan Campbell's castle keep to gain
    He presses steadfastly.

Full well the hoary warrior knows
Submission to his haughty foes
    Alone can safety bring;
And he whose eye with fervour bright,
Erst gleamed the foremost in the fight,
Must swear before to-morrow's light
    To serve an alien King.

" Campbell," said he, " with heavy heart
I come to play a recreant part,
    A nobler cause to rue ;
Far from my misty mountain home,
Twice twenty tedious miles I roam,
To save my 'minished clan I come
    To swear allegiance true."

" Alas ! the day of grace is past,
Why tarried thou, Glencoe, the last
    Thy tardy vow to take ;
Argyle is mad with hate and scorn,
Lord Stair a fearful oath hath sworn,
Ye mountain wolves, your cubs forlorn
    Shall perish in your lair."

That eye inured to martial deeds,
With unaccustomed tear now pleads
  His helpless tribe to save.
" Whoe'er," said he, " in wild Glencoe
Against the King his blade shall draw,
Shall meet McIan's self as foe ;
  The Glen shall be his grave."

With pity moved, Sir Colin said—
" Tho' tardily thy vow be paid,
  The King accepts thy plea.
Henceforth, McIan of the Glen,
Thyself, thy bairns, thy hardy men,
Secure may roam o'er moor and fen,
  O'er mount and vale and sea."

And now the chieftain turns his face
Towards the hamlets of his race ;
  The vale of frequent fears,
Where tardy spring doth visit last,
Where winter blows its chillest blast,
Where autumn's mistiest cloak is cast—
  'Tis called the " Glen of Tears."

Oh ! fiercely blows the blinding storm,
As o'er the mountain's awful form
  The old man wends his way.
Sad omens of disaster seem
The raven croaking by the stream,
The lonely eagle's piercing scream,
  The fen's delusive ray.

Secure at length the chieftain trod
The heather of his native sod ;
  Nor sought he yet to rest ;
For round his form the clansmen drew
With eager love their chief to view,
And soon the welcome tidings knew—
  The safety of their nest !

But hark! the tramp of armed men
Is heard adown the lonely glen—
   The soldiers of the King!
" We come," cried they, " this clan to greet,
McIan's friends as friends to meet;
No harm to thee or thine we seek;
   But peace and love we bring."

For full twelve days and nights they stay,
And feast the fleeting hours away;
   No stinted welcome there!
And vows of amity are made,
The plighted cup to friendship paid,
And hand to hand in kindness laid
   O'er hospitable fare.

But oh! McIan's dreams are sad;
And dismal thoughts and omens bad
   Oppress his weary brain.
He nightly feels unwonted fears,
He nightly sheds unwonted tears,
And dismal sounds afflict his ears
   With unaccustomed pain.

One awful morn the guests arose
To hurl their unsuspecting foes
   To their appointed doom.
Not mine the pen to trace aright
The horrors of that fearful sight—
The sun of heaven had veiled its light
   In melancholy gloom.

The palsied grandsire in his bed
Before his slayers bowed his head,
   Nor 'scaped the cruel blow.
The mother to her heaving breast
In vain her clinging infant pressed—
The dagger of her cherished guest
   Laid babe and mother low!

Strong men in agonising rage,
Unarmed, a vain resistance wage
    Against the recreant foe;
And 'ere MacIan's foot had trod
His threshold, on th' encrimsoned sod
His soul was sent to meet his God—
    He died without a blow.

'Tis done! That morning's work is o'er,
And on the bleak and silent moor
    The bloated ravens feed.
But in that ruin stricken vale
The bard shall chant the mournful tale,
Nor shall successive ages fail
    To curse the ruthless deed.

YE LABOURERS OF ENGLAND.

Ye labourers of England!
    Ye children of the soil!
With ready skill, and steadfast will,
    How patiently ye toil!
'Tis yours, with yellow waving corn
    To make the landscape shine,
To pluck the metals from their home,
    And tempt the dismal mine.

Ye labourers of England
    Who make our country great;
With fruitful vales and pleasant dales
    Who deck the brave old state;
Whose gallant hearts and sinewy hands
    Beneath far distant skies
Still raise new homes, still till new lands
    And bid new England rise.

Ye labourers of England
  Who make our country wise,
Whose sons though born to lots forlorn
  To highest honours rise ;
The shining talents of your race
  On countless pages glow,
Comes genius from a lowly place,
  Comes poesy from the plough.

Ye labourers of England
  Who make your country brave,
Your fathers' dust, in quarrel just,
  Filled many a nameless grave ;
And how they fought, those stalwart men,
  The breath of fame attests ;
The bulwarks of our country then
  Were British workmen's breasts.

Ye labourers of England,
  Your grateful country's pride,
Long may the great, who rule the state,
  Retain you by their side ;
Your homely faith, your hardy life,
  And simple valour prove
That England ne'er need fear the strife
  With you to guard and love.

INTEGRITY.

Hast thou against grim poverty
  A silent fight sustained ?
Hast borne thy evil fortunes here
  With heart and hands unstained ?
And hast thou ever spurned the thought,
  By servile arts to stand,
Thy simple manhood guiding thee ?
  Then let me grasp thy hand.

Dost thou, by secret pity moved,
　Bestow an alms by stealth?
In light of day dost thou refuse
　To cringe to upstart wealth?
Then poor thou art and poor shalt be,
　Small pelf at thy command!
But thou hast riches of the heart
　So let me grasp thy hand.

Canst thou for thine integrity
　A healthy motive prove?
Hast thou done the right because 'tis right,
　Unswayed by fear or love?
Then hast thou missed thy meed of praise
　E'en from the good.　Yet stand,
That I may claim thee as a friend,
　And let me grasp thy hand.

Canst thou admire the perfum'd rose
　Nor pluck it from its stem?
Dost value all created things
　And love thy fellow men?
Canst thou forbear thy just revenge,
　Thy neighbours' wrongs withstand?
Then I would brave all human ills
　To grasp thee by the hand.

And hast thou real humility
　Thy virtues to enshrine?
Then hath the world true benefit
　From every act of thine;
Part of thyself each deed remains,
　And beacon-like will stand
To guide us to thy destined home;
　There let me grasp thy hand.

Richard Abbot.

ICHARD ABBOT was born at Burton, in Westmoreland, in 1818. The Lancaster and Kendal Canal was being extended to Tewit Field at that time, and the poet's father was a sub-contractor on the works. Losing that best of guides, a mother, when he was only three years old, he was left to the rugged care of a parent whose life had been moulded by the hardest toil with the rudest class of men as associates. At the age of four he was sent to what was known until only recent years as an Old Dame School. His father had removed to the borders of Shap Fell, and later, pursuing his shifting avocation, he settled at Galgate, near Lancaster; shortly afterwards, however, they were stationed at Ingleton, where the poet was kept at school until the age of eleven. His father having married again and added farming to his other occupation, Richard became his shepherd on the slopes of Ingleborough. Some years later he came further north, working in the construction of railways in Scotland and elsewhere. For the past twenty-three years or so Mr. Abbot has managed the extensive limestone quarries at Forcett, between Darlington and Richmond.

In 1876, Mr. Abbot issued his first volume of verse with the title of "War, and other Poems," and again in 1879, he published "The Pen, the Press, and the Sword."

Byronic in structure, chiefly; massive and thundering in execution, his verse rings of the rocks and seems to beat time to the music of hammer and pick. He is quaint and double-edged in humour, rasping and peppery, almost fierce, in satire; gentle and soft as early motherhood in pathos and pity and love. He still resides in the beautiful Forcett dale, white and straight and seventy, an oak with the top leaves frost-nipt.

JOHN ROWELL-WALLER.

THE SONG OF INGLETON BELLS.

Come listen ye people, the song from the steeple,
  Dingle-ding, dingle-ding, dingle-ding, ding.
A spirit is singing and through the bells ringing,
  Dingle-ding, dingle-ding, dingle-ding, ding.
    " Hearken the voice of me ;
    " Come and acknowledge me ;
    " Come and rejoice with me ;
    " Come and made holy be."

Through the sweet chiming of Ingleton bells,
    Musical bells,
Through the sweet chiming of Ingleton bells.

Oh! God of the mountains!
    Oh! God of the dales!
Thou fountain of fountains
    Who spread out the vales,—
Established the caverns those archives of Thine,
    Where truth has been stored for all ages to come;
Permit me to draw, as from heavenly mine,
    A small precious portion my soul to illume.
Dingle-ding, dingle-ding, dingle-ding, ding,
    Musical Ingleton, Ingleton bells,
Hark! 'tis the music of Ingleton bells!

Oh! fountain of beauty, of music and song!—
The might of the mighty—the strength of the strong,—
Who raised up the hills, made the rivers to flow
Through the land for the use of Thy creatures below,—
Inspire me, I pray Thee, to sing with the bells
Whose music this moment resounds through the dells;
Listen the bells! Ingleton bells!
The music is charming, its influence warning,
It strengthens your souls as onward it rolls,
Far up the valley and down through the dale
Where it dies in the distance like Philomel's wail.
Dingle-ding, dingle-ding, dingle-ding, ding.
Musical Ingleton, Ingleton bells,
Hark to the music of Ingleton bells!

Come, come do you hear it?—
    The voice of the spirit—
" Come old men and women;
    Come young men and maidens."
The bells softly ringing
    With sweet mournful cadence;

Come beautiful children,
  With bloom on your faces,
  And heavenly graces.
(Your numbers bewild'ring.)

  Approach ye the altar,
  Come, come, do not falter,
The bells are inviting, the spirit inditing
  The song of the bells.
  Ingleton bells—sweetest of bells
    Heard on the hills,
    Heard on the fells,
    Heard by the rills,
    And heard in the dells,
  Beautiful, musical, Ingleton bells.
Oh! come from the mountains,
  And come from the valleys.
Dingle-ding, dingle-ding, dingle-ding, ding.
  Come ye by the fountains,
    From lanes, streets and alleys,
Come at the calling of Ingleton bells.
  Come, come with decorum, and with the bells sing,
    Come, ye from the woodlands,
    And ye by the river;
    Come birds from the cloudland
      Sing praises for ever,—
Sing praises for ever with Ingleton bells,
    Sweet Ingleton bells,
A song to the Saviour through Ingleton bells!

O, TURN ASIDE THY LOVING EYES.

O, turn aside thy loving eyes,
  They shoot into my very soul;
'Tis not thy wish to victimize,
  But now my heart is past control.

Is this a modern paradise?
  Art thou life's glorious, mystic tree?
O, turn aside thy loving eyes,
  Nor bend their powerful light on me.

O, turn aside thy loving eyes,
  Who can resist their influence?
Their darts my utmost power defies,
  They wound my frail heart past defence.
I fear thou never can be mine,
  Then why should I but wear love's chain?
A slave unto thy eyes divine!
  Nay! rather kill me with disdain.

O, turn aside thy loving eyes,
  Or teach them some repulsive art;
Teach me thy beauty to despise,
  And how we may be pleased to part.
Alas! it is not in thy power,
  Thou art attraction all in all,
And I must, till my latest hour,
  Before thy glorious image fall.

FADING BEAUTY.

Fading beauty, bending o'er thee,
  Here before high heaven I swear,
Doubt me not, love, I adore thee,
  Thou art still my joy and care.
Still devoted and unchanging,
  Through all change my heart shall be,
Nor, through all my fancies ranging
  Can it rest on aught but thee.

Fading beauty! nay, not fading,
　'Tis but change of loveliness,
And my heart needs no persuading,
　To believe thy charms no less.
True, the rose is turning whiter,
　True, thy locks are silvery now,
But thy loving eyes, once brighter,
　Still with love to me o'erflow.

Fading beauty! still unfaded,
　Still the charms of riper years
Keep the light of love unshaded,
　While thy beauty brighter wears;
And, though time at length succeed in
　Leading captive thee, my bride,
Shall not I the same path tread in,
　Linked for ever by thy side?

William Billington.

ILLIAM BILLINGTON, who is colloquially known in Lancashire as "The Blackburn Poet," was the son of a man who discharged the important function of road contractor, and at the same time, to eke out his livelihood, worked at home both at basket-making and hand-loom weaving. His "cottage was a thatched one," and situated in the quaint, old-world hamlet of Samlesbury, midway between Blackburn and Preston. Here William first saw the light some sixty-two years ago. He was the eldest of three brothers. The father died when William was seven or eight years old, and left the family, as the poet puts it, to "scrat on as they could." William got very little schooling and at an early age went to a neighbouring mill to learn throstle spinning. But he had a share of the "imperishable stuff of genius" in him, and having learned to read, assiduously applied himself to studies of various kinds. The family removed to Blackburn when he was fourteen, and while working first at one mill and then at another, he made considerable progress in self-education. He especially prided himself on being a good grammarian, and at a later stage of his life taught evening classes of young men in the rules of syntax. He also early manifested a disposition to cultivate the Muses, and before he was twenty-one began to contribute verses to a local journal. Having by his steadiness raised himself to the better paid work of taper in a cotton mill, he was able to save sufficient money to commence business as a publican. Not a very literary calling, certainly, but his house, the Nag's Head, Northgate, Blackburn, became the resort of such *literati* as Blackburn could boast. Subsequently he removed to another house, which he called the "Poet's Corner." He was a frequent contributor both of verse and prose dialect sketches to Lancashire journals, and in 1861 published his first volume of poems, entitling it "Sheen and Shade." This met with a favourable reception, and was noticed in a highly complimentary way by many journals. In September, 1883, he published a second volume of verse, "Lancashire Songs, Poems, and Sketches." But he did not live long to enjoy whatever fruits he might have reaped from this book, for on January 3rd, 1884, in his 57th year, he fell a victim to bronchitis, an old enemy, from which he had suffered much all that winter. He was twice married. His first partner proved a suitable helpmate to him, and two children were the issue of the union, whom he describes in one of his poems as "a boy and a girl, a rose and a lily, a pink and a pearl." His second matrimonial venture was not a happy one. Some idea of Billington's political views may be gathered from the fact that he called the only child whom his second wife bore him, John Bright Billington. During the later years of his life Billington suffered from vicissitudes of fortune and he died in comparative poverty. He was buried in Blackburn Cemetery, and a simple monument was erected over the spot by local admirers. Much of his verse is in the Lancashire dialect, which he wrote very fluently, but his productions in orthodox English also contain some fine word painting. His poetry has been compared to that of John Critchley Prince; in some respects Billington showed more poetic power than that writer, though his verse lacked artistic finish. He wrote both descriptive and introspective pieces, some of the latter dealing with his own theological doubts and difficulties.

JESSE QUAIL.

THE SINGER.

A singer there dwelt in a city of yore—
  A populous city and proud !
And his spirit was love, and his speech lit with lore,
But, bashful and timid, he trembled before
    The gaze of the gaping crowd ;
And he sang like a seraph at heaven's blue door,
And his aim and his hope were to sing and to soar
    Like a lark in the heart of a cloud.

That city grew rich with the sound of his praise,
    And the wealthy, soon, everyone
Seemed hanging with rapture and love on his lays,
And would wish him God speed, ever fanning the blaze
    Of his fame, which so brightly had shone ;
And they called him *Our* singer and poet always,
Little deeming how fleeting and few were his days,
    And how soon would the singer be gone.

He wove in his life with the woof of his lay,
    And that *good* city gave him its breath,—
Its emptiest homage, the poet's sure pay ;
From its loftiest spire, in the sun's golden ray,
    He suspended an evergreen wreath,
Far out of the reach of those sleepless and gay
Destroyers, Old Time and his kinsman, Decay,
    And too high for the arrows of Death !

One morning, as wont, when the world had awoke,
  And the people were prying for news,
The blue, bending heavens were dimmed by the smoke
Which in dark wreathing columns rose threatening to choke
  .The pure air from a forest of flues ;
On the ear of that city a rumour there broke,
Like the autumn wind sighing through forests of oak,
  'Twas the death of that son of the Muse.

    ✵   ✵

That city *then* draped it in mourning most deep,
  And said " Since our light, which had shone,
Like a midnight lamp from a castled steep,
For the guidance of travellers bound by that keep,
  Through the desert where path there is none,
Hath faded too soon, it is meet we should weep,
For, alas ! many ages may over us sweep
  Nor behold such a Luminous One !

" Our bard was our brightest and daintiest dower,
  But the richest robes soonest will soil !
O that we had but the magical power
To rekindle our lamp, even but for *one hour*,
  Whatever the cost of the toil !
It should flame on the top of our regalest tower,
Secure from the wind, from the wintry shower,
  And the storm, nor be stinted of *oil.*"

Thus ever the Christ hath been crucified,
  Our chalice of joy ever spilt !
Our hearts are with Evil so strongly allied,
Until they thought the Curtains of Death are descried
  Our Gods must be branded with guilt !
The grave yawns before thee, deep-throated and wide,
Sweet poet, enthroned on the heavenward side
  Sitteth Fame : freely choose which thou wilt.

FRAUD : THE EVIL OF THE AGE.

With what unutterable shame and scorn,
    Humiliation and indignant rage,
The bosom of the honest man is torn,
    Who contemplates the evils of this age—
Light weights, short measures, packing, paint and gloss—
One half the world kept by the other's loss—
    Chicane, cheating, bankruptcy, liquidation,
Clayed-cloth, damped yarn, short counts, and wasted weft.
With antiseptic's scientific theft—
    All trades worm-eaten by adulteration !
What folly—what short sightedness—what sin—
Enough to make the very Devil grin !
By cheating, one may win some paltry pelf ;
But, as a whole, the World can only cheat itself.

Oh ! Commerce, thou hast much to answer for,
    Cold, callous King of Trade's unconscion'd mart ;
No bolt of Jove, no hammer-stroke of Thor,
    Could singe or dint thy adamantine heart ;
    From morals, from religion far apart,
Thy God is Gold, thy Gospel selfish gain,
Thy bastard twins, pale Poverty and Pain,
    Foul imps by thee begotten upon Fraud,
Infest our cities, fill our cots, and fain
    Would shrink from our existence, or have thawed
The heart of Avarice, blocking Pity's way !
When rings and corners—swindling guilds- hold sway—
When vices rise which pulpits fail to reach,
The poet, not the parson, then must claim to preach.

CAPITAL AND LABOUR.

Once Capital and Labour pulled
   Together, both one way;
Till one demanded profit and
   The other wanted pay;
The point to be arrived at was—
   That each should have his share.
But Capital was master and
   Would not divide things fair.

Then Labour yoked with Union
   And gathered greater strength,
And wrestled long with Capital
   And won his rights at length.
The world became much wiser then,
   And Wealth obtained respect,
For Work had gained his guerdon and
   Came forth with soul erect.

Joseph Readman.

HIS widely known contributor to the Northern press is a native of Ripon, and was born on the 16th February, 1860. He was educated at the famous Grammar School of his native city. From boyhood he had a taste for literature and wrote many poems and sketches, but it was not until 1878 that he submitted to an editor any of his productions. Since that time he has contributed very freely to the press, and in 1884, a volume of his verse was issued by Heavisides and Son, Stockton-on-Tees, under the title of "Sunbeams and Shadows of Life, and other Poems." It contains many pleasing verses and was favourably received. Mr. Readman is engaged in business at Stockton-on-Tees, and for recreation takes a keen delight in authorship.

WILLIAM ANDREWS.

SHAROW BELLS.*

The day's turmoil is ended,
　The tranquil eve hath come—
Each son of toil hath wended
　His way to peaceful home,
As Luna in the starry sky
　Sends down her fairy light,
To lend a charm to even's calm
　From out her fretted height.

The old Yore sings in cadence sweet,
　As o'er wide pebbly bed
He flows, his lover Skell† to meet—
　Long centuries since they wed;
Across the water softly floats
　The chimes of Sharow's bells,
And music near, enslaves the ear
　As on the breeze it swells.

* The sound of these bells, floating as it does across the river Yore to Ripon, is heard to great advantage on a still night.

† The river Skell flows into the Yore about half a mile from Ripon.

The heart is thronged with gladness,
The mind hath joy anew,
No ling'ring touch of sadness
Doth course the senses through,
As on this night, when all is calm,
O'er Ripon city floats
The music soft, kind zephyrs waft
From Sharow's mellow throats.

Long years have flown since last I heard
Those simple village chimes,
Yet often is my memory stirred
With those dear by-gone times,
When like as from some fairy realm
The silvery voices o'er,
All touched with glee, with notes so free,
Flew 'cross the limpid Yore.

AWAKENED MEMORIES.

I sing of a charm which to music is wedded,
That holds o'er the feelings a magical sway.
A power quite resistless to mem'ries embedded
With records of actions in years far away.

Though memory perchance will e'en slumber for years,
Yet cometh the time when its powers will awake,
Bringing back to the mind's eye past pleasures and fears,
Illumed by the vividness fancy can make.

An air it is simply, with concord unblended,
Possesses the spell of some magical thing,
Unlocking the feelings from which are descended
The joys and the sorrows that unto men cling.

How sweet are the moments when fondly surveying
    Those early impressions of life's rapid stream,
That crowd on the senses, fresh gladness conveying,
    Divine as the workings of youth's brightest dream.

By this tend'rest of powers the veil o'er Time's hollow
    Seems lifted again to our wondering gaze,
And old friends and faces then quickly do follow
    The dictates of Fancy's mysterious ways.

Sweet are the memories of those who no longer
    Do mingle their cares with the rest of mankind;
Though Death hath divided—affection is stronger—
    More deepened the pathos that lingers behind.

Rev. Richard Abbay, M.A.

HE Rev. RICHARD ABBAY is a true Yorkshire poet. He is the son of Thomas and Elizabeth Abbay, and was born in the parish of Aldborough, in the West Riding (the Isurium of the Romans), on the 11th February, 1844. His education proper, that is the scholastic part of it, may be said to have begun at St. Peter's School, York, and since entering that ancient foundation, he has gone on taking degree after degree, and winning distinction after distinction. Here are some of his achievements. At St. Peter's he obtained a Free Scholarship, 1858, and a Foundation Scholarship, 1861 ; Open Scholarship at Exeter College, Oxford, 1863 ; First Class Mathematics, 1865 ; Proxine Accessit, University Mathematical Scholarship, 1886 ; First Class Final Mathematical Examination, 1867 ; B.A., 1867 ; Lecturer and Demonstrator in Natural Science, King's College, London, 1868 ; Elected to Fellowship in Natural Science, Wadham College, Oxford, open to both Universities, 1868 ; M.A., 1869. He has been somewhat of an athlete, having played two seasons in his college eleven, and won several prizes in his college sports.

After all these achievements, it is not surprising to find that Mr. Abbay is able to write M.A., F.R.A.S, and other capital dignities after his name. He has been a great traveller, and has left useful records of his observation and research in the numerous communications made by him to the several societies and to periodical literature both abroad and at home. His papers, embracing an extremely wide range of topics in Botany, Geology, Astronomy, Meteorology and other scientific fields, relate chiefly to matters of interest in the various countries visited by him. It is chiefly as a poet, however, that we are now concerned to consider him, rather than with his scientific researches in New Caledonia, Ceylon, Java, Australia, New Zealand, and California.

His poetical works are contained in a volume of 340 pages, 270 of which are occupied with a narrative poem in octosyllabic verse, entitled " The Castle of Knaresburgh." This poem therefore is Mr. Abbay's *opus magnum*, and besides it we have in the volume a number of short poems of a more reflective kind, and a legendary rhyme entitled " The White Mare of Whitestone Cliff." " The Castle of Knaresburgh " is spirited throughout, and often rises into passages which have the true poetic ring. Mr. Abbay seems to have an almost Homeric fondness for battle scenes, and urges his heroes to the conflict with all the enthusiastic energy of a poetic major-general. Amongst his miscellaneous poems are some exquisitely tender things, notably, " The Dying Naturalist," " Love," " Life and Death," &c. Mr. Abbay's volume is eminently enjoyable throughout, and that is what we cannot say of many volumes of verse of so large a size. Messrs. Kegan Paul, Trench & Co., are the publishers of Mr. Abbay's work, which merits a place in every Yorkshire library.

GEORGE LANCASTER.

TEMPLUM VENERIS.

[Claude.]

Oh, for the touch of that deft hand which drew
This stately splendour on the Baian shore,
The dreamy landscape and the waters blue
With azure skies for ever vaulted o'er,
The wealth of drowsy foliage and the store
Of shadows cool, beneath tall, slumb'rous trees,
The sunlit cliffs on distant mountains hoar,
The clouds above, so light and full of ease,
And clear air resonant with summer melodies.

Here slowly wends, amid the ivies cool,
The glad procession, tuneful, laurel-crowned ;
And two fair suppliants for the sweet control
Of love half recognised and half disowned,
On timid feet with doves and fruits are bound
To pay the tribute Love demands from all,
Peasant or prince, in lofty palace found ;
Love met them, in a guise ethereal,
And threw around their breasts his soft yet ruthless thrall.

There, on the marble steps, the wreathed faun
Holds drowsy panthers in his listless thrall ;
And, bearing wands with vine leaves deckt at dawn,
The eager suitors mount unto the hall,
Nor heed the pipes that for their worship call ;
And on the terrace stand the shrine of Love,
And white-robed priests with praises musical
As spring-time birds within the neighbouring grove,
While Venus and her boy bend lovingly above.

Oh, for that ear to hear, that eye to see
The spirits, moving in the summer air,
To know that gladness such as theirs can be,
And sift the sadness from our landscape fair,

And in all lovely things to have our share ;
With ear attuned unto a wakeful eye
To hear the music of the evening star
And all earth's glad and various minstrelsy ;
Young lives were always ours, and summer ever by.

THE DYING NATURALIST.

I care not for splendours that man can achieve,
  The pomp and the pageant of power ;
Their glitter may dazzle, it does not deceive,
It cannot console, it will not relieve
  My sadness of heart for an hour.

I heed not the praise and the plaudits of men,
  The honours that fame can bestow ;
They ravish the heart that is honest, and when
We dream we are blest as immortals, oh, then
  They satiate, sadden, and go.

Oh, give me the joy of unclouded skies,
  The smiles and the raptures of earth,
When she wakes from her sleep in a glad surprise,
And, uplifting her myriad of laughing eyes,
  She bursts into innocent mirth.

Oh, give me the hope of the lengthening day,
  The childhood and youthtide of flowers,
The hawthorn bud on the drooping spray,
Ere the bloom is touched with its soft decay,
  And the sombre hue that is ours.

Let me watch the pale primrose unfolding its bloom,
  Let me swoon in the violet's breath ;
They can lure my heart from its pensive gloom,
My immature hope from its early tomb,
  And my love from its lingering death.

Let me list till my fancy can hear the sweet strains
    They sing to each other whilst growing ;
They will soothe me to rest from my desolate pains,
Till my spirit shall burst from its shadowy chains
    With joy of their song overflowing.

Oh, give me the joy and the sadness of earth,
    The sunlight and shadows I love,
When the flow'rets come to a timely birth,
And the summer falls with its sweet young mirth
    From the overfull skies above.

ADVICE.

Gan yam, gan yam, ma bonnie lass,
Thoo mawn't be oot alaane ;
There's mony a man 'll deea tha wrang,
They've nowt bud hearts o' staane.

Gan yam, gan yam, ma bonnie lass,
Ah'l see tha doon to 't dike ;
There's waästril Tom, Will Louse-i'-t-heft *
An' hauf a scoor o' sike.

Gan yam, gan yam, ma bonnie lass,
Wharl thoo's an honest naame ;
They've bonnie wods an' bonnie deeds,
An' then there's nowt bud shaame.

Gan yam, gan yam, ma bonnie lass,
Thoo mawnt come here an' stot ; †
Thee faather'd lowp fra oot his graave
If owt sud deea tha hot. ‡

Ah will gan yam, at yance, Ah will,
Thoo's better nor a brudder ;
There's naan sall saay, Ah yance gat wrang ;
Ah'l bide at yam wi' mudder.

* Loose in the haft—a worthless, unreliable fellow.
† Walk jauntily.   ‡ Hurt.

Thomas Burns.

HOMAS BURNS was born on the 15th September, 1848, at Cessford, a farm situated in the parish of Eckford, Roxburghshire. He was sent to the parish school of that place at the age of five, and after four years of school life he was compelled by a hard necessity to grapple with the stern realities of life, his mother being widowed some time previously. At the age of thirteen he crossed the Border to Ford, Northumberland, being hired to farm work by Mr. Elliott of that place. Very bright and grateful are his recollections of this good farmer and his family, for here he was brought under such religious influences as tended not a little to mould his after life, and to produce in him those trustful Christian traits that well up to the surface of everything he has written. In the early part of 1876, tired of and dispirited with the monotonous drudgery of agriculture, he sought to extricate himself by joining the police force at Newcastle-on-Tyne. Only three years, however, did he remain in that position, when he was appointed to an office in connection with the School Board, which post he yet occupies. Many of his poems have appeared from time to time in the newspapers of the Borderland during the past few years; it was not, however, until the autumn of 1887 that he ventured into publicity in anything like substantial form. This was the red-letter period of an uneventful life, the publication of his first volume of verse with the title of "Chimes from Nature." It includes noble sentiment vigorously expressed, and much sweet and pure sympathy purely and sweetly spoken.

JOHN ROWELL WALLER.

COME, SING A SONG TO ME, MY LOVE.

Come, sing a song to me, my love,
    Thou knowest how I long,
Resume thy harp again and give
    Another melting song.
I've listened oft with secret joy,
    And half-veil'd swimming eyes.
Unto the soaring minstrel boy
    Who sings with such surprise.

Men shall adore thee, I contend,
   Of every creed and clime,
And forth thy name on history send
   Throughout the course of time ;
The wise in speech, in sense, and mind,
   The soldier, sage, and priest,
King, prophet, hero, bard, will find
   Within thy lays a feast.

The old, the young, the rich the poor,
   Coy maiden, and strong youth,
Shall draw sweet pleasure from thy store,
   And praise its flavoured truth.
When Time's grey wing shall winnow all
   Base metal from life's gold,
And every warranty appal,
   And love herself grows old.

The rising wavelets of your song,
   Light as galactic air,
Will dance on every human tongue
   Dame Nature doth prepare.
The boundless elemental whole
   Of incarnation's train,
Tears from the socket of its soul
   Will on thy memory reign.

That rich, mysterious gift divine,
   Self-conscious of its life,
Imbues itself on every line
   Without a sign of strife.
Around thy wide-spread disc of fame
   Shines honour's blazing star ;
Spite, lust, and pride quake when thy name
   Sounds on the field of war.

A brainless mass of copyists
  May flicker, flash, and vie,
But soon their laboured, rayless lists
  Beneath time's gaze will die.
Like shifting shadows in the sun,
  Or waves that mark the sea,
They'll sigh the syllables undone,
  And shift with woe is me

THE HUMAN MIND.

How facile and free is the mind,
No fetters forg'd by man can bind
    Or bar its spacious way;
It skims this wide terrestial sphere,
As light as winged elysian air,
      As jubilant and gay;
  It drinks the cordial from love's cup,
    And leads the victor's train;
  It lifts embrown'd industry up
    On honour's throne to reign.
    So quaintly and gently,
    Singing as it goes,
    Aye flashing and dashing,
    Revealing what it knows.

The mind has secrets to reveal
That yet lie under God's own seal;
    What wonders of research
Is in its well-fledged, downy wings;
What light from Heaven's court it brings
    Down yonder starry arch.
  It wanders where the silvery sun
    Has never sent one beam,
  Unswerving onward it doth run
    By hallow'd joy's sweet stream.

Inspiring and firing
Devotion's upward glance,
Still watching and catching
At every passing chance.

It sounds Eraca's rocky dells,
And rings imperial Salem's bells;
    It wakes the minstrel's song,
The Great Creator's Name to praise,
Draws down on earth fair glory's rays
    Upon the blood-wash'd throng.
The choicest gems in nature's mould,
    Or dark Golconda's mine,
Pales down before the lustre bold
    That from the mind outshine.
    It's charming and warming
    The nations with its bliss,
    Soft blushing and flushing,
    With animation's kiss.

William Longstaff.

ILLIAM LONGSTAFF was born at Soulby, a small village in the county of Westmoreland, in October, 1849. The name, which is essentially Saxon in its origin, has long been recognised as a north country one; and variously spelled Langstaffe, Longstaff and Langstoft, has been associated with the counties of Northumberland, Durham, Cumberland, Westmoreland and York, for hundreds of years. We have it on record that a person named Langstoft published a volume in the city of York in the 17th century : and since then more than one individual of the name has rendered himself conspicuous for literary talent.

The immediate progenitors of William Longstaff appear to have been of a wandering and unsettled disposition, a characteristic inherited by their present descendants. William's grandfather, who was at one period a gamekeeper, removed from Durham county to Cumberland, where he acted in that capacity to the Musgraves, at Edenhall. Having married " a Cumberland lass " locally famed for her vocal powers as a singer, thus presumably introducing musical talent into the family, he ultimately settled down as a small farmer at Soulby, in Westmoreland.

It is a well known fact that towards the latter end of the last and in the beginning of the present century, many of the small farmers were forced to succumb to adverse circumstances, which then, as now, specially affected the agricultural interest. This proved to be the case with the *quondam* gamekeeper, and it was in consequence of such adventitious circumstances that the father of our poet, a man widely known for his musical talent, was under the necessity of commencing life in a position little better than that of an agricultural labourer. His early death at the age of 30, leaving a widow and four young children, of whom William was the third, plunged them into absolute poverty, against which the widow bravely battled for years in the endeavour to provide for her helpless family. The recollection of this unfortunate period of his existence and the reminiscences recalled by the kindness and sympathy of humble friends in their adversity, have tinged with sentiments of melancholy and pathos some of William Longstaff's poetical effusions. rendering them singularly effective in their appeal to the affections and the finer feelings of the heart. At an early age, William was sent to school, the necessary fees being paid by local landowners and others, whose charitable aid to the distressed family is deserving of all praise. Under the old-fashioned tuition then in vogue, he made rapid progress in his reading lessons, which consisted almost entirely of scripture history and narrative, supplemented by the catechism of the Church. When five-and-a-half years old he was presented with a copy of " The Wharton Bible " for having successfully repeated seven of the Psalms of David, comprising 111 verses, and the Church Catechism aforesaid.

At the age of twelve he quitted school to work as "nipper lad" on a railway then in process of formation in the Eden Valley. Leaving this employment, he engaged himself as a boy gardener, &c., to the Rev. John Collinson, M.A., formerly incumbent of Lamesley, in Durham (but then living in retirement at Soulby), This excellent clergyman, a man of parts and a scholar, though a strict disciplinarian, was kindly and benevolent; and from him William Longstaff received lessons in moral rectitude and upright conduct, for which he has ever since expressed his indebtedness and grateful acknowledgment.

Leaving this employment, his next occupation was that of a hired farm servant, when, like Robert Burns, he followed the plough with happy musings "along the mountain side."

His next venture as a navvy on the Settle and Carlisle extension of the Midland Railway, was not at all to his taste: broken time and irregular wages, principally due to the rainy weather, disgusted him with the work, though he found his fellow-workmen, as a rule, the most generous hearted and genial body of men with whom he had yet been associated. Making his way to Shildon—the cradle of the railway engine—and then to Gateshead, with the intention of qualifying himself as a fireman, and with the idea of becoming an engine driver, he met with a series of disappointments. In 1873 he found himself, after fulfilling minor duties, promoted to the responsible position of relief signalman in the services of the North Eastern Railway Company, in which capacity he is still employed.

In 1887 Mr. Longstaff published his first *brochure*, a small collection of poems, which was favourably received by the public. This collection contains an ode on Her Majesty's Jubilee, and received the acknowlegment and thanks of the Queen through Sir H. Ponsonby, after publication.

As a contributor to the "Poets' Corner" in the local press, Mr. Longstaff is well and favourably known in the north. As a humorous and sarcastic writer of poetry, he has recently gained a wide celebrity in that extensively circulated comic Annual, known as "Fraser's Blyth and Tyneside Comic Illustrated Almanac," for which some time ago was purchased the copyright productions of the late firm of Chaters, comic publishers of Newcastle-on-Tyne. In the prize competitions for honours in Fraser's Almanac Mr. Longstaff has secured both the gold and silver medals awarded by the judges. Some of his satirical pieces are of a high order of merit. They are easy in versification, playful in fancy, and display a fine sense of humour.

His more serious pieces are highly creditable to his humanitarian feelings, and possess the sterling ring of poetry.

JAMES TROTTER.

THE WILD HELM WIND.

My own, my bonnie native hills,
　The Helmcloud gathering on your crest,
Hath settled there again and fills
　My musing mind with sweet unrest;

A pall from Stanemores height above,
  Far down the Pennines lengthy range,
Is weird, as mists together wove
    Seem seethed in masses wild and strange :
      Hark ! wails the wind in many a gust,
  See ! rolls the scudding whirling dust ;
  The Helm is on ; as blows a gale,
  Adown the mount—adown the vale ;
  But every sound my bosom fills
  With love for ye, my native hills.

Down Crossfell's breast, with maddening roar,
  The gusts commingle, race, and growl ;
Each grander, wilder than before,
  O'er crumbling shale and stones to howl
Around the pikes. Now *Knock to creep,
  Now from the peak of * Dufton skim,
Down higher *Murton next to sweep,
  With mocking voices harsh and grim ;
    Rocks many a tree, and many a wall,
  As many a gap is seen to fall,
  And many a bush, and many a tree
  Is bent, as if to bend the knee ;
  But every sight my bosom fills
  With love for ye, my native hills.

The cowering sheep instinct hath taught
  In sheltering nooks again are found ;
A cairn, a hedge, a rock is sought ;
  A hollow deep behind a mound.
  The croaking crow, the rooks soft caw,
Seem silenced, as with weary wing,
  The magpie and the saucy daw,
Behind the fences seem to cling.
    The blast assumes a mightier power :
  'Tis gathering strength from hour to hour ;

* These picturesque conical hills—Knock, Dufton, and Murton—are
seen from the Vale of Eden.

Leaves are upturned, as forests pale
Before the yet increasing gale ;
While every blast my bosom fills
With love for ye, my native hills.

From *Meerlaw Hill, to †Stanemore Fell,
  Where is there aught to this akin ?
Where clouds regather and reswell
  And now disperse in wildest din ;
Reborn with every gift of wealth,
  The boisterous gale—say not 'tis death ;
For cheeks and lips show ruddy health
  Who brave the Helmwind's giant breath.
Nor sights, nor sounds in other lands
Have grandeur such as this commands :
Nor breeze, nor winds like this can wreathe,
Wild charms like these for me to breathe ;
O, every breath my bosom fills
With love for ye, my native hills.

WHEN THE SWALLOWS COME AGAIN.

When the swallows come again,
As they journey o'er the main :
  Who hath not a willing welcome
  For their airy flitting wings,
  For the light and merry twitter
  The approaching summer brings ?
  Beauty's heralds, bright and joyous,
  At the close of winter's reign ;
  Hath the summer ever being
  Till the swallows come again ?

* Meerlaw Hill, in Cumberland.
† Stanemore Fell, Westmoreland.

When the swallows come again,
In the April's sun and rain ;
  If the primrose and the snowdrop
  May together speed away,
  Then we look for other flowers,
  For the hawthorn's scented spray,
  For the rosebuds to develop,
  Which to look for, 'twere in vain,
  Till the summer's glowing sunshine,
  When the swallows come again.

When the swallows come again,
Winging like a living chain ;
  With a light and loving message
  From the southern sunny shores,
  Coming nigh us, to us, with us,
  Building high above the doors ;
  Clinging to the eaves and windows,
  What can summer's smile attain
  Till the starting of their houses,
  When the swallows come again.

When the swallows come again,
Skimming o'er the grassy plain ;
  We have joying at their presence,
  Swifts and martins free and gay,
  Bright and happy in the morning,
  Never weary through the day ;
  Fleet, nor halting in their flitting,
  Life hath longing, and would fain
  Haste the spring a little onward,
  Till the swallows come again.

Rev. James Gabb, B.A.

HE REV. JAMES GABB was born at Ebley, in Gloucester-
shire, on the 3rd of February, 1830. He was educated at
Dame Schools till 1839, then at the endowed Parish
School until 1845. During the later years of this period
he received free instruction in Latin and literature from
the incumbent curate of the parish church, and in Euclid
and algebra from the incumbent of the district church.
By the influence of the former, in 1845 he obtained an
appointment at Dawlish, in the office of Mr. J. T. Harrison, brother of Mr.
T. E. Harrison, of the N. E. Railway, a principal resident engineer on the
South Devon Railway, then in course of construction, where he was soon
joined by his younger brother, Samuel. In 1848 he was promoted to a post
in the immediate employment of Mr. Brunel, the eminent engineer, in ful-
filment of a promise made by the latter to Mr. Harrison in 1845 that if his
protegé continued to give satisfaction in the performance of his duties he
would befriend him. A year afterward, in 1849, chiefly induced by religious
feeling, and at the suggestion of the latter of the two reverend friends already
mentioned,—both of whom are still living—he left the service of Mr.
Brunel, and returned home for six months to read for the University, to
which, after reading another six months at Matlock Bath Vicarage, he
proceeded in Oct., 1850, at the cost of friends who were mostly strangers to
him. He was entered at Gonville and Caius College, Cambridge, where, in
the following year, he was second mathematical prizeman, and obtained an
exhibition. In his second year he obtained a similar prize, and a scholar-
ship, followed in his third year by the Chapel Clerkship. He read mathe-
matics with Mr. Ferrers, now the master of his college, and with Mr.
Todhunter, the eminent private tutor and writer of mathematical class
books for the University, with whom he was a favorite. In the degree
lists, at the beginning of 1854, he passed as a wrangler, and in June was
appointed to the curacy of Barton-le-Street, Yorkshire, being ordained
deacon in York Minster by the Bishop of Madras, on behalf of Archbishop
Musgrave, on which occasion, by reason of his standing in the Bishop's
examination, he was appointed by him to read the Gospel in the Minster.
Taking up his residence at Coneysthorpe, in the parish of Barton-le-Street,
he found himself very near to Castle Howard, the family from which
regularly attended the little village chapel, in addition to attendance at the
service held in the Castle chapel, where their own chaplain officiated. In
the autumn of this year, 1854, Lord Carlisle returned from the Turkish
and Greek waters; and in the following year, 1855, on the death of his
chaplain, his lordship requested Mr. Gabb to take the office, remaining still
at Coneysthorpe. Here he began again to write verses. He also went out,
as a volunteer helper, to preach and speak for the Church Missionary

Society, of which his rector, the Rev. Charles Hodgson, was then the secretary for Yorkshire. Still later, he went out in the same way for the British and Foreign Bible Society. During the few years which followed his settlement at Conevsthorpe he had several livings proposed for his acceptance, all by Archbishop Musgrave ; but finding himself possessed of much less physical vigour than a heavy sphere of labour demanded, and being happily placed in other respects, he declined these. In 1864 he was offered the curacy of Bulmer-with-Welburn, also on the Castle Howard estate, within sight of the Castle, and to be held with the chaplaincy, which, with Lord Carlisle's approval, he accepted. A few months later his lordship died, his latest public act having been to attend service at the Welburn Church, where Mr. Gabb officiated, to a seat in which his lordship was with difficulty assisted, after having already attended the Castle Chapel service, which Mr. Gabb had performed as his chaplain. Mr. Gabb continued to reside at Welburn until 1867, when his rector died, having been more than half a century incumbent of the parish. Mr. Gabb had previously married, in 1866, Jane, the youngest daughter of Prebendary Hird, of Low Moor, and of York, and youngest sister of Mr. Wickham, formerly member for Bradford. In 1875 Mr. Gabb's attendance at the Castle Chapel ceased, it having been determined to re-arrange the structure, and employ a higher ritual than had been previously in use there. Mr. Gabb's muse lay comparatively dormant during this later period, but has reawakened during the last three years. He published, however, "The Welburn Appendix of Original Hymns and Tunes," in 1875; "Hymns and Songs of Pilgrim Life," in 1871; and "Steps to the Throne," in 1864; having previously adjudicated, in 1861, in conjunction with the late Dean Champneys and Bishop Alford, four essays, of £50, £20, &c., on the subject of "Missions," which were published, with an introduction by Dean Champneys, under the title of "The Golden Opportunity;" also a visitation sermon, entitled "Church Reform," preached at Malton in 1869.

Mr. Gabb's brother Samuel left Dawlish at the same time as himself, and afterwards, having executed engineering works in a subordinate capacity in South Wales and Belgium, he received from the Russian Government the appointment of chief resident engineer in the Caucasus, for the construction of the Poti and Tiflis railway, dying of erysipelas at the latter place after the construction of the railway, in 1880, at the age of 48 years, having received a liberal salary during the long period in which he served that Government, and also a decoration from the Emperor.

The only sister of the two brothers has recently commemorated, in conjunction with many of her former scholars, her jubilee anniversary as a Sunday School teacher, in association with the only religious community to which she ever belonged.

W. A. ASHTON.

WELCOME REST.

Beyond the hill I watched the bright-haired sun
Weary, and stooping as he neared the west,
Sink down, as if he would in climes more blest
Cease from the course which yet he had to run.

Of thousands that beheld him, there was one
Who yearned like him for some fit place of rest,
Some downy couch, on which to lean his breast
And think with joy " The day's work now is done."

How strange that all things here so droop and fall!
That men so earnest, and with aims so high—
The cheerful birds that rouse at morning's call—
The very sun that leaps into the sky—
Should crave for rest, and night's descending pall,
That bring such deep unconsciousness to all!

RECOLLECTION.

I sometimes sing a weak and broken song,
As if a linnet, in a leafless grove,
Attuned his lay, still mindful of his love,
In drear December! hoping that among
My scattered notes, by breezes borne along,
Some may be wafted to the world above,
Where, in Elysian fields, for aye will move
One whose dear love to me on earth was strong.

Nor all in vain! I hear her far away
Answer me sweetly from that happy land;
The strain breaks on my heart, as in a bay
The low sea-music breaks upon the strand,
Or as the voices of an angel band
Heard in the dawning of some holy day.

SPRING BREEZES.

Blow, winds, blow,
O'er the winter's snow ;
From the south and west
Blow, blow, blow ;
Bid the flowers spring,
And the sweet birds sing,
Till, in beauty drest,
Earth with music ring !

Haste, winds, haste
O'er the barren waste !
With your bugle-horn,
Haste, haste, haste ;
Call to field and wood,
Where the trees have stood
All too long forlorn
Of their leafihood.

Breathe, winds, breathe,
And with verdure wreathe
All the rural scene ;
Breathe, breathe, breathe :
Hence no longer roam,
But, returning home,
Clothe the fields between
In accustomed bloom.

Come, winds, come,
Bearing sweet perfume ;
From your foreign bowers
Come, come, come !
Hither speed, and bring,
On your downy wing,
Soft and sunny showers
To the opening Spring !

TO-MORROW.

On bright to-morrow much we love to dwell,
Thinking of all the good that shall befall ;
Of bright to-morrow many a tale we tell,
As if that good would come to one and all !

But soon we put to proof dark-dealing Time,
Aye on the wing, mysterious, fateful, weird,
Whether we call to mind last evening's chime.
Or think how fair this present morn appeared.

The morrow's here ! Yet, even now, how sad
His face appears ! Then, other morrows loom
Large on our inward sight, and make us glad,
For Bows of Promise span the distant gloom.

These say to us, " Be cheerful still, and live
For fairer days to come ! To-morrow may
More than fulfil its promise—loth to give
Scope to the storm that gathered at noonday."

Still trace we, then, Heaven's bow on every cloud,
The faithful sign of God's continuing love !
Yea, see one shining on the very shroud
That briefly holds us from our home above !

LIGHT IN DARKNESS.

Time flies, and from his waving wing
  Flash beams of light upon us here.
As on a dark embosomed spring
  The noon gleam flashes clear.

And though they flash to fade again,
  They lighten up the narrow span
Of those brief years that come to men,
  In wondrous Nature's plan.

From the vast Infinite they come,
  Clear sunbeams from a Source Divine,
The smile of Heaven, to cheer our gloom
  And make earth's darkness shine !

Nor do we think of them amiss,
  If God looks down on those He made !
Nor of their end, were it but this—
  To gild each earth-born shade !

For when the heart is dark with care,
  Deep, anxious care, to act aright,
They shed a radiance brighter there
  Than comes with morning light.

Thus, while the years successive go,
  And men are born, and doubt, and die,
They know the bliss, and feel the glow,
  Of heavenly sympathy.

And all these smiles one day shall fall
  On some bright spot in realms above,
Where souls that trust shall, one and all,
  Live on for aye, and love !

George Oswald Wight.

EORGE OSWALD WIGHT was born in Sunderland, on the 10th August, 1853. He is the third son of the late Mr. William Wight, head of the firm of Robert Wight & Son, forge masters and iron founders, Sunderland and Seaham. He was educated at Mill Hill, near London, and Richmond Grammar Schools. He resided in Spain from November, 1871, to May, 1874, at Garrucha de Vera, in the province of Almeria, at which rising port he was acting, when only nineteen years of age, as British Vice-Consul, when the Intransigente Cartagena insurgents, under Galvez, visited the place. After his return home, he lived in Sunderland till September, 1878, and from that time till October, 1881, he travelled over Spain and Portugal, France, Ireland, etc., for a Welsh Colliery Company. Since that time he has resided in Sunderland, where he carries on a flourishing business as an iron merchant. He is likewise Belgian Consul and Secretary to the Local Chamber of Commerce. He takes a deep and intelligent interest in social and political questions ; is a Radical Reformer or Advanced Liberal of the most genuinely enlightened type ; is a good platform speaker, without a particle of either bounce or bunkum ; takes a prominent part in every important local movement ; and is highly esteemed by sensible men of all parties for his gentlemanly bearing and conduct. He is the author of several pamphlets of a miscellaneous kind, including one entitled " Life, Whence and Whither," which deals critically with a difficult metaphysical subject ; and synopses of some of his popular lectures on Spain, Home Rule, Equitable Taxation, etc., have appeared in sundry papers and periodicals ; but hitherto he has published no elaborate work. It is worthy of mention that his maternal grandfather, Mr. John Murray, was one of the Secretaries of the Glasgow Emancipation Society, instituted in 1833, with the object of bringing about the universal abolition of slavery and the slave trade, the protection of the rights of the Aborigines in the British Colonies, and the improvement of the condition of our fellow subjects—the natives of British India. His grandson may be said, in Scottish law parlance, to have duly served himself heir to his grandsire's principles.

WILLIAM BROCKIE.

BLINDNESS COMING ON IN YOUTH.

And I am growing slowly blind, and feel
The twilight ever darkening, day by day,
Into a night which throughout life must last.
At first there faded from me distant views ;

But now the foe attacks my chiefest love,
And having shut from me th' unthinking world,
Which lies in others' view, but not in mine,
Would close entirely up that world of thought
In which my mind has revelled until now,
Relying for the work on the eye's strength,
Which, poor slave ! is, alas, nought but a tool,
And like ought else wears out with overwork.
Henceforth I must sink back into myself,
With what more I may have caught from out
The minds of those who've thought on life and death ;
With whom I've journeyed o'er too little ground,
And feel that much there is beyond my grasp.
(Perhaps beyond the grasp of all who live !)
Still though since the world began, life's aim
Has been the riddle which has puzzled all,
Yet would I ne'er give up th' unravelment,
For we do know that oft the first who'd cross
A country wild, and then before unknown,
Dies in the trial, so may be the next,
But comes a third and does fulfil the task,
By taking heed from failings of the rest,
And aid from sayings which they left behind.
Yet, I through failing strength must cast aside
All hopes of aiding in this work of life.
My mind, untarnished, eager for the fray,
Scorns the base tools which cannot go its pace,
Yet feels without their help its uselessness.
" O God ! Is this life ? and is this being ?
When I cannot control this body mine,
But on my road with halting steps must creep,
With drag unlifted from my wheel of life ? "
And in reply there comes a voice which says :—
" This is not life.   You are but in the womb.
Death is the birth-pang which shall open out
A new existence, boundless, grandly free,

In which the mind, unfettered by the needs
Of a poor shell, shall work for soul alone,
With strength unfailing, and with task as wide
As is the universe, with time to work
Long as the durance of eternity."
At this my heart leapt up and gladly sang,
As one of old, " Where is thy sting? O Death !
O Grave ! o'er me thou hast no victory."

THE SEA

Oh changeful mirror of the skies how dull thy look !
Thy cheerless face of cold, grey blue does not invite
A voyage o'er thee, nor a swim athwart thy waves ;
And as I watch thy white crests tossing to the shore,
They gleam with vicious menace, like the iv'ry teeth
Of some wild beast, which, sudden roused from dreamy rest,
Shows, by the quick withdrawal of the curling lips,
The fierce revengeful nature couching deep within.
I do accuse thee thus, and this is thy reply :—
" My nature is not wild nor restless, but reverse ;
I would that I could lie unbroken and becalmed,
And ever show the brilliant, phosphorescent blue,
Which in the South my waters offer to the sight.
But I am like unto thyself, oh changeful man :
I am no master, but am moved by ev'ry wind
Which bloweth o'er me.   The hue which thou upbraidest
Is reflex—not mine own.   Look upwards to the sky :
If it be bright, then so am I ; if it be dull,
Then I but shadow back the coldness I receive."

So spake the sea to me, and straightway I reflect
Our hearts are like the sea, for they responsive are
To what there is about them, and we each express,
In our emotions, things beyond our wish and thought,
Which make us what we would not be—unkind—untrue,
And leave it hard to bear the weight of daily life.

Rev. John Bernard Mc.Govern.

[J. B. S.]

MONG poets of the Northern Counties John Bernard Mc.Govern J. B. S., novelist and prolific sonneteer, justly claims a place. A native of Liverpool, he was born August 16th, 1849. His father, Bartholomew S. Mc.Govern, a member of a well-known Irish family and a successful shipbuilder, died in 1861, leaving two sons, the subject of our notice and J. H. Mc.Govern, a well-known architect in Liverpool, and the author of several works on architecture and kindred subjects. John Bernard Mc.Govern, after a preliminary education in his native city, finished his studies in Belgium and took orders. From an early age literature had fascinated him, and when only twelve years of age he had published a little work entitled "Jacob's Ladder, or Steps to Heaven," which was followed seven years later by a similar work, "Thoughts at the Foot of the Altar." These puerile effusions were printed for private circulation. When stationed in Ireland and discharging his duties as a clergyman, he contributed fugitive pieces to the *Limerick Reporter* and other Irish papers, but it was not until 1880 that he commenced regular literary work. In that year he published a translation of "Lamartine's Graziella," and he was the first, we believe, to present in English that pathetic story. Three years later he published a novel, "Imelda, or a Romance of Kilkee," which was favourably received; and in 1884, under the title of "Cupid's Darts," a collection of celebrated love letters. In addition to these works he has written several short stories, and (in conjunction with his brother) "An Irish Sept," being a history of the Mc.Govern or MacGauran Clan. This work, which was unfortunately printed for private circulation, is a valuable addition to early Irish history. Mr. Mc.Govern is a frequent contributor to periodical literature, and to *Notes and Queries*, and its French counterpart *L'Intermédiare*. As a poet he has devoted himself of late years to the cultivation of the sonnet. Many of these have appeared in the columns of Northern newspapers, where they at present lie buried with a mass of ephemeral literature, and it is to be hoped that Mr. Mc.Govern may be yet induced to publish a collection of his sonnets, many of which show more than ordinary poetical ability. We append four specimens. It may be added that Mr. Mc.Govern at present discharges the duties of curate of All Saints' Church, Manchester.

E. E. E. PARTINGTON.

KEATS.

[1796—1820].

Not Britain, but the land the Tiber laves
Shelters the mortal frame—now long since cold—
Of Keats, the poet of Hellenic mould.
He rests not where we keep our heroes' graves,
'Neath that high dome where sleep his country's braves,
But lies where Roman tribunes trod of old,
His ashes mingling—oft the story's told—
With those great Dead of whom the schoolboy raves.
Why, gifted youth, why did'st thou leave so soon
This orb to soar aloft to worlds unseen ;
And leave us 'ere thy life was scarce begun ?
Yet I am grateful for that priceless boon
That thy few works for me have ever been,
Which for thy brow a poet's laurels won.

THE TOMB OF SCOTT.

'Mid Nature's beauties and a fane's decay,
The poet sleeps.   Pierced not by shafts of sound,
The lucent air hangs tranquil all around,
Save but by music from the Tweed and lay
Of tuneful birds.   Calm Peace doth here alway
As sovereign reign supreme; 'tis sacred ground,
Where pilgrim hearts, full often thrilling, bound
At thoughts that seem at once both sad and gay.
Fit spot, O ! Dryburgh, for great Walter's frame,
Where Art and Nature struggle for the best—
Both types of him who's laid in thee to rest.
Thy crumbling ruins figure what here lies,
Whilst Nature, ever living, typifies
Those works that gain'd for him a deathless name.

OUR WEDDING DAY.

'Neath chancel arch we stood ; without, a sea
Of golden sunlight gleam'd ; unseen, within,
A brighter stream of lovelight did begin
To lave our souls, for there it was that we
Knew all our fears were o'er, henceforth to be
But shadows of the past ; and bliss akin
To poets' dreams began for us to win
Unclouded hopes for all futurity.
The binding words that trembled on our lips,
From deepest awe and consciousness of love,
But ratified the fusion of thy soul
With mine ; not then the panting heart first sips
Love's nectar ; it but asks the pow'rs above
To bless the fact—such sanction is love's goal.

I E R N E .

Thou, Niobe of Nations, sad Ierne,
What storm-clouds eddy round thy marble brow
Erst deck'd with gladness but with sorrow now ;
Long centuries of wrong have cast a stern
Grave look athwart thy face ; thy poor eyes burn
With scalding tears ! How could great Jove allow
Thy crownless head in woe so low to bow.
And on thy foes his lightning shafts not turn ?
Yet, mother, raise thy face and smile !
Mark'st not yon writing on the walls of time
In fiery letters which the blind may see ?
" Thus saith at last, white wingèd Hope : O Isle
Of Destiny, throughout thee soon shall chime
The bells, long muffled, of thy liberty ! "

Abraham Stansfield.

BRAHAM STANSFIELD, botanist and poet, was born on the 12th February, 1838, at Platt's House, in the romantic Vale of Todmorden, and was brought up amid surroundings most favourable for the development of the poetic temperament. He had been for many years a contributor to the provincial press, before he appeared as a verse-writer, by the publication, in 1876, of a volume of original poems and translations, under the title of "Ground-Flowers and Fern-Leaves,"—which was well received both by critics and public. All Mr. Stansfield's best work, however, in the way of verse, has been done subsequently to this ; and a considerable portion, at least, has appeared at intervals in various magazines and periodicals. Of the original poems, and they are numerous, his longest effort is his " Death of Sir Philip Sidney," a poem which has been much and widely admired. But it is by his masterly renderings from modern French and German poets, especially the latter, that Mr. Stansfield's name is best known; and in this department he has probably no rival in the North Country. In fact, apart from his claims as an original poet, Mr. Stansfield's permanent place in English literature is assured by his exquisite translations of the works of modern European poets.

With respect to the general character of Mr. Stansfield's original poetry, all who read it must be impressed with the absolute truthfulness and sincerity of the author, in treating his many and various subjects: there is nothing strained, all is natural and spontaneous—his poems are so many impromptus. Perhaps the prevailing tone is one of melancholy ; yet it is no morbid but rather a pleasing melancholy. It is the utterance of a man whose thoughtful habit has led him to ponder too often and too deeply the everlasting problem. But the solace which the poet himself obtains he indicates to others, and this solace he finds in nature, his descriptions of which are as accurate as they are simple, and beautifully written, " O Nature ! " he says,

———through all years thy lover I ;
Thee have I followed still; upon thy breast
Have lain secure, when the rude, pelting storm
Did rage without! Thy sweet society
To me is all-sufficing. I have friends,
Faithful and kind, dear to my heart, and true
As ever Earth did bear ; but even they to me
Are less than thou, O mistress of my heart!
Beneficent Nature ! Bearer of the Balm !
And Sovereign Healer of all earthly wounds!

We believe it is Mr. Stansfield's intention to issue shortly a second volume, containing all his more important poems, sonnets and translations up to date (1889) ; and as he is still in the prime of his powers, we hope it may be followed by many another volume from his facile pen. Resident for thirty years in his native valley, Mr. Stansfield removed twenty years ago to Manchester, where he at present resides, connecting himself actively with various literary and scientific societies of that city.

Among his more recent prose-writings which, through their direct local connection, are of special interest to North Country readers, may be mentioned his "Mossgatherers : a Lancashire Specimen," "Rambles in the West Riding (with a glance at the Flora)," "A difficult Lancashire place-name," and "Folk Speech of the Lancashire and Yorkshire Border." In addition to these, Mr. Stansfield, within the last few years, has contributed to the transactions of the Manchester Literary Club, and other societies, a number of papers on various literary and scientific subjects of the highest interest, and implying on the part of their author a most unusual acquaintance with ancient and modern literature. Mr. Stansfield is also editor and founder of the *Northern Gardener*, a weekly journal of wide circulation.

W. D.

'ERE MARCH ARRIVE.

'Ere March arrive, must roll another moon —
    Another moon, 'ere yet the snowdrop peeps ;
    Still, nestled in the earth, fair Flora sleeps,
And far remote, indeed, is leafy June ;
And yet my heart is in a merry tune ;
    For love, late chilled, hath woke to life anew ;
    The spring has come before the spring was due —
My spring has come, but is it late or soon ?

Are whitening locks, and the still-deepening line,
    Graven by Care and Time, emblems of spring ?
And though, like as of old, this heart of mine
Carol its joyance, in a festive lay,
    Within the leafless woods, a thrush will sing
As blithe a song, upon a winter day !

AMOR REDIVIVUS.

Air made sweeter by her breath
    Have I breathed again to-day ;
Though to breathe it be my death,
    Still I cannot keep away.

Songs I heard her sing, once more ;
   Thrilled my heart her every tone :
Ah, so like that voice of yore !—
   Scarcely I repressed a groan.

Though the years have rolled away,
   Stands She here in all but name :
Love, why dost thou vex me, say,
   When I cannot be the same !

Cruel Love, to come so late !
   Envious Time, thou art to blame :—
When the birds in winter mate,
   I may hope to do the same !

ON A BOOK-WORM.

[F. S.]

A man of middle size, and middle age,
   (From out the " middle ages " come, to see
   What this much-boasted age of ours may be !)
With flowing beard, and glittering eye, whose rage
Is still to turn o'er some quaint-lettered page.
   Deep in the ancients, you shall see him pore—
   A pensive statue, 'mid the city's roar—
Whilst you proceed upon your pilgrimage !
A man of learning, cold, impassive ? no ;
   By nature gentle : tender still, his heart
Hath pleasant places, where the sweet herbs grow
   Of Love, and Friendship, and all herbs of grace :
A poet he, without the poet's art,
   Whom all must love that look upon his face !

THE SHEPHERD.

[Translation of " Der Schäfer," of Uhland.

The youthful shepherd, tall and fair,
    He drove so near the royal tower,
Him saw the royal maiden there,
    And loved him from that hour.

And sighing, thus she softly spoke :
" Oh, could I come to thee, my dear !
As white as snow thy gentle flock,
    But love lies bleeding here."

The youthful shepherd thus replied :
" Oh, wouldst thou come to me, my dear !
That I might press that hand so white,
    And kiss thy cheek so fair ! "

And as, each morn, he meekly drove
His woolly flock the castle by,
Upon the turret, far above,
    The maiden he did spy ;

And greeting her with friendly word :
" O welcome, the king's daughter fine ! "
Her gentle answer soon he heard :
    " I thank thee, shepherd mine ! "

The winter sped, the spring, so fair,
Was blooming richer than before ;
The shepherd with his flock was there,
    The maiden——never more !

Yet sadly thus on her he calls :
" O welcome, the king's daughter fine ! "
A voice it issues from the walls :
    " Adieu ! thou shepherd mine ! "

JOURNEY BY NIGHT.

From the German of Uhland.

Into the gloomy land I ride,
No light of moon or star to guide,—
   How bitter blows the wind !
Here have I journeyed many a day,
When golden sunshine lit the way,
   And the breeze was soft and kind.

I ride the gloomy garden by,
The naked trees are tossing high,
   The seared leaf doth fall.
Here, 'mid the roses, oft I strayed,
With her I loved, the darling maid,
   When love was all in all.

Extinguished is the sunlight now,
The roses long have ceased to blow,—
   My love is lowly laid !
I ride into the gloomy land,
'Mid winter's storm, no light at hand,
   Enwrapped within my plaid.

Fred. Pratt.

T is pleasant to think that the Ideality of life is not incompatible with its Reality ; pleasant to observe that the sunny slopes of Parnassus can be and are ascended with equal facility by the feet that are accustomed to pace the busy streets of a commercial city ; pleasant to know that the higher functions of the mind can be cultivated without detriment to mercantile pursuits. And it is well for the Republic of Letters that literature has long ceased to be a monopoly of professional *littérateurs* ; were it otherwise, many priceless gems of thought in prose and verse would have been irretrievably lost to it. To say that Cottonopolis, despite her proverbial smoke and inky rivers and general unloveliness, stands amongst those votaries nearest to the divine Pallas, would be to assert a truism : the literary streams that flow from her into the river of English thought are as numerous as the gigantic buildings in which those bales repose that give to her her somewhat matter-of-fact soubriquet.

Not the least amongst these is the subject of this sketch. Born at Hendham Vale, Manchester, Mr. Fred. Pratt was educated at Alma Hill Academy, Cheetham Hill, where he carried off several prizes for Latin and drawing. His career since then has been varied and useful. He was apprenticed for five years to Messrs. James Mc.Laren and Nephews, home trade and Canadian merchants, at the expiration of which term he made an engagement with the well-known shipping house, Messrs. N. P. Nathan's Sons, with whom he has remained twenty-one years as buyer and manager of one of their departments. His business capacity is much enhanced by his practical knowledge of German.

Mr. Pratt has also for many years been actively engaged in church work in connection with All Saints' Church, Chorlton-on-Medlock, of which he was four years sidesman, and is in his eighth year as warden, in addition to which he is one of the signing managers of the All Saints' National Day School, and an active member of the Committee of the Adult Deaf and Dumb Institution in the same parish. Nor is he unknown in the arena of politics, being one of the founders. and first (as also present) Chairman of the All Saints' Ward Working Men's Conservative Club.

The art of war has likewise had an attraction for him from an early date, and he holds at present the post of lieutenant in the First Manchester Rifles, now the Second Volunteer Battalion of the Manchester Regiment ; he is also a good shot, and the winner of numerous regimental prizes, company challenge cups, etc.

But it is as a man of letters that he will be chiefly interesting to the readers of this monograph. His versatility is on a par with his activity.

He is as much at home in the company of the Celestial Nine as he is in the society of hard-headed men of business, brother officers, or church officials, and how he finds time amidst his multifarious avocations to worship at their shrine is a wonder to those who know him. Poems, songs, and anthems for children's services, drop from his pen with marvellous rapidity; nor does their frequency impair their vigour. They lie for the most part hidden away in the poets' corner of local and metropolitan periodicals, from which obscurity it is to be hoped they will one day be rescued, and enjoy a less ephemeral existence in book-form. The subjoined selections will serve as specimens of his muse. Mr. Pratt's poetry is remarkable as much for its admirable conjunction of the intellectual and emotional as for clearness of expression. Nor does he follow any exemplar in the distribution of his lines, but yields himself to the guidance of his fancy and the genius of his subject. One of his songs, "The Streamlet," has been set to music by W. J. Young, and many of his volunteer effusions have been sung by his comrades at their regimental gatherings.

Amongst our author's prose writings I may mention his "Sketches of Camp Life," and "For Marion's Sake," a clever comedy-drama in three acts, which has been performed with much success several times in Manchester, and neighbouring districts. I may add, in conclusion, that Mr. Pratt has been from boyhood an omnivorous reader, having, *inter alia*, devoured all the Waverley novels on entering his teens, and that his literary life is a consoling witness to the fact that neither a commercial, nor political, nor military calling, nor all these combined, need unfit a man, if he be so fashioned by Nature, for deeds of literary prowess.

J. B. S.

THE BROKEN COLUMN.

Circled the sea-mews o'er the fishers' haven,
    Each fluttering shadow dashed across the waves
And leapt the church, girdled by fishers' graves,
    Where rose a column with a legend graven.

How to the hamlet came, as winter ended,
    Two happy souls from out the world's rough way,
To dream a short sweet dream each passing day,
    Their tender whisperings with the surges blended.

Rippled the ocean with a face so smiling,
    That little wist they of its envious wrath,
Its gentle murmurings seemed to bless their troth,
    And tempted them from shore, with dreams beguiling.

Sprang out a tempest, high the wild spray driving,
　Each crested wave grew white, with passion toss'd
Aloft with treacherous power the light bark cross'd,
　And madly seethed against their hopeless striving.

Clasp'd in its folding arms, the jealous foaming,
　With hungry haste parted the stricken twain,
Then toy'd awhile with sweet possession's gain,
　Flinging the troth-bound shoreward in the gloaming.

THE LITTLE FOLK.

By the window there they stand,
Such a happy little band—
　　One, two, three—
Gazing through the evening shades,
Waiting, as the twilight fades,
　　Just for me !
Such a pattering of feet,
Then from rosy lips so sweet,
　　Many a kiss.
Now the slippers, now a chair :
Welcome from such faces fair
　　Who would miss ?
As they gather all around,
Sweet their little voices sound,
　　Talking fast ;
Never music's grandest strain
Echoes such a fond refrain—
　　Too soon past !
Do they bother—never mind :
Love so boundless, if you're kind,
　　Will they give ;
And they creep within your heart,
Nevermore from thence to part,
　　While you live.

Join then in their little pleasures,
Let them bring their tiny treasures,
      And you'll find
That their joyous, merry faces
Quickly hasten gloomy traces
      From your mind.

THE AVALANCHE.

The sun had set, and dark'ning shadows crept
Along the mountains' sides, the shades of night
Were deep'ning in the valleys, while the hills
Were wrapt in gloom, far off the heav'ns above,
The air between, and in its mighty course
The earth seem'd hush'd to deep repose; while soft
The moon stole forth from fleecy clouds, its rays
But adding to the deep solemnity,
And Alpine's highest peaks, in snowy robes,
Grand in their majesty, reflected back
Those silv'ry rays, e'en now more silv'ry still :
No handiwork of man was there,—below,
Deep in yon gloomy valley could be traced
The smallness of his craft ; above, around,
Were the creative powers of Godhead shown
Sublime in their own vastness.
      All was calm.
No breezes swept that mighty range of hills,
Nor coursed the valleys through, the Switzers lay
(Secure in thought, beneath the homely roof
Their toil had raised, their daily task long done)
In midnight's deepest sleep, no less profound,
E'en for the calm around.
      But rudely they
Were doom'd to be awaken'd,—from above
Came thund'ring o'er their homes a pond'rous mass,

Terrific in its course, it sped its way,
And where the village and its inmates were
Nought could be seen, deep buried in the vale,
'Neath loosen'd snows from off the mountain heights,
Which, gath'ring force and mighty impetus
The dreaded avalanche its form assumed,
And in majestic grandeur onward roll'd.
Swift o'er crevasse, and down the deep abyss.
With crashing speed it tore o'er craggy rocks,
And staid but when with its own weight 'twas hurl'd,
All wildly crushed upon those peaceful homes.
Those who that night within their cots reposed,
Now sleep death's dreamless sleep; and then the wind
Arose, and on the midnight air it bore
The wail of death along that mountain range:
Then hush'd again, and all was peaceful,—still.

Thomas W. Little

HOMAS W. LITTLE is the eldest son of Mr. Samuel Little, grocer, of Mickley, in the county of Northumberland, by his wife, Mary Ann Pattison, third daughter of the late Mr. Thomas Pattison, formerly of Old Ridley, Stocksfield, who was an influential and successful Tyne-side farmer.

Thomas W. Little, the subject of this notice, was born at Mickley, on July 25th, 1858. He went to the village school of Mickley when he was only five years old. The schoolmaster was his uncle, who at the present time holds an important position at Rockhampton, in Queensland. From there he went to the Royal Grammar School at Hexham, where he soon became a favourite pupil with the then head master, the late Mr. Thomas Dobson—a gentleman who stood very high as a mathematician. This gentleman exerted a great influence over the gentle and timid character of his pupil. To this day Thomas has a profound respect for his memory, and speaks of him "as a capital master, and a good friend to me."

When he finished his schooling he joined his father in his business; as his brothers grew up they also joined the firm. From comparatively small beginnings, the firm of Samuel Little & Sons, as general merchants, has become a large concern. They have a wide reputation for integrity and honourable dealing.

While diligent in business, he still continued his studious habits. His chief delight was the study of the poets, Milton, Cowper, Thomson, Byron, &c.; he also became a collector of rare and curious books. As a boy, he was of a shy, retiring nature—probably from overtaxing himself with study and business. After leaving school, he became subject to frequent severe attacks of dyspepsia, which produced (as it has done in the case of many of our illustrious poets) a very depressing effect upon him, mentally and physically, for some time, and gave his naturally gentle disposition a sedate and melancholy turn.

It was at this period of his life that he first felt the true inspiration of poetry. Fortunately, unlike many of our illustrious poets, who in their early struggles were similarly affected, he had not to trust to literature for his living—he had ample means at his disposal. He gave up both study and business for a while, and it was during his rambles in search of health through the beautiful valleys and rugged hills of his native county that many of his earliest and best pieces were composed. These were only distributed to his intimate friends; but with returned health and spirits he took renewed courage, and published numerous pieces in the leading journals of the district, notably in the *Hexham Courant*, *Newcastle Courant*, and the *Newcastle Chronicle*, and which met with most favourable notice. He early established for himself a high local reputation, not only for his literary ability, but for his kind and genial disposition. The first volume of his poems, published under the title of "North Country Lyrics," has been most favourably noticed in the critical press. The volume forms one of "The Moray Library," published by Stancsby & Co., London, and Frank Murray, Derby.

ROBERT WALLIS.

BAMBOROUGH CASTLE.

Hail! lordly castle on this rocky steep,
Scorning the lion breakers of the deep
That dash with thundering sound upon thy base,
And lash with spray thy brown, majestic face.
Stupendous castle, let the wild waves roar.
Thou standest firmly on the rugged shore
Of bold Northumbria, heeding not the sea
Moaning, because it can't o'erwhelm thee.
Here Saxon kings govern'd with stubborn will
Northumbria's powerful warriors, until
Came cunning Danes, and robb'd thee of thy vast
And valued treasures, soon though they were cast
Out by the Saxons, men of iron frame;
Then scores of years roll'd over, and there came
The keener Norman, with his flashing eye,
Who held thee bravely: ages have gone by
Since first his coming; often hast thou been
From that time sore defaced, yet still thy mien
Strikes the beholder as a glorious scene.
And listening, too, the sea's tremendous roll,
His spirit soars, and strengthen'd is his soul.

I THOUGHT OF THEE.

As on yon bank I calmly lay,
  And look'd upon the grassy lea,
And view'd the closing of the day,
  Oh! maid benign, I thought of thee.

I thought of thee as golden Sol
  Lit up with fire the western sky,
And ting'd the walls of Bywell Hall,
  And Tyne's fam'd waters gliding by.

I thought of thee in yon calm nook
  Where boughs bend down to kiss the stream ;
Where joins the Tyne the rippling brook,
  Where blossoms glow, and insects teem.

I thought of thee as up I cast
  Towards the foliage dense mine eyes,
And heard the breezes as they past
  Breathe forth their mild, melodious sighs.

I thought of thee when all around
  Was full of soul-delighting glee,
And when I heard the welcome sound
  Of evening bells come soft to me.

I thought of thee with soul serene
  As Bywell* sisters came to sight,
And as I view'd the ivy green
  Upon the castle walls that night.

Delightful girl, where'er I turn'd
  My roving eye these joys to see,
And beauteous though they were adorn'd,
  I thought of thee ! I thought of thee !

COUSIN LILLIE.

Across the sea, across the sea,
A slender form appears to me,
Yes, Lillie, still I think of thee.

* The two Churches.

And Lillie, still thy sad-like face
Comes back to me, and I can trace
A portion of thy mother's grace.

Thy gentleness, thy breathings high,
Thy touching look, thy pitying sigh,
Come even yet before my eye.

And that last morning comes again
When parting gave the bitter pain,
And down thy cheeks tears fell like rain.

Though just a thoughtless lad was I,
Thy tender hand-touch made me sigh,
And tremblingly I said "Good-bye."

Since then what ups and downs I've had;
I am no more a boisterous lad—
The world tempestuous makes me sad.

And thou hast had thy load to bear
Of sickness, and of wearying care,
Yet thou art bless'd with children fair.

What pleasure now 'twould be to me
To voyage o'er the mighty sea,
Thy dear ones, and thyself to see.

I fear though on Australian land
My weakly form will never stand;
In fancy then I'll grasp thy hand,
And greet each blossom of thy band.

AS SOOTHING AS THE ZEPHYR'S ROLL.

As soothing as the zephyr's roll,
As tranquil as the brooklet's flow
Were those soft eyes, which cheer'd my soul
Beneath yon shade, long years ago.

And oh! that sweet, transporting voice,
   Which oft I heard with willing ear,
No longer bids my soul rejoice,
   No longer draws from me the tear.

Pure innocence upon yon brow
   Displayed itself with lowly grace,
But now to bitter fate I bow;
   No more I'll see that matchless face.

No more I'll see those chasten'd eyes,
   No more that touching voice I'll hear;
And memory will awake the sighs
   For one who had no earthly peer.

A PATTERDALE LEAF.

To the " Maid of Wansbeck."

I cull'd this leaf by the Silver Lake,*
   Near the great wild crags, for you,
Which I hope you'll keep for the giver's sake,
   And the lovely spot wherein it grew.
Oh! how sweet is the vale of Patterdale,
   And the charming scenes around;
And the 'witching grace on its striking face,
   Is the same that on yours I've found.

Then maiden, I pray you keep this leaf,
   That grew in a hallow'd dell;
Maybe if you're troubled with pain or grief
   'Twill act as a soothing spell.
And your thoughts maybe it will sometimes wing
   To the friend who cull'd it there;
But, maiden, may never its presence bring
   A frown to your features fair.

        * Ullswater.

Rev. J. W. Kaye.

JOHN WILLIAM KAYE was born February 20th, 1840, of parents who were members of the Society of Friends. His father was a direct descendant of the Kayes of Totties Hall, Wooldale, near Holmfirth, Yorkshire. The subject of this notice was educated at the Friends' School, Rawdon, near Leeds, afterwards at Spring Street Academy, Huddersfield, and subsequently by private tutors at home. His favourite study was the languages. From his youth he was accustomed to write verses, and his parents treasured up many a scrap of paper on which his early rhymes were written. Mr. Kaye's first scholastic appointment was that of French Master at Tickhill Academy, near Bawtry. He afterwards commenced a private school at Crossland Moor, near Huddersfield. In December, 1860, he was married to Miss Whittenbury, daughter of Mr. W. C. Whittenbury, and grand-daughter of Dr. Whittenbury, an eminent physician of Liverpool. About this time Mr Kaye began to have a strong desire to enter the ministry, and removed from Crossland Moor to Nottingham. During his residence in Nottingham, Mr. Kaye attended the theological lectures of the Congregational Institute, for about eighteen months. He then was induced to undertake the management of a private school at Bentham. The desire for the ministry still followed him, and he determined to enter St. Bees' College. After passing the full course of study he was ordained by the Bishop of Brechin, to the curacy of St. Mary Magdalene, Dundee, in 1873. In the following year the reverend gentleman removed to the curacy of St. Mary, Ilkeston ; and in 1876 he became Curate of St. Philip's, Bradford Road, Manchester. Here he remained for six years, when he was preferred to the Rectory of Derrybrusk, near Enniskillen.

Mr. Kaye has been a contributor to various magazines and newspapers—frequently writing over *noms-de-guerre*. Being diffident and distrustful of his own genius he has hesitated to collect his fugitive pieces, and issue them in book-form. At the urgent desire of many of his friends Mr. Kaye, at no far distant period, hopes to issue a volume of his verse.

J. POTTER BRISCOE.

LIVE TO A PURPOSE.

Oh ! rouse you from slumber,
And wake to the day ;
For hours without number,
Are lost in delay.

Forbear more to murmur,
  And cast off its mood;
And live to a purpose,
  That's noble and good.

Ah ! Time is a treasure,
  Of value untold;
Then waste not in pleasure,
  Its moments of gold. ·
But bravely endeavour,
  Whate'er is withstood,
To live to a purpose,
  That's noble and good.

Despise not your station,
  Whate'er it may be;
The world is the nation,
  Of brave men and free.
What though you may labour,
  In field or in flood;
Still live to a purpose,
  That's noble and good.

Beware of allurement—
  'Twill need all your might,
And powers of endurement,
  Life's battle to fight.
Yield not to temptation,
  Through fire and through blood;
But live to a purpose,
  That's noble and good.

One aim be your token,
  One end still in view;
One purpose unbroken—
  To that ever true.

Where'er you may wander,
By mountain or wood ;
Still live to a purpose,
That's noble and good.

Oh ! fear not the battle,
But struggle right on ;
And heed not the rattle,
Till victory's won.
Then rise o'er each failure,
Nor fretfully brood ;
And live to a purpose,
That's noble and good.

THE BLUE FORGET-ME-NOT.

'Tis said that once upon a time,
A lover and a maiden fair,
Had pledged their troth, for weal or woe,
By heaven and all that's holy there.

The lover was a valiant knight,
The lady was of high degree ;
They sat beside the river's brink,
Beneath a favourite trysting tree.

" 'Tis hard," he said, " to leave my love,
Perhaps to see her face no more ;
Yet I must go withstand our foes,
And fight upon a foreign shore."

" What dearer pledge can I yet give ?
What further may your lover do,
To prove his heart is all your own,
For ever faithful still to you?"

" On yonder rock," the lady said,
  " There grows a little flow'ret blue,
Give me but that, and in my hair
  I'll wear the pledge your heart is true."

He climbed the rock, which far o'erhung
  The river's brink and water's flow ;
He plucked the flower, but plucking—fell
  Amidst the deep, dark waves below.

And grasping still his flow'ret pledge,
  He struggled hard to reach the shore ;
The tide was strong, his strength grew weak,
  He could, alas ! hold out no more.

The flow'ret to the brink he threw ;
  She caught the prize—unhappy lot,
" The pledge is yours, my love," he cried,
  " Forget me not "—" forget me not ! "

His strength was gone, his life ebbed fast,
  He sank beneath the flowing tide ;
And there she vowed, come weal or woe,
  Till death to be his faithful bride.

The flower she braided in her hair,
  Ere yet she left that mournful spot ;
And called it by that tender name,—
  Love's parting word—" Forget-me-not."

And e'er since then the flow'ret's been,
  The pledge of all fond hearts and true ;
Then, for that ancient story's sake,
  We still will love the flow'ret blue.

MAKKIN' IT UP AGEEAN.

Whoay Sally lass, what's happen'd thee?
What mak's thee look sa queer?
Tha's getten, mun, sa foine and prayad,
Oa hardly dar come near.

It nivver ust ta be loake this,
Ther's summat wrang o'm suer;
Dooan't turn thee owd sweetheart away,
Befoor tha's fun a truer.

This huffin fairly caps me mun;
Its not at all loake thee;
Tha tell'd me we them bonny lips,
Tha'd geen thee heart ta me.

Tha ust ta link thee airm e moine,
Bayaght makkin' sich a fuss;
An' on me shoolder laid thee heead,
Just wol oa stale a kuss.

True love they sea ne'er runs sa smooth,
It has its bits a jars;
Oa think its true—but nowt but deeath,
Mun pairt two hearts loake yars.

That chap 'ats been an flattered hard,
Ta turn thee heart thro' me,
He's troay'd his hand we other fooak,
Befoor he coom ta thee.

Ne'er 'eed him lass—just let him gooa,
An' sweep his doorston cleean;
But come into me airms, moa love,
An' be me own ageean.

Shoo crept up to his soide, an sobb'd—
Wol he hush'd all her fears,
An' claspt his airm arayand her waist,
An' kusst off all her tears.

ME DEAR OWD WOAFE AN' ME.

Ah ! Sally lass, it's trew enough,
  We'er growin' owd an' gray ;
But bless thee, mun, tha'rt bonny yet,
  An' bonnier ivv'ry day.

We've seen some ups an' dayans together ;
  We'en known what trubble's been ;
But throo it all, a better woafe,
  Moa lass, O've nivver seen.

Throo rough an' smooith, we'en struggled on,
  Still joggin soide be soide ;
An' lass tha'rt dearer ta me nayagh,
  Nor when tha wor me broide.

When hard toimes coom, an' when we felt,
  We knew nowt what ta do ;
The lovin' smoiles, an' wopful words,
  They cheer'd me all t'way throo.

For yers an' yers, we'en toddled on,
  Loake childer hand e hand ;
An' still ta ha' thee be me soide,
  Seems reight loake fairy land.

Me dear owd woafe, tha's allis been,
  Me best an trewest frend ;
God bless thee lass ! an' bless us booath,
  An' keep us safe ta th' end !

H. Ernest Nichol.

ERNEST NICHOL is a native of Hull, and was born in 1862. Up to his twenty-third year he was engaged in a civil engineer's office ; after which time he devoted himself to the study of music, for which he has always had the strongest love. In 1888 he took his degree of Bachelor in Music at Oxford, and is now a teacher of the art. He is the author of a cantata entitled "Our Father's Love," both the words and music being his own composition, and he has also composed a number of songs, piano pieces, part-songs, carols, &c. ; and in the case of some of these he has also written the words, thereby proving how in him "music and sweet poetry agree."

Mr. Nichol's natural taste has inclined him towards the serious and reflective in poetry, yet he has shown his capabilities for the humorous in a capital series which he contributed to *Rare Bits* under the title of " The New Ingoldsby Legends." The merit of these was fully recognised. He has been an occasional contributor to *Chambers's Journal*, and *Great Thoughts*. Mr. Nichol's serious verse—of which we give some selections—has many excellencies. Whenever he writes he has evidently something to say which is worth saying, and he has the ability to say it well. This we think will especially apply to " The Artist of the Sunset," and " The Snowflake." The Rondel commencing. " Let us go home, my love," is an exquisite little poem, and if our author had written only " The Artist of the Sunset," it alone would have proved him to be a genuine poet.

J. R. TUTIN.

THE ARTIST OF THE SUNSET.

" Behold," said Fancy, pointing to the sun.
" Behold, the Artist by his picture stands ;
He waits until your rapture is begun,
Then blushing, hastens down to distant lands."

" Believe her not," said Truth ; " the Artist dwells
Deep hidden in thy spirit's inmost core :
And cloud on cloud he day by day dispels
That thou mayst worship him for evermore."

A RONDEL.

Let us go home, my love, the sun is low,
Our shadows slant along the fallen snow,
   And on the distant hill, across the gloom,
Our own hearth-fire shines out with waiting glow ;
     The white wan moon among the clouds hath clomb ;
       Let us go home.

Let us go home, my love ; thus, year on year,
The dwelling of our mingled lives grows dear ;
   Out on the world's wide sea the striving foam
May seek to mount the rocks all steep and sheer,
   For fame and gold the foolish crowd may roam ;
       Let us go home.

Let us go home, dear love, for we are blest
That we have found the perfect calm of rest,
   Where all who work and trust at last will come ;
The love of Love within each quiet breast,
   And o'er our heads the silent starlit dome—
       Let us go home.

MENDELSSOHN'S "GONDOLA SONG."

[Lieder ohne Wörte, No. 6.]

A boat is sleeping underneath the moon,
   Caressed by the ripples which at every plash
   Collect the scattered light in one long flash
Of quivering fire. Across the air of June
The boatman's call is borne ; then faintly, soon,
   Two maiden voices sing ; and like a dash
   Of dewdrops from the swaying of an ash,
The notes of a guitar are lightly strewn.

The gondola glides onward, and we hear
One sweet voice singing lonely ;—low and clear
   It fades into the distance like a dream ;
A dying echo of that wild, sad song—
Then all is still ; save for the boatman's long
   Low cry that creeps upon the silent stream.

THE SNOWFLAKE.

O Snowflake, whirling and dancing,
      Whence do you come ?
   With a rush and a dart,
   And a sleep and a start,
With a swift, subtle sliding like fairy queen gliding,
   O Snowflake, whither advancing ?
      Where is your home ?

" From the Spirit living and loving
      In heaven I come ;
   I dwelt in His light,
   And so I grew white ;
Then clad in His beauty I came to my duty,—
   O man, to your heart I am moving,
      That is my home."

Richard Le Gallienne.

ICHARD LE GALLIENNE was born in Liverpool on the 20th of January, 1866. He was educated at the Liverpool College, and then, being intended by his father for a business career, he was apprenticed to a firm of accountants in his native city, and by them initiated into the mysteries of balancing, auditing, and winding-up estates. His tastes were, however, literary. The books he loved were not ledgers and journals, but Elzevirs, and, while still in his teens, he gathered about him an excellent library, which includes many of those scarce volumes that delight the bookworm; for, though a book reader, Mr. Le Gallienne is still more a book lover. He early developed a more than ordinary taste for poetry and poetical composition, and in 1887 he issued through the press of Messrs. W. & J. Arnold, of Liverpool, a " privately printed " volume entitled " My Ladies' Sonnets and other Vain and Amatorious Verses." This was well received by the critics, the limited edition was soon disposed of, and the author found himself safely placed on the first step of the ladder of literary fame. " We do not think there will be much difference of opinion," wrote Mr. James Ashcroft Noble, the accomplished critic of the *Manchester Examiner*, himself a poet, " concerning the poetical quality of the contents of this dainty little volume, and there can be no difference whatever concerning the artistic quality of its external appearance. . . The tiny tome is one which will charm the connoisseur who buys his books simply to gaze at and fondle them. Mr. Le Gallienne is unmistakably a poet, and his verse is at once so artistic and yet so human, so finely wrought and yet so obviously spontaneous, so rich in elaborate daintiness and in winning simplicities, that it finds the man in us not less surely than it charms the critic." Since then another work, entitled " Volumes in Folio," has been published. It consists of the " bookish " pieces that had already appeared, together with some others. Of the sonnets which will be quoted presently, the first was written for Mr. Alexander Ireland's always delightful " Book-lover's Enchiridion," and reproduced in " Volumes in Folio." It is, in my opinion, though not, I believe, in the opinion of its author (but authors cannot always judge), the best sonnet Mr. Le Gallienne has yet composed. The second was printed in the *Academy* at the time of Matthew Arnold's death. " The Song of the Morning Wind " is taken from the pages of " My Ladies' Sonnets," &c.

Mr. Le Gallienne, though primarily a poet, has a good prose style. Grace of form distinguish the essays of his which have appeared in the magazines. They make no pretensions to be profound. They are the essays of the poet, not of the student. Doubtless, if Mr. Le Gallienne were permitted by Father Time to choose his own place among the prose-immortals, he would prefer to rank with Lamb, Hazlitt and Leigh Hunt, than with John Locke, Adam Smith and Herbert Spencer.

It is safe to affirm that Mr. Le Gallienne is one of the most promising of our young poets. He is not the man to hide his light under a bushel, and, well-endowed as he is with literary tastes and fine talent, if the motive force prove sufficient he will surely become famous.

WALTER LEWIN.

A BOOKMAN'S CONFESSIO AMANTIS.

When do I love you most, sweet books of mine?
In strenuous morns when o'er your leaves I pore,
Austerely bent to win austerest lore,
Forgetting how the dewy meadows shine;
Or afternoons, when honeysuckles twine
About the seat, and to some dreamy shore
Of old Romance, where lovers evermore
Keep blissful hours, I follow at your sign?

Yea! ye are precious then, but most to me
Ere lamplight dawneth, when low croons the fire
To whispering twilight in my little room,
And eyes read not, but sitting silently,
I feel your great hearts throbbing deep in quire,
And hear you breathing round me in the gloom.

MATTHEW ARNOLD.

Died 15th April, 1888.

Within that wood where thine own scholar strays,
O! Poet, thou art passed, and at its bound
Hollow and sere we cry, yet win no sound
But the dark muttering of the forest maze
We may not tread, nor pierce with any gaze:
And hardly love dare whisper thou hast found
That restful moonlit slope of pastoral ground
Set in dark dingles of the songful ways.

I

Gone! They have called our shepherd from the hill;
   Passed is the sunny sadness of his song,
      The song which sang of sight, and yet was brave
   To lay the ghosts of seeing; subtly strong
      To wean from tears and from the troughs to save ;
And who shall teach us now that he is still ?

THE SONG OF THE MORNING WIND.

The morning wind came whispering by,
With breath as soft as maiden's sigh,
And voice as sweetest lullaby ;
But seemed a sadness in his tone,
As one who liveth life alone,
And for the death of fairest hopes makes moan.

And so I said :—" O ! wind of spring,
Why goest thou a-sorrowing
While all the vales for gladness sing
And all the little hills rejoice ?
Why liftest not a gladsome voice,
Why makest thou this melancholy choice ? "

Then came the answer, soft and low—
" Not mine the choice that thus I go
So sadly sighing to and fro.
Alas ! I would rejoice with all
These gladsome voices musical,
But sorrow knows no merry madrigal."

And then the voice was hushed again
With deep intensity of pain,
And silent was the sad refrain ;
Then feeling all his depth of woe,
I cried in ruth—" O, weep not so,
But let a sorrowing heart thy sorrow know."

But still no answer came to me,
No sorrow for my sympathy,
For the sad wind had silently
Stolen away to weep his fill ;
And soon I found him sobbing still
In the seclusion of a little hill.

" Nay, nay ! " I cried, " why this despair ?
Come, tell me ; never yet was there
A woe beyond a sweet repair."
Then the sad voice that spoke before—
" Nought can avail of all thy lore,
Loveless am I, and must be evermore.

" All know the sweetness of love's power ;
The bee may love the meadow-flower
And kiss her many a golden hour ;
The mountain has the valley's love,
The river wooes the skies above,
And only I, alas, must loveless move.

" Hard, even, is the lot of those
Whose face and form must ever close
Love's path that only beauty knows ;
But harder still, it seems to me,
To win Love's smiles, and then to be
Condemned for ever from those smiles to flee.

" And such my fate, for every day
Some flower smiles, and bids me stay
And pass my life with her alway ;
So sweet, says she, is it to feel
My breath into her bosom steal,
And all its dower of loveliness reveal !

" But when I fain would stay with her,
And whisper through her dewy hair
Low melodies to comfort care,

Straight comes my fate and stills my tongue,
Breaks off the burden of my song,
And bears me loveless winds and clouds among.

" And then the flower will breathe a tale
Of heartlessness, and her sad wail
Float mournfully down mead and vale—
' Beware, beware the wind of spring,
Heed not his tender whispering,
But to ensnare he doth so sweetly sing.' "

. Sudden he paused, but not from woe,
But joy; for in the vale below,
Drooping across the river's flow,
Just waking to the storms and stress
Of life, from dreams of nothingness,
A rosebud blushed at her own loveliness.

Soon are the tears of memory dried,
Soon was he wooing for his bride
That rosebud by the river-side;
And soothly very sweet the song
That fell like honey from his tongue;
What maiden could resist such accents long?

And she, sweet innocent young thing,
Unused to lovers' whispering,
Knowing nought of the wind of spring,
Smiled sweetly at his fatal lay,
Gave him her love, and bade him stay
And make for her such melodies alway.

Then a great joy shook all his soul,
As when some great despair shall roll
From off the heart its dread controul;
The love he mourned for ever past
Had dawned upon his life at last,
And all his sorrows far and wide were cast.

His love's white arms were round him pressed,
His head was pillowed on her breast,
And all his soul was steeped in rest ;
As when some fierce delirium
Is laid to sleep by opium,
And the soul dreams in sweet elysium.

Ah, me! from dreams so sweet as this
How bitter the awakening is,
And wind and flower knew that, I wis.
Why should we dwell upon their pain?
The wind soon lost his love again,
The flower listened for his voice in vain.

Whether or not she pined away,
Waiting her lover day by day,
Comes not within my roundelay ;
Or whether she took heart and thought,
As all forsaken maidens ought,
That lovers plenty remain to be caught,

I know not, for I strode along
Heedless amid the flowery throng,
Hearing nought but that sad sweet song,
Like waves on a desolate shore—
"Nought can avail of all thy lore,
Loveless am I, and must be evermore."

John Thomas Barker.

JOHN THOMAS BARKER was born at Bramley, near Leeds, on January 19th, 1844, and is the son of Mr. Benjamin Barker, an amiable and much respected gentleman, and an excellent business man. His uncle was the celebrated Joseph Barker, a man of versatile and extraordinary talent, whose reputation was high, for many years, as a preacher, lecturer, and subtle debater. In this three-fold capacity, he was a thorough master of pure Saxon English. Some of his ability is possessed by his nephew, the subject of this notice. Although engrossed in business pursuits from the age of fifteen, when his school life was cut short, his leisure moments have produced a large amount of literary matter, in both prose and verse. A good deal of this first appeared in the "Bramley Almanack," and the "Bramley Parish Magazine." He has been a frequent contributor to the *Yorkshire Post*, and other papers and periodicals. In 1880, he edited and published a charming autobiography of his uncle, Joseph Barker, which was highly commended by the leading reviews.

His first poetical venture, published separately on his own account, was "A Midsummer Day's Dream," which appeared in 1869. In 1886, there followed a collected edition of his poems, entitled "The Pilgrimage of Memory, and other Poems." The longest poem in the collection," The Pilgrimage of Memory," is in irregular, unrhymed metre, like that of Southey's "Thalaba." It displays considerable inventive power. He is most successful, however, in his use of the West Riding dialect, as exemplified in the "Bramla Band," the "Cottar's Setterda Neet," &c. Here he is at home. These poems are very pleasing presentations of the vocabulary, idioms and peculiarly quaint humour of the artisans of Leeds and its neighbourhood.

JOHN WOOD, B.A.

BRAMLA' BAND.

Who hesn't heerd o't'Bramla' Band,
   That's famous far an' near?
An' wins sich honor for aar taan,
   Wi' ivvery cumin' year.
At Gala, Feast, an' Flaar Show,
   At Chris'mas, an' May-day,
At Contests tew, aar Band is suar
   Ta carry t'prize away.

Wi' bran' new clothes an' instruments,
  All shining bright an' clear,—
An' lads an' lasses craadin' raand,
  The Big Drum in the rear,—
The men all marching breast ta breast,
  Wi' martial stride an' pomp,—
Who can withstand thur stirrin' strains,
  As daan the taan they tromp?

Nah, whether, t'Band chaps played ta mich,
  (For t'trumpets didn't rust,)
I cannat say, but suar enif,
  They blew 'em till they brust.
T'poor chaps wor o'most fit ta roar,
  For all thur brass wor spent,
But t'taan clubbed up, an' bowt each man,
  A bran' new instrument.

Sum wor silver, an' sum wor brass,
  An' nicely curled i't'middle,—
An' sum they went,—trom, trom! bom, bom!
  An' sum did nowt but twiddle;
An' sum hed keys, an' hoils, an' lids,
  An' wun, a queer consarn,
Wor two yards long, or theer abaat,
  An' slotted up an' daan.

But when they played 'em all at wunce,
  An' mixed 'em weel together,
An' when the chap upon t'Big Drum,
  Thum, thum! began ta leather;
T'effect wor rayther startlin', and
  A Captin from the wars,
Enlisted 'em as soudgers, in
  The "Prince of Wales'" Huzzars.

Nah, sum hed nivver ridden a horse,
 Except at Bramla' Tide,
An' then upon the willy-gigs
 They'd hed a haup'ny ride ;
So when thur regimentals com',
 An' they began ta don,
They cuddn't tell what t'spurs wor for,
 Unless ta hod 'em on.

They thowt if they wor fastened tight
 Ta t'horse they'd somehow stick,
An' then they cuddn't be thrawn off,
 If it began ta kick ;
So off they went full trot ta York,
 Though nearly josst ta jelly,—
They stuck ta t'pummil, an' kep' thur spurs
 Weel under t'horse's belly.

An' when they gat ta t'City walls,
 They pooll'd up in a raw,
An' "See the Conquering Hero Comes,"
 They all began ta blaw ;
An varry weel they played it tew,
 When t'horses didn't prance,
But when they heerd a lively bit,
 They seemed abaat ta dance.

At last that chap wi' t'slottin' thing,
 Wi' cheeks puff'd fit ta crack,
He thrust it aat sa varry far,
 He cuddn't pooll it back ;—
An' t'horse bein' freeten'd at it tew,
 An' feelin' summat prickin',
It started off a raunin' up,
 An' then began a kickin'.

First t'instrument flew on ta t'graand,
　An' jingald fit ta breck ;
Then he wor fotched all on a lump,
　Reight on ta t'horse's neck ;
But t'warst of all, a spur cam off,
　An' t'chap bein' aat o'plumb,
T'horse sent him flyin' like a shot,
　Heeard first into t'Big Drum.

They pooll'd him aat bi his coit-tail,
　An' sum began ta chaff,
But t'chap wor suar, he'd ne'er been thrawn,
　If t'spur hed nut cum off.
So readers, nivver use a thing
　Ye dunnat understand ;
An' if yer tempted so ta dew,
　Remember t'Bramla' Band.

BUBBLES.

Suggested by Sir J. E. Millais's Picture.

A lovely boy of child-like grace,
With golden locks and upturned face,
　Blows bubbles in the air ;
His ruddy cheeks and parted lips
Are like the bubbles that he slips,
　So round and plump and fair.

The upward glance of his bright eyes,
Watches the globules as they rise
　Into the sunny sky ;
Like mimic worlds they float away,
The playthings of a summer's day,
　And then collapse and die.

We are but bubbles of the earth,
Thrown off by Nature at our birth ;
    And down life's glittering river
Full gaily on our course we glide,
Buoyant and sparkling, till in the tide
    We melt like foam for ever.

Our schemes and plans of daily life,
With checks and disappointments rife,
    Our very cares and troubles,
Ambition's heights, all beauteous things,
And joy and hope with silver wings,
    What are they all but bubbles ?

The wealth we have amassed in vain,
Rank and position to obtain,
    And fickle fortune's smile ;
Esteem of friends and woman's love,
The shouts of men and gods above,
    Abide but for a while.

And what is knowledge, fancy's flights,
The passion's glow, and love's delights ?
    Subjects for a poet's theme ;
Poems are but bubbles of the mind,
Filmy, evanescent, and refined,
    A vision and a dream.

THE NEWSPAPER BOY.

Dirty and ragged, with matted hair,
His elbows out and legs all bare,
Blear-eyed, shivering wretch of a child,
" Nobody's bairn," unkempt and wild ;

His papers tucked up under his arm,
Blowing his fingers to keep them warm,
Hear his cry as he runs on his mission,—
" Evening News here !   Special edition !"

Hoarse he cries through the crowded street,
With fluttering rags and pattering feet ;
Hungry and naked, wet and cold,
And still his papers are not sold ;
Till, fagged and weary, down he squats
And counts his pence, and plays and chats ;
Or coils himself in his rags of state
On the warm and savoury cook-shop grate.

He sniffs the tantalising fumes,
Then, warm and rested, he resumes
His daily fight for daily bread,
Though pinched and hungry, still unfed ;
Out he stretches his skinny arm,
With staring eyes and wild alarm,
Crying,—" Appalling railway collision !
Extery special !   Last edition !"

How strange the streets' familiar sights !
There is a *blind* man selling *lights* ;
In the noisy, clattering thoroughfare
The organ grinds its noiseless air ;
Ignorant boys and girls dispense
The brains of men of light and sense ;
Like crickets cry the merry mites,
" Football edition, sir ?   Box o' lights ?"

At last the garish sight is o'er,
The lights put out, and closed the door ;
The trams and 'buses all have gone,
The streets are silent, dim and lone.

Sad and weary, we thankful come
To well-earned rest, our own sweet home,
'Tis then our thoughts to others flow,—
O God! where do these children go?

To the squalid hovel, the filthy den,
A place more fit for beasts than men ;
To blows and oaths, and what is worse,
A mother's cries, a drunkard's curse ;
To straw and rags, a fever bed,
On which they hang their aching head ;
To foul disease, such home is his,—
Better the open streets than this.

Joseph Philip Robson.

HE poets of Newcastle, to borrow an expression from one of them, are as " thick as curns in a spice singin' hinnie," but, though numerous, there are not more than two or three who have risen above mediocrity and produced work of much literary value. Akenside, whose " Plea-sures of Imagination " even Dr. Johnson—the great Pomposo of style—could never read through, was for a long time the only representative of his native town in the Republic of letters. He, however, never gave poetic utterance to Northumbrian thought and feeling. It was not until the advent of J. P. Robson that the reading-world knew anything of the humour and pathos concealed in the heart of Tyneside. This amiable poet was born on the 27th of September, 1808, almost beneath the shadow of the Norman keep, in Bailiff-gate—a rickety old street, which has recently been removed to make way for railway extensions,

> But now they're tumblin' a' things doon
> In spite o' ancient grace, man.

His father, who had been educated at Stoneyhurst College for the Roman Catholic priesthood, kept a paint shop at the time in Pudding Chare. Here the future poet, when ten months old, narrowly escaped being poisoned by sucking paper which had contained yellow arsenic. His mother died in 1814 and his father in 1816, and their children, three boys and a girl, were left to the care of a grandfather. At the age of eleven young Robson was taken from school to commence the battle of life as an errand-boy to a grocer. Five years later, when apprenticed to a plane-maker, the impulse to sing came upon him, and the bottoms of his planes were soon filled with verses. Macpherson's translations of Ossian cast a spell over his imagina-tion at this period, and he versified every line of them. At the early age of seventeen he wrote his fine, swinging song, " The Tyne Exile's Return." In 1819 he was nearly drowned in the river he had celebrated, and was only saved by remembering Dr. Benjamin Franklin's advice to persons in a similar predicament. In 1830, spraining himself severely by lifting a heavy log of wood, he gave up the making of planes to become a school master. In 1831 appeared his first volume, entitled " Blossoms of Poesy." From this time forward most of his leisure time was devoted to literary composition. He published " Poetic Gatherings " in 1839; " The Mono-maniac and minor poems " in 1847; a collection of fourteen " Tyneside Songs " in 1848; " Life and Adventures of Billy Purvis " in 1849; " Bards of the Tyne," in which appeared several of his own songs, in 1850, " Poetic Pencillings " in 1852. For sixteen years, our poet, by reason of the " lack of pence, which vexes public men," showed how Apollo might serve Admetus in a novel fashion by writing a weekly puff for a firm of tailors.

In 1854 he left Newcastle and settled in Sunderland, where he assisted in the compilation of a shipping register. In 1857 he published "Hermione, the Beloved, and other Poems," and received, through Lord Palmerston, a grant of £20 from the Civil List. In 1859 he versified "The Song of Solomon" in the Lowland Scotch and Tyneside dialects for the philological collection of Prince Louis Lucien Buonaparte. He contributed from 1862 to 1871 to Chater's "Tyneside Comic Annual," and wrote a weekly local letter to the *North of England Advertiser* under the *nom de plume* of the "Retiort Keelman"—a letter which formed quite a new feature in north-country journalism. About the middle of 1869, while his last work, "Evangeline," was passing through the press, he was seized with a paralytic stroke. A painful illness supervened, and on the 16th of August, 1870, the "Bard of the Tyne and Minstrel of the Wear" died in Clayton-street, Newcastle. Robson married in 1831, and had a family of six children, only one of whom survived him, and but for a short time.

The poetic fame of J. P. Robson does not rest on his longer and more ambitious poems, readable as they nevertheless are. He was too much of a lyrist to excel in a sustained work. The terrible tale of jealousy and baffled vengeance which is told by the "Monomaniac" in a letter to his daughter, abounds in fine passages—I would instance that one describing the effect of music in turning for a time the would-be murderer from his purpose—but exhibits too much the influence of Byron to be considered a characteristic work of Robson's. It is in his shorter poems and songs that we see Robson at his best. Pathos and humour were equally at his command, and he had a delicate and graceful fancy which garnished a subject with lovely images. With an almost feminine sensibility to suffering and misfortune, his sympathies went out to the helpless, the crushed and the unhappy in songs of such beauty as "The Auld Wife's Plaint," "My Bonnie Bairn," "The Wail o' the Fallen," and "The Sichtless, Mitherless Bairn." The labour question is passionately represented from one point of view, in "The Song of the Coal-Mine Sprite." Robson's songs in the vernacular are the best of their kind. They are brimful of that broad, though quaint and homely, humour to which the dialect of Tyneside seems to lend itself. He touches many a tender chord in the heart while bringing a merry twinkle to the eye, investing his subject with a kindly human interest. A note like the following was rare on Tyneside till Robson's time.

> When we were at the skuel, my lads,
> We oft wished to be men ;
> We gat our wishes ; now we lang
> To be at skuel agyen.

There being so much that is excellent in Robson's work, it is difficult to make a judicious selection. The claims of such poems as "The Dial of Life," "The Sichtless, Mitherless Bairn," and "The Pawnshop Bleezing," are not readily set aside. Space, however, being limited, the genius of our poet may not unfairly be represented by the following three songs, which are printed in this work by the kind permission of Messrs. Allan, of Newcastle-upon-Tyne, and Mr. John Fraser, of Blyth, the owners of the copyright.

W. W. Tomlinson.

THE AULD WIFE'S PLAINT.

I hae naebody now; for my bairns are a' gane,
And a' the day lang I sit sabbin' alane :
I hae naebody now; like a weed on the wave
I am driftin' awa' to my bed in the grave.
When, weary wi' weepin' I sink to a slum,
I dream that my bairns to their mither hae come,
And I feel their saft lips, and their tears fa' like rain :
But I waken to find that the tears are—my ain.

I hae naebody now, as in days o' lang syne,
When Robie was wi' me—ah ! wha could repine ?
Then the lang simmer days cam as blythe as could be :
Now Robie is gone, and a's winter wi' me.
Ah ! there hings his bonnet, but law lies his head ;
His staff canno' guide his cauld feet frae the dead ;
And his auld elbow-chair to decay maun sune fa'.
Oh ! in grief how it moulders—its maister's awa' !

I hae naebody now : I'm a puir helpless thing—
Like a tree in the desert, forsaken by Spring ;
I hae naebody now to console my heart's cares,
E'en the breeze whistles past as it lifts my white hairs.
The cloud on the hill, wi' its dark-mantled brow.
In the smile o' the mornin' shall bonnily glow,
But the gloamin' that shadows a lane widow's day
Increases to darkness that lingers for aye.

I hae naebody now: a' my joy's in the tomb :
Like a lamp I am wastin' 'mid silence and gloom :
I hae naebody now to enkindle its flame
A' is cheerless and mirk in my heart an' my hame.
But my time sune maun come for my spirit is wae,
And langs for its pillow o' death in the clay.
Oh ! it langs for the land where my bairns now abide,
Where the tear of the heart-broken mourner is dried

THE WAIL O' THE FALLEN.

I canno' come to thee, mither ;
    My hame I daurna seek ;
I ken no' where to flee, mither,
    My heart is like to break ;
The pet I was o' a', mither,
    The youngest wean o' ten ;
An' why I fled awa', mither,
    I wish I didna ken.

The warnin' an' the dree, mither,
    Like snaw upon the flood,
Were wasted things to me, mither ;
    My ears were deaf to guid.
But the bird is sure to fa', mither,
    That spreads a wilfu' wing ;
The snare or vulture's claw, mither,
    Destruction sune maun bring.

Wi' sloe-black, glitt'ring een, mither,
    The tempter smiling came ;
Ca'd me his winsome queen, mither,
    And whiled me frae my hame.
The silken gowns and gowd, mither,
    Uncounted, were my ain ;
An' though he fondly wooed, mither,
    My spirit sank in pain.

I thoucht o' hame an' thee, mither,
    As tears gushed frae my een ;
My love proved fause to me, mither,
    As ithers aft had been.
I wake as frae a slum, mither,
    The gowd and gowns are gane ;
Thy words o' truth hae come, mither,
    I'm dyin' here alane.

I canno' come to thee, mither,
  My weary limbs are weak ;
The grave my hame maun be, mither,
  What ither dare I seek?
My brow is red wi' shame, mither,
  That ance was pure as snaw ;
Oh ! how can I come hame, mither,
  That broucht disgrace on a' ?

THE TYNE EXILE'S RETURN.

From wandering in a distant land, an exile had return'd,
And when he saw his own dear stream, his soul with pleasure
    burned ;
The days departed, and their joys, came bounding to his breast,
And thus the feelings of his heart in native strains expressed :

Flow on, majestic river,
Thy rolling course for ever ;
Forget thee will I never,
  Whatever fate be mine !
Oft on thy banks I've wander'd,
And on thy beauties ponder'd ;
Oh, many an hour I've squander'd
  By bonny, coaly Tyne !

Oh, Tyne ! in thy bright flowing,
There's magic joy bestowing ;
I feel thy breezes blowing,
  Their perfume is divine !
I've sought thee in the morning,
When crimson clouds were burning,
And thy green hills adorning,
  Thy hills, O, bonny Tyne !

When stormy seas were round me,
When distant nations bound me,
In memory still I found thee,
  A ray of hope benign.
Thy valleys lie before me,
Thy woods are waving o'er me ;
My home, thou dost restore me !
  I hail thee, bonny Tyne !

John Emmet, F.L.S.

OHN EMMET was born in 1822, at Final Royd House, Birkenshaw, at which place his forefathers acquired a large property and settled during the latter part of last century. He commenced drawing and Greek and Latin when eight or nine years old, and completed a thorough classical and mathematical education at Elam's Academy, Birstal. He then enjoyed the advantages of his excellent father's large library, and became enamoured of Natural History by reading Gilbert White's "Natural History of Selborne," and Waterton's "Wanderings in South America," at the same time intellectually devouring all the poets and prose writers on his father's shelves.

His first pilgrimage was to Rydal Mount in 1845. The poet Wordsworth, and his sister Dorothy, shewed him round their well-known garden, and the afternoon was passed with Hartley Coleridge—a happy day was spent. The second pilgrimage was to Selborne, when he made the acquaintance of Mr. and Mrs. S. C. Hall, who were very kind to him ; and soon after, an invitation to Walton Hall introduced him to that prince of naturalists, Charles Waterton, and an acquaintance began which lasted through life. In a letter we have seen, the veteran ornithologist says of a monograph our poet had sent him, "Poor Jack! you have indeed given me a most interesting account of his short life. I have never read an account of any winged favourite more amusing, sad, and touching. Such little pets almost always have an untimely end."

Soon the feeling for literary expression developed itself, and verses were strung together which were accepted by the Leeds, Bradford, and York newspapers. In 1848, a series of articles called "Ruralia," with the *nom de plume* of "Paul Puzzlecraft," became popular in the *Bradford Observer.* Various contributions to the *People's Journal* and *Hogg's Instructor* followed, during which time Mr. Emmet held a post as reviewer on one of our chief Yorkshire newspapers which continued over twenty years.

A joint volume, "Lays of the Sanctuary," appeared in 1859, to which our author sent four poems, one of which, "A Litany," is now appended. It took Dr. Winslow's fancy, who inserted it in one of his books, and the critic and sonnet writer, Samuel Waddington, has given it a place in his "Sacred Song." Another old favourite, "Golden Stairs," appeared in the *Bradfordian,* was successful, and highly appreciated at penny readings and other gatherings. Of another piece included in this small collection, viz. : "Love and Beauty," Eliza Cook says " It is a sweet lyric." This is now printed for the first time.

Mr. Emmet does not often write verse—sometimes ten or fifteen years elapse without a line. His various studies have taken him into botanical, conchological, antiquarian, and other inquiries, and contributions, in prose, of course, will be found in the " Archæological Journal," " Science Gossip," " The Naturalist," and elsewhere; but he chiefly confines himself in his prose articles to *Chambers's Journal*, to which he is a frequent contributor. He often, too, employs himself with water colour painting, and John Ruskin has passed a high eulogium upon some of his work.

Although not publishing much on his own account, Mr. Emmet has often helped other authors, particularly the editors of several county " Floras," the " Life of Eliza Hessel," " Clark and Roebuck's Handbook of Yorkshire Vertebrata," &c., &c., and he may be found in some thirty newspapers, from the *Standard* downwards.

In 1878, Mr. Emmet visited Rome and the classic sites of Italy, and had the pleasure of being introduced to Pope Leo XIII, and Victor Hugo —very dissimilar men! During the earlier part of his life, Mr. Emmet frequently met James Montgomery, who had great influence over him in matters of taste and culture. P. J. Bailey, of " Festus," also helped him with generous praise in early years.

Mr. Emmet had the honour of being elected a Fellow of the Linnean Society in 1855, and he has resided at Boston Spa, more or less, for over thirty years. He enjoys his *otium cum dignitate*, and has not an enemy in the world. He lives in a house smothered with roses and filled with old china bric-a-brac, antiquarian and other curiosities—as Waugh would say, " Crom full o' ancientry an' Roman hawpennies," and books and pictures, old and new. He leads a cultured life, varied by travel, retaining his intellectual tastes in all their freshness, enjoys life and his churchwarden pipe, and is never better pleased than when offering hospitality to old friends of similar tastes—and, indeed, with his quaint, happy way of looking at things, his inexhaustible fund of apt anecdote and vast general information, a more entertaining companion or genial host would be hard to find.

His love for every living creature wins in return the fearless confidence of all animals, who seem at once to recognise him as a friend.

In Mr. Emmet's neighbourhood he is regarded as a sort of walking encyclopædia, and whenever coins or trophies, shells or rare flowers, curious stones or old books are discovered, he is supposed to know all about them and name them as did Adam in Eden!

We have pleasure in knowing that there is a pile of MSS. waiting for the printer, with the title, " Marguerites and Marigolds," verse, old and new. There is the right ring about the work, and those who like what we have now given will welcome the coming guest.

                                             E. HELEN BARLOW

GOLDEN STAIRS.

There is a cottage by the stream,
  Whose thatch is near a century old ;
'Tis never scorched with summer's beam,
  With winter's ice 'tis never cold

I often watch them in and out,
    The children, and the good old pair;
For in that cot, beyond a doubt,
    There is an unseen golden stair.

Whilst sang the thrush one sultry night,
    Amongst the roses round the door,
They laid a gentle girl in white,
    I never heard or saw her more—
But those who watched her smile at last,
    And those who heard her latest prayer,
Aver, that up to heaven she passed,
    Passed upward by that golden stair.

An autumn morning, cool with mist,
    Brought its raw wind amongst the trees,
And, just as God's new red light kisst
    The frost-flowers from the lattices,
A boy lay on his sister's bed,
    He quite as gentle, cold, and fair,
Some called it death—but he, then dead,
    Went upward by that golden stair.

And others; some were in their prime,
    Just wedded when that thatch was new,
Went in and out a little time,
    Lived, loved, and lost, like me and you—
And went away, unseen by me,
    They went, you need not ask me where,
They went where we oft wish to be,
    Right upward by that golden stair.

And now whilst pulling vernal flowers,
    And now whilst sings the same old thrush,
And now whilst fall the autumn showers,
    Upon the beaded hawthorn bush,

The loved ones left will gather round,
  Low listening to the dear old pair,
Who point them to each lowly mound,
  And point them to that golden stair.

You never saw that rosy cot,
  Or sunned yourself amongst its blooms.
Or knew the treasures it has got,
  The wealth that lines its cosy rooms ;
But you would see and hear them oft,
  Still climbing up if you were there,
And soon they all will be aloft,
  Gone upward by that golden stair.

Mayhap the cottage where you dwell,
  Is bright with bloom and prankt with green,
And oh, if you would search it well,
  There may be golden stairs unseen,
For if to you the grace be given
  To love the God who hears your prayer,
Be sure you have the road to heaven,
  Your cottage has the golden stair !

A LITANY.

Lord, leave us not to wander lonely,
  Through this dark world unloved by Thee ;
All other friends are helpless only,
  Though full of love as friends may be.
Drear are the fondest homes around us,
  Sad like our hearts when Thou art far.
When Thou hast sought us, heard us, found us,
  How sweet Thy consolations are !
    Hear us, cheer us,
    Lord, and leave us not !

Leave us not when pride and anger
  In the heart would dare rebel;
Claim us in our utmost danger,
  Calm us at the mouth of hell.
Leave us not till we inherit
  Charity that works no ill,
And we hear Thy gentle spirit
  Inly whisper, " Peace, be still! "
    Hear us, cheer us,
    Lord, and leave us not!

Leave us not in days of trial,
  Let us act at duty's call,
Though it lead to self-denial,
  Though we have to give up all.
Raised on high, or humbled lowly,
  Praised or scorned from land to land,
Bear us up, our Father holy,
  Bear our burdens in Thy hand.
    Hear us, cheer us,
    Lord, and leave us not!

Leave us not when all have left us,
  Health and vision, strength and voice;
When of friends death hath bereft us,
  Let us still in Thee rejoice:
Near us, when in doubt, to guide us;
  Near us, when we faint, to cheer;
Near in battle's hour, to hide us;
  Nearer ever, and more dear.
    Hear us, cheer us,
    Lord, and leave us not!

Leave us not when foes come nigher,
  Cheer us when the grave looks cold,
Lead us onward, upward, higher,
  Forward to the gates of gold.
Leave us not when ailing, failing,
  Sore depressed, and bending low;

Be Thy love then most availing,
  Then to aid us be not slow.
    Hear us, cheer us,
    Lord, and leave us not !

Leave us not, till Thou hast brought us
  To the holy, wealthy place,
There to see Thee who hast bought us,
  Fought our fight, and won our race ;
There to hear no more the shouting
  And the thunder of our foes ;
Dangers past, and past all doubting,
  And the grave's austere repose !
    Hear us, cheer us,
    Lord, and leave us not !

LOVE AND BEAUTY.

Love makes love where'er it be
Of all we hear and feel and see,
Of all things fair or grand or good ;
The grove, the rainbow or the flood
The flowers below, the stars above—
All things give us love for love !

Love and beauty o'er the land
Everywhere go hand in hand ;
Where there's love, there's something fair.
Where there's beauty, love is there—
Nothing fair in heart or mind,
Who to love would be inclined ?

Loving one, we feel to move
Circled by a world of love -
Looking upward, there's the sky
Greets us with its laughing eye
Looking downward, love is seen
Ambushed in the rural green.

Loving one, a thousand songs
Echo from a thousand tongues,
Tongues that burn with heavenly fire
To enchant us and inspire—
Thus, whilst loving, all things seem
Loving, like the lover's dream.

Love makes love, if love it be
Of all we hear, think, feel or see—
Of all things fair or grand or good,
The grove, the rainbow, or the flood,
The flowers below, the stars above,
All things give us love for love !

AFTER THE RAIN.

After the rain and the swirl,
    The wind, the rain and the roar,
Come to my garden, my girl,
    The girl I love and adore—
Who sees thee, never forgets
    Charmed roses and violets.

And thou art my violet,
    And thou art my blushing rose,
And thee I never forget,
    However the weather goes—
After the roar and the rain
    And wind—thou art mine again.

O violet—rose—so shy,
    Let the rain pelt, the wind roar,
The wind will whirl the world dry,
    For us to love and adore—
Who sees thee never forgets
    Sweet roses and violets !

Mrs. Tonkin.

MRS. TONKIN (*née* S. E. Jones) is a lady well-known to a large circle of friends in the neighbourhood alike of Manchester and Stockport. She was born in the first-named town, June 12th, 1831, of parents distinguished for their uprightness and amiability, and grew, with other children, to be a joy and solace to them to the end of their days. In July, 1855, she gave her hand to Mr. Joseph Tonkin, a native of Buryan, Cornwall, and in due time became the mother herself of a son and daughter. A warm admirer of the beautiful county where he first saw the light, Mr. Tonkin delighted to familiarize the mind of his much-loved wife with the varied and always romantic charms for which it is renowned. Her visits to Cornwall were frequent, and it cannot be doubted that the richly poetic abilities of her mind were stimulated, in no slight degree, by the scenery and associations to which she was there introduced. Very much of what is nearest and dearest to her heart, in its memories, and brightest and fairest as a living element of her imagination, is linked for ever with consecrated Cornwall. Mr. Tonkin was a man of singularly energetic, prompt, and skilful business character. Hence he acquired, while still quite young, a position of distinguished value and responsibility in one of the very highest classes of Manchester warehouses. He held his position for more than a quarter of a century, resigning it, at last, with the sincere regret of all who knew him, and most particularly of his employers, by reason of severe and protracted illness, from which, after several years of patient suffering, he was released by the hand of Divine mercy, August 6th, 1882.

From the days of her early womanhood, onward, unbrokenly, Mrs. Tonkin has charmed her friends with sweet and elegant verse; not in any kind of continuous stream, but in that very agreeable way which pleases the more by its unexpectedness. She makes no pretension to be a poetess in the lofty sense of the term. She compares herself to a little singing bird of the hedgerow, whose notes may perchance enter the ear of the tired wayfarer, and become to him another form of "Traveller's joy." Her outbursts of song, very numerous, were an accurate counting to be made of them, are to be regarded as the natural outflow of a spirit ever alive to the beautiful in creation. Capable of appreciating, if not of fully comprehending, the grand chords of human life; sensitively quick to the appeal of human emotions, and taking an almost child-like delight in the simple and common, so that it is pure and comely, she weaves her thoughts and fancies into tunes of never failing melody. Many of her contributions appeared originally in the columns of the *Manchester Weekly*, and some were supplied to the Cornish press, and among these last are assuredly to be found some of the very best pieces that ever appeared in print. "Corn-wall, my Country," may be adduced as one of the most delectable. In 1866 she published a little volume, called from the name of the opening piece, "Rostherne Mere, and other poems." The whole edition was rapidly taken up by the public, and it is unquestionable that were a second series to be brought out, it would meet with quite as cordial a reception. Very remarkable, too, is the diversity of style and subject in this little volume. Pieces that breathe an earnest and simple piety, and that are worthy of a place in any collection of sacred poetry, stand side by side with others that overflow with fun and humour, for Mrs. Tonkin is no weeping sentimentalist. The best characteristic of a truly happy genius is that it enjoys a laugh every bit as much as any votary of the comic.

In Mrs. Tonkin we thus have one who combines the pleasant realities of amiable emotion, honoured mother, esteemed friend, and contributor to our keenest intellectual enjoyment. The stream, happy to say, continues to flow, bright and refreshing as ever. It reminds one of those beautiful springs in the Holy Land, for which the ancient Hebrew poets found no name so suitable as that of the "eyes" of their lovely land.

G.

WIMBERRY RIPE.

" Wimb'ry ripe! Wimb'ry ripe! " Well done, old man!
Go vend thy juicy wares about the street ;
Awake the " Seven sleepers," if thou canst,
With thy loud, tuneless voice. I love its ring
This summer morning. It has awakened me,
And set me musing of the summer time
When I was young and rambled on the moors
About my home, in search of " wimberry ripe."
O bonnie berries! bountiful and blue !
How doth my spirit leap at sight of ye !
I am not old and grey this gladsome morn,
But blithe and lissome as the moorland maid
Of fifty years ago, erewhile the mirk
And toil of city life had robbed mine eyes
Of the bright sparkle that belongs to youth,
Or Time's chill touch had bleached my sunny locks,
And weary made my once untiring feet.
Nay, but I am not foolish, though I feel
The warm tears gushing to my happy eyes.

Pictures are floating o'er mine age-dulled brain :
I am a child upon my native moors,
And the long fifty years seem but a day ;
The blue-bells nod once more about my feet,
And purple heather blends with golden gorse ;
The oak boughs crouch and spread their leafy boughs,
As to protect the brown-winged brood below ;
The mountain ash trees rear their slender stems ;
Sporting their feathery leaves and scarlet crests
Beside the tassel'd birch in silver grey ;
While, under and about, the sturdy shrubs
Spring free and cultureless, and deep-hued fruit
Yield to the youngsters without loss of pence,
Or sanguinary tithe by bramble claimed,
When, with rash hand, the glossy balls are seized
And cruel thorns demand a recompense.
Come, loved companions of my childish days !
Come once again, with baskets as of yore !
Let us to our beloved blue-shadowed moors,
To breathe again the freedom of the hills,
And fill our spirits with the murmurings
Of thyme-blessed bees, and butterflies made glad
With scented sunshine and the hymns of birds
And arching heavens. Ah ! let us once again
Mount our beloved grey scar, moss coronaled,
Or in the brook below build minnic mills
Of magic power, to make the wheel of life
Roll smoothly round, as in the little space
That shines above the mist of long ago.
Here comes the man, with Minnie by his side .
I hear her chattering like a magpie bold :
" Now, go and ask my grandma ; she will buy ,
For she loves wimberries. I know, old man :
And we all want a pudding for to-day
As big as a cannon ball, with lots of juice
To stain our lips and teeth, and make us laugh.

Do they stain yours, old man?"　"Naw, naw, my lass,
They dunna stain Phil's grinders now-a-days;
And for good reason why.　Bu' fotch a bowl
While I shout ' Wimb'ries!' just to let folk yer
As I'm a-comin'; it's nigh pudding toime;
Ay, missus, sure they're fresh, just fresh fro' th' moors.
And see yo', they're as big and blue as grapes,
And mebbe full as sweet—they're gradeley fruit—
None better grown than Owd Phil's wimb'ry ripe.
Here come th' young childer!　Bless us, what a troop
Of laughing little 'uns!　Gi' me th' bowl to fill
Reet up to th' brim; good measure yo' shall have
For your bright faces and th' owd lady's sake.
Hoo minds Owd Phil when he wur but a boy—
How strange things come abeaut!　Ay, who would think
Owd Phil wur bred upo' her fayther's moors,
And worked for years within owd Carrbrook Mill?
But, sithee, th' folk are out wi' bowl in hand,
While I'm a-gapin' o'er th' long buried past.
Good mornin', missis!　Toimes is changed since then.
Good mornin', childer!　Now for wimb'ry ripe!"

CORNWALL.

Cornwall, my country! the home of my childhood,
　Land of my forefathers, land of the free,
Land of the mighty, the wild, the majestic,
　Land of the beautiful, land of the sea!

Ever-loved Cornwall! though rugged thy mountains,
　How fair and how fruitful thy valleys beneath;
How memory recalls the bright haunts of my boyhood—
　Thy wild moorland country, empurpled with heath!

Ocean-bound Cornwall! still home of the sea-bird,
　Thy rocks,—once the haunt of the Druid of old,
Still wondrous thy caves, and thy boulders of granite,
　Still wondrous as first o'er thy mountains they rolled.

Where are thy champions, famous in history?
    Where are the free-hearted, where are the brave?
Where are the bards, and the minstrels poetic?—
    They found in loved Cornwall, a home, and a grave.

And ever the waves of the ocean are hymning
    A requiem sad for the noble and free;
And full of strange cadences, mournful and tender,
    They sing 'neath the rocks the wild song of the sea.

But, Cornwall, thy glory has not yet departed;
    Though gone are thy bards, and thy heroes of old,
Still proudly the sun sets upon thee, loved country,
    Brightly tipping the peaks of thy mountains with gold.

Cornwall, my country! the home of my childhood,
    Land of the brave, how my heart pants for thee!
Land of the mighty, the wild, the majestic,
    Land of the true-hearted,—Cornwall for me!

ONLY TWO LITTLE SHOES.

Only two little shoes!
Such a shabby, worn-out pair!
And yet they are gazed on fondly,
As if they were passing fair.
        Worn and old,
        A mine of gold
Would not purchase those two little shoes.

Only two little shoes!
Once they were brilliant red,
Now they are sadly faded,
But they speak of a darling, dead.
        And tears like rain,
        Again and again
Have dropped on those two little shoes.

Only two little shoes !
But where are the baby feet
That made them twinkle with beauty,
As they danced, and made music sweet ?
  Joyous and clear
  To a mother's ear
Came the sounds from those two little shoes.

Only two little shoes !
Their music has passed away,
The nursery still sounds blithesome,
But not with their pattering play.
  There they lie
  All silently,
Speaking for ever, those two little shoes.

Only two little shoes !
A shabby and worn-out pair !
But the mother's lingering footstep
Is often heard on the stair.
  Softly she steals
  To a drawer, and kneels,
As she weeps o'er those two little shoes.

Only two little shoes !
That call forth many a sigh ;
But a beautiful vision is granted,
When she breathes a prayer to the sky.
  On bended knees
  The mother sees
Something fairer than two little shoes.

GROWING OLD.

Growing old ! growing old !
 Life lasts not for ever ;
Warmest hearts must cease to throb,
 Closest love-links sever.

Growing old ! growing old !
  Yes, in spite of yearning,
Not one day from buried years
  Ever comes returning.

Growing old ! growing old !
  Is the wide world better
For my drop of influence,
  Or am I it's debtor ?

Growing old ! growing old !
  Is my life progressing ?
Can I hope my latter days
  May be crowned with blessing ?

Growing old ! growing old !
  How the years are flying,—
Work unfinished, good unwrought !
  Will it be so—dying ?

Growing old ! growing old !
  O for great endeavour,
Noble aims and loving deeds
  That will last for ever.

Growing old ! growing old !
  Lord, be ever near me ;
When I tremble, weak and faint,
  Stoop from Heaven and hear me.

Growing old ! growing old !
  In Thy tender keeping
Why should I my sojourn pass
  In despondent weeping ?

Growing old, growing old.
  Need not bring me sadness :
Age leads to eternal youth ;
  Death to joy and gladness.

John Walker.

OHN WALKER was born on the 18th November, 1861, at Wythburn, in the Thirlmere valley. He was a scholar at the elementary school in the village, and afterwards at Richardson's School, St. John's-in-the-Vale. He is great grandson of the Matthew Jopson mentioned in William Howitt's "Rural Life in England," who was the friend of Charles Gough (immortalized by Wordsworth and Scott), and of John Dalton the discoverer of the atomic theory. At an early age he began to work for his daily bread, but the laborious and distasteful occupations which he followed at this time unfortunately left him but little leisure for reading or the developement of his education. Beyond evincing a strong love of botany, which led him into long and lonely rambles amongst the hills and vales of Lakeland, we do not learn that in early youth he shewed any marked inclination for poetry. At the age of sixteen, however, he began to write verses of a more or less emotional character: the solitude and impressive silence of the hills doubtless tended to foster the latent germ which existed in his mind, and the effervescent mountain blood inherited from a long line of "statesmen" ancestors asserted itself in song. As we have already intimated, he was at this time labouring under many disadvantages, but, when he had completed his eighteenth year, he was fortunate enough to secure more congenial employment in the busy town of Bury, in Lancashire, where, since then, he has held an appointment in a large woollen-manufacturing firm. This change has been favourable to his undoubted talent for literary work, and for some years past he has been a frequent contributor of poems, sonnets, tales, &c., to various magazines and newspapers.

His longest published poem, "Love Unreturned," appeared in the *Red Dragon of Wales* for March, 1886. It is based upon the legend of King Arthur's rescue by the Queen Morgana, after the battle of Camlan. In this poem the influence of Dante G. Rossetti is very strongly marked, and it has met with favourable notice from several well-known English writers. His "Lyrics of Lakeland,"—being sketches of rustic life written in the local fellside dialect—have met with hearty appreciation at the firesides of the people. One of the longest of these pieces, "Lost i' t' Sna" is said to be a very powerful delineation of the tragic side of the life of the Cumberland "statesman."

Mr. Walker has been favoured in his literary efforts with the counsel and advice of some eminent workers in the world of letters, amongst whom Miss Christina Rossetti has been especially helpful. From the brief specimens of his writings which are here given it will be seen that he holds no mean place in the anthology of North Country Poets. With youth on his side, and an ardent, enthusiastic love of nature and the best models in verse, we may reasonably look for more valuable work from him in the future.

E. E. MINTON.

EVEN TRYST.

A deep grave dug by Time holds all
The happy early years of Love,
When youth first felt the joy thereof,
And life was sweet ;—the cuckoo's call
Reminds me of those early days,
And of the wildering woodland ways.
　　O lilies, budding in the dusk,
　　Dear were those days !

A deep grave dug by Man holds her
Whom I have deemed earth's fairest prize ;
But in the shadow there her eyes
Did surely smile on me ?　(The stir
Of wandering winds amid the blue
Wood-hyacinths adrip with dew.)
　　O bluebells, budding in the dusk,
　　Dear were her eyes !

Sweet Phyllis dead and gone ! Ah me !
Stretch out thy fair right hand :—for Heaven
Is surely round us in the even
When Spring hath wrought her witchery ?
And Heaven being round us, surely thou
Art near thy lover even now ?
　　O hawthorn, budding in the dusk,
　　Dear is this even !

The green boughs touch me, her warm breath
Plays on my forehead, and I see
By that rapt look she wears, that she
From the far Heaven travelleth.
Thy spirit answers to my moan,
My fair, sweet Phyllis, dead and gone.
　　O green boughs, budding in the dusk,
　　Dear was her breath !

To melt earth's sorrows into song,
My soul will struggle through deep grief
Sunwards : therefore, my love, though brief
Our trysting time may be, along
The briar-lined path, when I leave thee,
I shall go chanting joyfully.
   O sweetest mystery of the dusk,
   Dear soul of song !

THE HOUSING OF THE HAY.

ANNIE.

" The gloaming shadows gather,
   The rooks fly swiftly home,
The mountains wear their sunset crowns
   And cattle cease to roam ;
We labour on 'mid laughter,
   Our work akin to play,
For who would not be merry
   At the housing of the hay?

The one whose laugh is loudest
   Is he whose eager eyes
Speak thousands of the sweetest things
   We maidens dearly prize :
His tongue speaks ne'er a love-word,
   And little does he say,
But brown eyes speak to blue eyes
   At the housing of the hay.

My Willie's eyes are bonnie,
   And when he looks at me
I tremble at the gentle glance
   From which I cannot flee :
I see my face reflected
   Whene'er I look his way ;
I know my Willie loves me
   At the housing of the hay.

O have you seen the brown pools
  That lie in Stanley Ghyll,
When the sunlight flits and fleckers
  Through birches on the hill?
If so, you've seen the lovelights
  That never pass away
From those brown eyes of Willie's,
  At the housing of the hay.

No wild bird in the woodlands
  So free from care can be
As my dear, light-hearted Willie
  Who lives at Beckerby;—
The wild birds pipe in springtime,
  He whistles ev'ry day,
And sings and laughs the loudest
  At the housing of the hay.

In haytime or in harvest
  His whistle's sweet and clear,
And his voice is rich and mellow
  Through all the happy year;
He is so strong and supple,
  That love him well I may,—
Who is there like my Willie
  At the housing of the hay?"

WILLIE.

" The sun forsakes the valley
  But lingers on the hills,
Yet he has left a bonnie beam
  Whose light the meadow fills.
My Annie rakes besides me
  And sings a merry lay
That fills my heart with gladness,
  At the housing of the hay.

The oatcroft in late autumn
　　Glows golden with the corn,
But brighter is my sweetheart's hair ;
　　And never queen was born
Whose face was filled with beauty
　　Like that which beams to-day
In my true-hearted Annie's,
　　At the housing of the hay.

The ripe, red rowan berries
　　That cluster on yon tree
Are envious of her laughing lips
　　Whose kiss is ecstacy ;
The thrush's song in springtime,
　　When songbirds charm the May
Is not so sweet as Annie's
　　At the housing of the hay.

O, she is good and gentle,
　　Her love is all for me,
It is pure as mountain-streamlets
　　And as full of melody
No love-word has been spoken
　　But what is there to say
I know my darling loves me,
　　At the housing of the hay !

Those eyes of hers are bright tarns
　　In which the heaven's blue
Has mirrored all its magic glow
　　And tenderness of hue ;
In looking in their fair depths
　　My soul is borne away,
And travels forth with Annie's
　　At the housing of the hay.

My golden-tressèd Annie !
  The great moon signals her
To take the homeward path again
  Through woods of fragrant fir ;—
To-night she'll say she loves me,
  For something will I say
Of Love, when all is silent
  At the housing of the hay."

YOUNG LOVE.

[At Sunset].

From the farthest shores of the farthest sea
  Young Love with his smile has come,—
With a passionate face to thee and me ;
  Then, little one, be not dumb.
Sing out, budding blossom of spring, sing out,
  Sing sweet by the golden shore,
For the shallop of Love may turn about
  And travel to us no more.

Happy Love will stay for an hour at least,
  An hour by the western wave,
Whilst the pale May moon in the purple east
  Looks down at the sun's red grave—
Whilst the tide flows in like a shimmering line
  Of emeralds flecked with fire,
Till it foams and falls in its mirth divine
  At thy feet, my heart's desire.

Happy Love, he has come through all the years,
  Like a tune that lives for aye,
That trembles from lover to loved with tears
  And laughter, then melts away ;

Like a flower that flames and fades and dies,
　But dying for what Death gives,
Young Love will upspring, with hope in his eyes,
　Wherever a maiden lives.

He will rise and bloom, he will blaze and fall
　Like a poppy in the corn,
And, in flashing his flaming face on all,
　Make evening seem the morn ;
Or the pale-faced morn seem rosy eve,
　Or the fleeting hours run slow,
Then the happiest heart will learn to grieve,
　And the palest cheek to glow.

John Thomas Baron.

OHN THOMAS BARON, of Blackburn, owes his excellent reputation chiefly to a series of " Rhymes in Dialect " which he has contributed to the *Blackburn Times* newspaper during the last three years under the *nom de plume,* " Jack o' Ann's." These vernacular verses show the author to be a prolific writer, thoroughly in touch with the joys and sorrows, the humours and eccentricities of the Lancashire factory folk, well acquainted with their pungent, idiomatic expressions, and capable of infusing poetic feeling into the most ordinary passages of everyday life. He was born at Blackburn, on March 1st, 1856, but taken to Blackpool during his infancy, and there educated at the National School. He has since picked up a wide knowledge of men and things by his assiduous attention to the writings of the best authors. At the age of thirteen he returned to Blackburn, and has lived in that town ever since. In his youth he won a few prizes in open competition. His first poem to a newspaper appeared in the *Blackburn Times,* in October, 1876, since which time his muse has been very prolific. In 1879, he won eleven volumes of Tennyson's works at a May-Day Festival in his native town. Among his literary signatures are " Jack o' Ann's," " Nora B." (his surname cleverly reversed), " J.T.B." (his initials), &c. Many of his more serious poems are tinged with a feeling of reverence for the mighty ocean, engendered during his youthful days at the seaside. His reputation is not merely local, for, although a regular contributor to the *Blackburn Times* for a long period, he has written far more verses for papers outside Blackburn, and has always found appreciative readers. We hope to see, ere long, his collected poems published in book form, and there can be little doubt that the appearance of such a book will at once place so versatile and gifted an author in his true position among the Lancashire poets.

J. G. Shaw.

JOHNNY'S CLOGS.

Howd on, theer ! Dunnot use 'em rough,
But put 'em gently deawn :
They're nobbut hawf-worn clogs to yo,
Wi' tops o' musty breawn :
To me, they're sacred links 'at bind
My thowts to one i' th' mowd :
Eawr Johnny wore those clogs afoor
Deeath med him stiff an' cowd.

They're but a pair o' little clogs,
   Wi' irons rusty red,
Yet thowts they wakken i' my heart,
   Ov a life-star 'at's fled !
For th' gloom o' grief seems darker neaw,
   An' life's nowt near as sweet
As when he used to welcome me
   Wi' hooam-smiles every neet.

Tho' th' sod's bin o'er him mony a while,
   To life he's gi'en a grace ;
Oft reawnd my cot aw wond'ring stare—
   There's summat cawt o' place !
Thad lad wur th' best mate 'at aw hed
   I' sunshine or i' storm.
Wur aw a king, my creawn aw'd give,
   To clip th' familiar form.

No other eye could shine like his ;
   His speech, so soft an' mild,
Fell o' my ears, like music-strains,—
   He wur my darling child !
No hand seemed hawf so nice to grip,
   Nor greetin' e'er so kind
As his ; an' neaw aw seem to hear
   His voyce i' every wind.

Last neet, aw see a little star,
   'At fairly pleeased my eye,
Id seemed o ov a flutter theer,
   Heigh up i' th' dusky sky.
An' then a thowt flasht thro' my mind
   'At med my eyeseet dim.
He wur my child ! aw stood on th' earth,
   An' looked tort Heaven, on *him* !

Con he be waiting for me theer,
    Hawf-way fro' th' gowden Throne ?
Wur them his wings 'at fluttered breet
    Heigh i' thoose realms unknown ?
His bonny face seems allus near,
    An' th' love for him shall be
Clasped clooase an' glorious to my heart
    Reight to eternity !

A COMFORTABLE SMOOK.

Awm bothered nooan wi' acres broad,
    Nor burdened mitch wi' wealth ;
For tried friends aw've a ready hand,
    An' for misel—good health !
When work is o'er, at hooam aw sit
    I' th' cosy cheer i' th' nook,
An' reach my pipe deawn to enjoy
    A comfortable smook.

There's doctors, nobs, an' simple fooak,
    Wi' faces long an' pale,
'At's fairly shocked at pun or jooak
    Or gradely merry tale.
They say 'at 'bacco's pisenous,
    An' dolefully they look
On every hearty cock 'at loves
    A comfortable smook.

It's nowt to me, they suit thersels,
    They've narrow hearts an' brains ;
They suit thersels—but nob'ry else,
    An' ged chaffed for their pains.

Mi grondad wur a veteran bowd
  'At fowt wi' th' "Iron Duke."
He oft enjoyd—an' sooa will aw!
  A comfortable smook.

When sorrows linger reawnd my mind,
  An' try to poo me deawn,
Aw' leet my pipe—a puff o' wind,
  An' troubles leave my creawn.
They ged i'th' draft wi't' smook; up th' flue
  They fly, an' quit my nook!
There's nowt 'at kills care sooner than
  A comfortable smook!

It's th' true philosophy o' life
  To tek things as they come;
An' if yo have a gradely wife
  An' childer reet at home,
Yo' needn't cry o'er th' Past, nor try
  To peer i' th' Future's book,
Use th' Present weel, an' calmly tek
  A comfortable smook.

I' winter time, when th' neets are dark,
  An' blustry winds blow cowd,
My pipe, lit wi' contentment's spark,
  Brings hooamly joys untowd.
When summer fleawrs i' th' sunleet gleeam,
  Aw ramble deawn by th' brook,
An' birds sing for me while I hev
  A comfortable smook.

Aw've oft watched th' smook arise an' curl
  I' queer shapes o'er my head,
But queerer thowts hev filled my brain
  Wi' th' fancies 'at they've bred.

Like 'bacco, Life soon burns away,
   Eawr ashes gooa to th' rook;
  So while Life lasts, live reight, an' tek
   A comfortable smook!

THE MOUNTAIN—NIGHTFALL

Yon kingly mountain, like a wearied knight,
   Hath slung the sun, his shield, behind his shoulder,
   And, heedless how the west fires burn and smoulder,
Prepares for silent vigils of the night.

Around him slow he draws his cloudy robe,
   All stern and solemn, tho' star-hosts are gleaming
   Like foemen's spears; of conquest he is dreaming
The while that darkness surges o'er our globe.

So will he dream, till Day—his trusty squire—
   Shall bear his shield on fields of Eastern splendour,
   Then will he greet fair Morn as her defender,
His crest aglow with her triumphal fire!

Bernard Batigan.

 OME pleasing contributions to poetry and prose have appeared in magazines and newspapers from the pen of Mr. Bernard Batigan, of Hull. He has edited several collections of recitals which have been widely circulated and well reviewed by the critical press. It is in Mr. Batigan's works for elocutionists that his best poetry appears. Not a few of his productions, however, have found their way into high-class publications and have been extensively quoted. In a great measure, writing has been Mr. Batigan's pastime, though, had he devoted more attention to it, he might have attained a high place. The work of his life has been that of a teacher of elocution, and in this he has been extremely successful. He is one of the chief popularisers of the art at the present time and by him not fewer than three thousand pupils must have been instructed, of whom many have gained distinction in the pulpit, on the platform, and on the stage. He is the teacher of elocution at the leading institutions and schools in Hull and district.

Mr. Batigan has won distinction as a lecturer on Shakespearian and other topics, and has appeared at many of the more important literary institutions of England and Scotland.

Mr. Batigan takes a great interest in the religious, social, and literary institutions of Hull, having founded several, and lent his assistance to others.

In his youth he came to Hull from Hanley, his native town.

WILLIAM ANDREWS.

RECONCILED.

OR, NOT IN THE PLAY.

You've heard, I dare say, of Ben Rivers, and the scene he enacted
    one night
That was not in the " book " of the author, though the audience
    cheered with delight.
No?   Do you mean it?   Why I thought that his story had
    travelled all round.
Well, just take a chair and I'll tell you—'twill go to your heart,
    I'll be bound.

You remember Bob Bateson, our "heavy?" He lately has
    won a big name
As writer of drawing-room dramas, that bring him both money
    and fame.
His earliest "hit" was at Blankton, a nice little place by the
    sea,
Where I was the managing spirit, so he owed its production to
    me.

Ben Rivers was cast for *The Father*, in the "Father and
    Daughter"—Ben's play—
And we knew he would play it with credit, if naught unforeseen
    blocked the way ;
But he had been ailing much lately, and looked sadly careworn
    and weak,
And several days at rehearsals there wasn't a smile on his
    cheek.

He always was close, and we couldn't discover then what was
    amiss,
Though some of our ladies in whispers referred to a daughter
    of his,
And said it was rumoured among them the girl (who was dear
    to his heart)
Had flown with a handsome young suitor, who'd acted a
    villainous part.

At length it was known that the sorrow of Rivers did really
    arise
From the flight of his beautiful daughter—his darling—the
    light of his eyes !
And broken in health and in spirit, he lay in his lodgings a
    ghost
Of the elegant fellow we knew him a few weeks before, at the
    most.

Now the piece of our talented "heavy" was billed for per-
formance just then,
And it was my benefit night, too, and our principal player was
Ben ;
So we went to his lodgings to see him, and asked him to tell
us out straight,
If he thought he could manage the business—or ruin would
else be our fate.

We almost were shocked by his strange look, as firmly he
answered us then,
" I'll be in *this* 'show' if I live, boys, though I never should
play part again."
He faithfully came as he promised, though he half staggered
into the room,
And, somehow, I felt it was cruel; though what could we do?
It was doom !

The piece was but crude and unpolished in plot, and in dialogue
too,
But *The Father* was cast to perfection ; his acting would carry
it through.
He looked, when he came on, inspired, and physical weakness
was nought
To his passionate, conquering spirit, and Art a true miracle
wrought.

Loud cheers for the play and the players resounded from
boxes and pit,
And Baker, a lessee from London, pronounced it "a glorious
hit."
He offered to buy it for money, that Bateson ne'er dreamed of
before,
And said it would soon be the town's talk, and certainly cause
a *furore*.

But just as we all were rejoicing, came news that forecasted
    but gloom ;
The runaway daughter of Rivers had forced her way straight
    to his room.
We knew very well, if he saw her, the play would be ruined
    outright—
Yes, ruined, when triumph seemed certain, and honour and
    riches in sight.

Then one of those sudden impulses that visit the good and the
    bad,
Came into the brain of Bob Bateson and made him unfeeling
    and mad.
The play was approaching the climax, when the wanderer comes
    to her home,
And flies to the breast of her father, and vows she will never-
    more roam.

The ruse was undoubtedly thoughtless, though Bob at the time
    saw no ill ;
And he instantly said that Ben's daughter should the rest of
    the story fulfil !
Poor Rivers grew grand with excitement, as the touching finale
    drew nigh,
And it now was the " cue " for " The Daughter " to crave his
    forgiveness or die !

He turned to embrace—not the actress—his child ; his own
    child took the part !
And the audience knew not 'twas *real*, as he clasped the frail
    girl to his heart.
But the terrible tone of " My Father," and the agony heard in
    " My Child,"
Raised the house to a tempest of cheering and tears for the
    twain—Reconciled !

'Twas a desperate trick of the author, and a dreadful ordeal for
 Ben,
Which ended all right, as it happened, though death might have
 followed it then.
But Ben had no mind for revenges ; his penitent darling at last
Had come to herself, and, rejoicing, he silently buried the past.

NOT ALL A DREAM.

I had a dream. The breath of beauteous Spring
Had come—had come with happy sunshine gay,
And life ran laughingly through all my blood ;
My heart upsprung like bird upon the wing,
And everything was joyous as the day,
Nor mingled evil with life's gladsome good.

But strangely soon the scene was all transformed,
And Winter's icy arms clasped me like death—
A dreary, dismal death, like frozen wretch
In winter wild on Arctic sea bestormed ;
The dread bleak winds o'erwhelmed my very breath,
And not a limb could my volition stretch.

But just as life was sinking into night,
And every hope evanished from my soul,
I woke to hear the Yule log's cheery roar,
My slippered feet upon the fender bright ;
Adown my spine a chilly blast had stole
And—*Mary Jane had left ajar the door* !

IMMORTALITY.

No surer guide than perfect analogue
Has man discovered yet, who gropes for light :
And by that guiding star the searcher sees
The mystery of Life—Immortal Life—

Lie all unfolded to his raptured soul
In Nature's world, the key to worlds unknown.
The Universal Soul transfuses all!
No unit so, but infinitely parts:
And, like the atoms of the Tangible,
Each part, dividable, completeness owns,
And lives a soul distinct for ever—clothed,
Or unclothed—perceivable to mortal sense,
Or only visible to spirit sight,
As HE may will who is the Affluent
Source of all: sometimes, perchance, as man;
Anon as beast or flower; devoid, or full
Of beauty, like the living soul within.
And when the living from the mortal flits,
It springs again (released) to other sphere,
But changed, may be, for better or for worse—
More beautifully fair, or loveless grown—
(According, as enclothed, it willed to be);
And then rejoins the conscious entities
In God's great commonwealth of Spirit Life!

Benjamin Preston.

ENJAMIN PRESTON was born August 10th, 1819. The great poetical faculty which he possesses seems to have been inherited. His paternal grandfather is said to have had talents for versification of no mean order, and it is to be regretted that his productions have passed into oblivion. An old woman, upwards of eighty years of age, once recited to the subject of this sketch a few lines of a satirical poem, called " The White Abbey War," which she had known in her younger days, and which, according to her statement, had been written by his grandfather on the occasion of some disturbance that had taken place amongst the dwellers in White Abbey. What a pity it is that these lines were not written down and preserved. The father of our poet was, in early life, a hand-loom weaver, and, in many respects, superior to his class. In the life of Dr. Steadman, pastor of the Baptist Church, Bradford, there is some allusion to a Mr. John Preston, a wealthy member of the congregation. To this gentleman the poet's father, who was left an orphan at an early age, was indebted for such schooling as he had, but death prevented the development of the plans for the welfare of his protégé. Brief as was that scholastic career, it begat in him a thirst for general information. From Bradford, the birthplace of the poet, his parents removed to a " Fold," called " Waterside," situated about a mile and a half out of town. When this change of abode took place, the future bard was but a few months old ; to him, therefore, " Waterside " has all the charms of a birth-place. Near as it now is to the great centre of the worsted trade, it was, half a century ago, a picturesque and quiet spot, consisting of the farmstead, with its outbuildings, and three cottages, tenanted, as such places mostly were at that period, by weavers and wool-combers. Some few years after the removal to Waterside, the father left the loom, and entered the warehouse of Richard Fawcett, in whose service he remained seventeen years ; but his advancement necessitated a change of residence—a sore trial to the son, who loved the green pastures better than the pavement. After a few years of town life, and town schooling, the bard was bound apprentice to the father's employers, and served six years to the trade of wool-sorting. It was during his apprenticeship that his rhymes first saw the light of day; the *Bradford Observer* inserting his maiden poem. Soon after attaining manhood, our poet entered the holy state of matrimony. Wool-combing was then on the decline, and as time and changes brought him more and more in contact with the world, he became a witness of the way in which purse-proud tyranny ground down the poor and weak. Scenes of this kind are calculated to awaken the ire of most men, but in the poet, wrath is intensified a hundred fold, and too often becomes undiscriminating. To experiences of this kind we trace that contempt for the "Factory Lord" which peeps out in "Aw nivver can call hur mi wife," which shows itself more plainly in "Uncle Ben," and which culminates in scourging, slashing sarcasm in "T' Short Timer." But twenty years and more of town life began to tell upon the poet's health. The close air of the warehouse, the dusty atmosphere, and the monotonous work, were all against him. At one time of his life, an inflammation of the lungs, at another, an ailment almost as serious, warned him off the ground. At last, after yearning as Abraham Cowley never did, for "a small house and a large garden," both were given to him. When the common lands of Bingley were enclosed, an allotment of two-and-a-half acres was awarded to Alfred Harris, jun.; this the poet bought, erected a house thereon, and to it removed himself and family, in May, 1865. Edward Sugden, in a lecture "On the Poetry of Common Life," after remarking that Benjamin Preston has, not inappropriately, been called "the Burns of Bradford," says that "satire, sentiment, vivid description, are all within the range of his powers; and in each he is equally at home." In several popular poems, expressed in the broadest Bradford dialect, and spelt in a way to reduce to despair any man but an habitual reader of the "Fonetik Nuz," he launches at some prevailing faults of the class to which they are addressed the shafts of his ridicule, feathered for flight with poetry, and pointed with keen wit, but never envenomed by malignity; for he is genial when most severe. He is also a master of the pathetic, and many a manly eye, "albeit, unused to the melting mood," has been surprised into a tear of sympathy with the patient sorrow of his "poor weaver, whom poverty has forbidden to marry." "Nature, and the author of these word pictures," says Edwin Waugh, "have evidently formed a co-partnership; let us hope that many years will elapse before the dissolution comes." However remarkable the dialect poems may be, Mr. Preston's great excellence is to be found in his other works—some of which have been pronounced unsurpassed in the whole range of English literature His "Adelphos," "The Mariners' Church," and lines "On the Death of James Waddington," are, perhaps, his finest compositions.

Mr. Preston sold his property at Gilstead, and now resides in a commodious and retired house near the upper part of Eldwick Glen. Here, at various times, he has written, *inter alia*, many articles on social and other questions, which have chiefly seen the light in *The Yorkshireman*. In 1880 the whole of his poetical works, so far as they could be traced, were gathered together by Mr. T. T. Empsall, and published in the following year by Thos. Brear, of Kirkgate, Bradford.

J. E. PRESTON.

AW NIVIR CAN CALL HUR MY WIFE.

Aw'm a weyver ya knaw, an awf decad,
So aw du all at iver aw can
Ta put away aat o' my heead
The thowts an the aims of a man !

Eight shillin a wick's whot aw arn.
　　When aw've varry gooid wark an full time,
An aw think it a sorry consarn
　　Fur a hearty young chap in his prime !

But ar maister says things is as well
　　As they hae been, ur ivir can be ;
An aw happen sud think soa mysel,
　　If he'd nobud swop places wi me ;
But he's welcome ta all he can get,
　　Aw begrudge him o' noan o' his brass,
An aw'm nowt bud a madlin ta fret,
　　Ur ta dream o' yond bewtiful lass !

Aw nivir can call hur my wife,
　　My love aw sal niver mak knawn,
Yit the sorra that darkens hur life
　　Thraws a shadda across o' my awn ;
An aw'm suar when hur heart is at eeas,
　　Thear is sunshine an singin i' mine,
An misfortunes may come as they pleeas,
　　Bud they nivir can mak ma repine.

That Chartist wur nowt bud a sloap,
　　Aw wur fooild be his speeches an rhymes,
His promises wattered my hoap,
　　An aw leng'd fur his sunshiny times ;
But aw feel 'at my dearist desire
　　Is withrin within ma away,
Like an ivy stem trailin it mire
　　An deein' fur t'want of a stay !

When aw laid i' my bed day an neet,
　　An wur geen up by t'doctur for deead—
God bless hur—shoo'd come wi a leet
　　An a basin o' growil an breead ;

An a once thowt aw'd aht wi' it all,
  Bud sa kindly shoo chattud an smiled,
Aw wur fain tu turn ovvur to t'wall,
  An ta bluther an sob like a child!

An aw said as aw thowt of her een,
  Each breeter fur't tear at wur in't ;
It's a sin to be nivir furgeen
  To yoke hur ta famine an stint !
So aw'l e'en travel forrud thru life,
  Like a man thru a desert unknawn,
Aw mun ne'er hev a hoam an a wife,
  Bud my sorras will all be my awn.

Soa aw' trudge on aloan as aw owt,
  An whativir my troubles may be,
They'll be sweetened, my lass, wi' the thowt
  That aw've nivir browt trouble ta thee ;
Yit a burd hes its young uns ta gard,
  A wild beast, a mate in his den ;
An aw cannot but think that its hard
  Nay, deng it, awm roarin' agen !

T'WEYVVR'S DEEATH.

Aw Mary, me heart's dlad an fain
  Once moar ta see t'shine o the ee ;
I darknass, an wakenass, an pain,
  Awve watched an awve waitad far the .
" Shool suarly be cummin " aw said,
  If it be bud ta bowster me heead,
It wor nobbud for this that aw stayed
  Soa long ameng t'deeing an t'deead.

Awe lenged wol e ardly cud bide
    Ta tell tha what's passin within ;
But nah, when tu't set be me side
    Aw cannot tell hah ta begin ;
Aw mud just as weel tell tha me case,
    Awve a doctor, a nurse, an all that,
Bud—don't let me breathe i' the face—
    All ther skill an ther care is ta lat.

Aw Mary, as dear as me life,
    Awve loved the this mony a year—
If aw ne'er tried ta mak tha me wife,
    Twor becos that aw felt tha sa dear ;
An awve thowt that tha's liked ma as weel,
    An that clasp o' the hand maks it knawn ;
Soa, lat as it is, lass, aw feel
    That it face o' two worlds thart me awn !

Thaw here aw wur nivir nowt worth,
    An's a pauper as hard as awve striven,
Yet suar as awve loved tha on earth,
    Soa suar aw sal love tha in heaven.
Does ta hear that queer saand i' me chest,
    It's a sign at me clock's at a stand,
Let ma leyn ma poar heead on the breast,
    An dunnot leave off o' my hand.

Iee'd a liked tha to sing ma that hymn,
    That sweet hymn tha sang me t'last May,
Bud my seet's getten claady an dim,
    An all things is fading away.
Still, still, aw can see the sweet face,
    As it sinks like a sun aht ot seet,
Bud a glory is filling this place,
    An the shadows grow rosy and breet.

Ta see what aw see tha'd be charmed,
  The fields where in childhood we trod ;
An my sowl feels all leetud an warmed
  Wi' the love an the presence o' God.
All's peaceful an breet as the morn,
    All faces seem fain that awve come ;
An softly an sweetly aboon,
  The angels play " Home, home, sweet home."

Aw dreamt that sore sorras awd knawn,
  That me lot wor to hunger an weep ;
Bud aw see nah, be t'leet o' this dawn,
  That my life wor a dream an a sleep ;
Awm near it, that bewteful land,
  Wear sweeat drops, an tears nivir fall,
Wear brother taks brother by't hand,
  An the Lord, like a sun, shines on all.

THE MARINERS' CHURCH.

Banks of the Mersey ! afar and on high
Masts, like a pine forest, crowding the sky !
Clouds on the waters and clouds on the shore !
This way and that way a rush and a roar,
Steamboat, and omnibus, each with its load.
Churning the billow, and shaking the road !
Crowds, like dead leaves, by the whirlwind uplifted,
Hitherward, thitherward, hurried and drifted ;
Hubbub and tumult for ever and ever,
Dust on the highway, and foam on the river.

Pleasure boats start to the sound of the fife,
Friends of dear friends, take the last look in life,
Labourer's sweat-drop, and Emigrant's tear,
Fall down together and darken the pier.

Harlots in satin, with graces untold,
Offer you friendship, love, all things for gold :
Harlots in tatters, too !—smelling of gin—
Wrecked long ago on the breakers of sin !
Merchant ! whose warehouse is half of a street,
Passing poor Lazarus, crouched at his feet.
Ladies and dandies perfuming the air ;
Troops of rank sweaters all heated and bare :
Numbers unnumber'd, and mixed with the throngs ;
Men of all nations, and kindreds, and tongues !
Spot on the world's deck, where pass in review
Types of the races that make up her crew !
Messmates that still thro' Time's watches employed ;
Man the great Air Ship, that sails thro' the void.

Thro' the dense multitudes,—handsome and brave—
Moved a stout sailor boy, fresh from the wave,
Dealing out freely the jest or the curse ;
Joy in his countenance—gold in his purse—
Riot, wild revel, and brawl in his plans,
Daring the sea's wrath, and laughing at man's !
Onward he goes, till a sound in his ears
Startles his soul, and he bursts into tears ;
Suddenly, softly, steal forth into air,
Words of thanksgiving, repentance, and prayer !
Lo ! near his feet, like a dove on her perch,
Sits on the still wave, the Mariners' Church !
There some poor seamen, each finding a brother ;
Sing of Christ Jesus, the God of his mother,
Sing too, the words, that in life's dawning years,
Lips silent now, sweetly sang in his ears !
Enters the prodigal, leaving without
Laughter and uproar, the curse and the shout !
Enters, and humbled, and melted, and shaken,
Turns to the Father, forgotten, forsaken,

Heeding not, hearing not, what men are saying,
Down on his knees he is weeping and praying;
Weeping and praying, while lovingly o'er him
Hovers an angel, the mother that bore him!
She, whose delight was to shield and caress him,
She, whose last words were a whispered " God bless him."
Home of the homeless one—found without search—
Blessings rain on thee, O Mariners' Church!
Friend of the friendless one, found without search,
Stand thou for ever a Mariners' Church.

The Earl of Carlisle.

T is a curious fact that so few members of our patrician families have distinguished themselves as poets. Our Chaucers and Shakesperes and Miltons, our Drydens and Popes, our Wordsworths and Coleridges and Tennysons, have all sprung from the middle class of society. Lord Byron is the one solitary instance of a peer occupying a front rank in poetry. The Duke of Buckingham, Lord Dorset, Lord Houghton, and a few other noblemen have written poetry of a high class, but compared with the above names, they can only be considered as second or third rate versifiers. To the same category may be assigned the Earl of Carlisle, who, although he has produced some pleasing poems, replete with sweetness of versification, beauty of utterance, amiability of sentiment and tenderness of feeling, he has written nothing that will live to after ages. His family present a remarkable instance of the heredity of literary genius and æsthetic tastes. Charles, the 3rd Earl, the builder of the palatial Castle Howard, was a statesman ; a man of artistic and literary talents, and is mentioned in Walpole's "Royal and Noble Authors" as "a poet of no mean ability." Frederick, the 5th Earl, was the author of several dramas and poems, and displayed a fine artistic discrimination by purchasing from the Palais Royal, during the French Revolution, the famous "Three Maries," of Annibal Caracci, which caused so great a sensation at the Manchester Exhibition, in 1857. The Earl, who is the subject of this sketch, was born in 1802 ; died earl. in 1864, and was buried in the mausoleum at Castle Howard. He was educated at Eton and Oxford. where he took the highest classical honours, and carried off the prizes for both Latin and English verse. He was a nobleman of great reputation as a statesman, an orator, and a man of letters ; he was equally esteemed for his amiability of character and virtue ; beloved by his tenantry, respected by the electors of Yorkshire, and revered by the Irish people. He represented Morpeth and West Yorkshire in Parliament ; was Chief Secretary for Ireland, 1835-41 ; Chief Commissioner for Woods and Forests, 1846-50 ; Chancellor of the Duchy of Lancaster, 1850-52 ; and Lord-Lieutenant of Ireland, 1855-58, and 1859-64. He was also Lord Rector of the University of Aberdeen in 1853, and was a Vice-President of the Bible Society. In Parliament, he introduced and carried no less than thirteen Bills, including the Irish Tithe Bill, Municipal Bill, and Poor-Law Bill. He travelled extensively in America and the East ; published a narrative of his Asiatic wanderings, and lectured at Leeds on his Transatlantic experiences.

On leaving Ireland, in 1841, he was presented with an address of satisfaction on 400 feet of parchment, signed with 257,000 names ; and the same year, when he lost his election for West Yorkshire, he was presented by the

Freeholders with a wine-cooler of bog-oak, mounted in silver, with the arms of the twenty-five polling-places engraven thereon ; and in 1853 was presented with the freedom of Edinburgh.

His statue has been erected in Carlisle and in Dublin ; his bust placed in Morpeth Town Hall ; a Grecian Column erected at a cost of £2061, on Bulmer Hill, near Castle-Howard ; and a monument fixed in Brampton Church, Cumberland, all by public subscription as memorials of the esteem in which he was held. His portrait was frequently painted, and his memoir is given in Lonsdale's "Worthies of Cumberland," 1872.

The following is a list of his Lordship's writings :—"Elensis," Latin Prose Poem, 1821 ; "Prestum," English Prose Poem, 1821 ; "The Last of the Greeks : a Tragedy," 1828 ; "America," Lecture at Leeds, 1850 ; "The Poetry of Pope," Lecture at Leeds, 1852 ; "The Poetry of Grey," Lecture at Sheffield, 1852 ; "A Diary in Turkish and Greek Waters," 1854 ; "The Second Vision of Daniel," in verse ; "Italy," a Poem ; "Poetical and Historical View of the Chief Scenes of Interest in York-shire" ; "Vice-Regal Speeches and Addresses," Posthumous, 1866 ; "Poems," selected by his sisters, Posthumous, 1869.

FREDERICK ROSS, F.R.H.S.

THE ABOLITION OF SLAVERY IN 1834.

Proudly on Cressy's tented wold
  The lion-flag of England flew ;
As proudly gleamed its crimson fold
  O'er the dun heights of Waterloo,
But other lyres shall greet the brave ;
Sing now that we have freed the slave.

The ocean plain where Nelson bled,
  Fair commerce plies with peaceful oar ;
Duteous o'er Britain's clime to shed
  The gathered spoils of every shore :
To-day across the Atlantic Sea,
Shout—shout ye, that the slave is free.

And eloquence in rushing streams
  Has flow'd our halls and courts along,
Or kindled 'mid yet loftier dreams
  The glowing bursts of glorious song.
Let both their noblest burden pour
To tell that slavery is no more.

Bright science through each field of space
　　Has urged her mist-dispelling car,
Coy Nature's hidden reign to trace,
　　To weigh each wind and count each star,
Yet stay, thou proud philosophy,
First stay to bid mankind be free.

And freedom has been long our own,
　　With all her soft and generous train,
To gild the lustre of the throne,
　　And guard the labours of the plain ;
Ye heirs of ancient Runnymede !
Your slaves—Oh ! could it be ! are freed.

'Mid the drear haunts of force and strife,
　　The ministers of peace shall stand,
And pour the welling words of life,
　　Around a parched and thirsty land ;
While spread beneath the tamrind tree,
Rise " happy homes and altars free."

Ye isles, that court the tropic rays,
　　Clustered on ocean's sapphire breast ;
Ye feathery bowers, ye fairy bays,
　　In more than fable now " the blest,"
Waft on each gale your choral strain,
Till every land has rent the chain.

O England, empire's home and head,
　　First in each art of peace and power,
Mighty the billow crest to tread,
　　Mighty to rule the battle hour—
But mightiest to relieve and save,
Rejoice that thou hast freed the slave.

NIAGARA FALLS.

There's nothing great or bright, though glorious Fall
Thou may'st not to the fancy's sense recall,
The thunder-riven cloud, the lightning's leap,
The stirring of the chambers of the deep;
Earth's emerald green, and many-tinted dyes,
The fleecy whiteness of the upper skies;
The tread of armies thickening as they come,
The boom of cannon and the beat of drum;
The brow of beauty and the form of grace,
The passion and the powers of our race;
The song of Homer in its loftiest hour,
The unresisted sweep of Roman power,
Britannia's trident of the azure sea,
America's young shout of liberty!
   O may the wars, that madden in thy deeps,
   There spend their rage, nor climb the encircling steeps;
   And, till the conflict of thy surges cease,
   The nations on thy banks repose in peace.

Anthony Buckle, B.A.

NTHONY BUCKLE was born in 1838, at Barden, in the parish of Hauxwell, where the father of " Sister Dora," the Rev. M. J. Pattison, was rector. He was educated at the Corporation School, Richmond, Yorkshire, and was trained as a schoolmaster at the Training College, York, under the late Rev. Canon Robinson, during 1857 and 1858, where he was appointed one of the assistant masters. In 1863 he was appointed by the Education Department as assistant to the Rev. F. Watkins, H.M. Inspector of Schools ; and took the degree of B.A., at London, in 1865. He was elected superintendent of the Yorkshire School for the Blind, in 1869. In 1883, in order to illustrate the history of the King's Manor, York, he took up, in leisure hours, the art of etching. After the work by the late Mr. Davies had been illustrated, he continued the bewitching art ; and then, Mr. Jackson, of Leeds, brought out a series of " Yorkshire Etchings and Sonnets," by him, some illustrations of which are here given.

R. V. Taylor, B.A.

SISTER DORA.

Heroic soul, with tenderest woman's heart !
　How, nobly listening to the Master's voice
　Thou yieldest all to Him, and didst rejoice
　That 'midst His suffering poor, to thee the part
Was given, by skilful hands to soothe the smart
　And ease the throbbing pangs of pain !　Thy choice,
　How far above the worldling's empty joys !
　In memories dear how deep enshrined thou art !
O happy soul ! thou didst attain the bliss
　Of following Him who walked in Galilee,
　Dark Galilee, all loving, all alone ;
His joys on earth thou surely didst not miss ;
　And when thy work was done, He sent for thee,
　And made thee yet more utterly His own.

KIRKSTALL ABBEY.

Deal gently, Time, with all these reliques grand
  Of ages gone. In their decay, how fair
'Midst nature's loveliest scenes they meekly stand,
  With all their wealth of ornament laid bare ;
And seem from out of windows blank to stare
  In every lovely vale throughout the land !
How many a weary heart found shelter there,
  And pining want and pain, the helping hand !
O heart of man, with frailties manifold !
  Like Time, be no harsh judge of glories gone,
  But ivy-like, with tender pity hide
The human weakness of those times of old,
  And let their beauties for their faults atone,
  And scenes like these in memory ever bide.

O CRUCIFIED !

O Crucified, with arms outstretched so wide !
  Those loving arms, that in their dear embrace
  Would fain enfold us all, we ask Thy grace,
  That we may take our stand Thy cross beside,
While from Thy wounded heart the cleansing tide
  Of precious blood upon our souls may fall,
  To wash from every sin and make us all
  Worthy within those arms for aye to bide ;
That, wearied with the toil and cares of life,
  We there may listen to Thy words of cheer,
  And lean our aching head upon Thy breast,
Awhile forget the vain world's worthless strife,
  Sooth'd by those tones of comfort, sweet and clear
  "Come unto Me, and I will give you rest."

YORK MINSTER.

Majestic pile ! O glorious house Divine !
  Of beauty-loving souls the witness grand,
  That tells of hearts devout and cunning hand,
  Skilful alike to trace those carvings fine,
And rear the stately shaft like graceful pine !
  In love of beauteous art how well they plann'd,
  And wrought, until, as though with magic wand,
  They raised God's house, so fair to shine
In morning's beam, or in the rosy light
  Of eve to stand, a joy for every eye ;
  Or 'neath the moonbeams pale in silent night,
Like fair white heavenly watcher standing by
  To speak to man of boundless hopes, all bright,
  That reach from earth into eternity.

HOME.

Blest word, thou dost recall the dearest place
  Our hearts have ever known or lov'd ; where we
  In childhood's years long past, so glad and free,
  Could always find that smiling, love-lit face
Of mother, in whose sheltering, warm embrace,
  Our childish griefs were hush'd all peacefully
  To rest. In her sweet love we seem'd to see
  That love which time nor death can e'er efface.
O memories dear ! To hearts cast down and tried
  Ye come like gentle breezes from above,
  To cool our aching brow at eventime,
And fill us with a longing deep to hide,
  Within the arms of everlasting love
  The cares and sorrows of our manhood's prime.

George Roberts Hedley.

F all our northern poets George Roberts Hedley is perhaps the nearest akin to that species of versifier which comes under the beautifully associative designation of Bard. He sings upon occasion. He recognises the soul-appeal, the suggestiveness of an occurrence, an aspect, a current sentiment, and straightway pours it forth in a lay that recalls in its spontaneous flow the grandly simple song-flood of Ossian, If it is done with secret labour we are rarely aware of it, and never does his verse impress its mechanism upon us. To *attempt* this style is fatal; it must be accomplished without effort, and in a great measure without consciousness. In this respect we may call Hedley a strong poet. To urge such a Pegasus as he rides would be (to repeat) fatal; to check him would be to mar and dock him to worthlessness. It is this last consideration—the example he furnishes that first thoughts are best—which gives us a true comparison for his poetry. We have spoken of that of Ossian,* but simply as a comparison of the unobstructed flow of the poetic fountain. Where we find the greatest similarity in tendency of thought, construction of language, and above all, in the undeleted record of first impressions, is in Herrick. Hedley is the Herrick of the nineteenth century. He has been compared with Burns—partly on account of his semi-amorous pieces—but lacks a blemish or two to make such a comparison in that connection just; that there are points of likeness, however, must be admitted—not that he's like Burns the less, but Herrick more.

It is a great thing for men as readers and thinkers that the achievements of their forefathers are permanently before them; but for the true poet of our day it is individually more a misfortune. As all things material are governed by relentless laws, scarcely less, does it seem, is the universe of ideas ranged by an orderly circle of rules into, not an exhaustible series, but a series whose ultimate differences are becoming evanescent or unworthy subtleties. Do we want other example than the enormous quantity of verse the world now produces; the tiny brooklets which have been overleaped to reach the fuller streams of Northern Poetry are evidence,

If we find Hedley in his robust course occasionally striking a sounding note upon a string which has been meant to vibrate associatively with the names of Burns, Herrick, or another, we shall also find that it is not more theirs than his, for Nature has given him a gamut in tune with her own. The proof of the melody is in the hearer.

We will not limit Mr. Hedley's merits to his pastorals, though they cannot be unmentioned. It has been said that they have the true byre-

* In questions of critical comparison of this nature, Ossian it should be, and no other name. A student of Macpherson's collections and compositions, if he will not believe that the spirit of those words was ever attuned to Ossian's harp, must fall back upon some Pythagorean theory.

whiff and hay-smell of the country ; a long and enjoyed rural experience
has rendered Nature's breath for him here almost an inspiration.

His songs to female beauty are delicate, though often glowing, pictures
that have no moral flaw. His narrative compositions—narrative rather by
suggestion and implication than by statement—are most touching, and
shew the gift of sympathy which should be in every man, but must be in
every poet.

He is happy in lines where satire reigns, and his pieces of chastise-
ment are marked by great powers of, and the unrestrained use of, invective ;
these character-cameos are valuable studies, and we could wish them more
numerous.

Mr. Hedley's verse includes the use of many archaic words and expressions, which would be a fault were it not that they are so well chosen,
being chiefly such as impart to the verse a dignity born of a chivalrous
origin.

George Roberts Hedley was born at Ovington, on the north bank of the
Tyne, in 1833, a scion of the fighting, farming clan of Hedley, of Reed-
water, and himself a typical Border lord in all but the lawlessness of that
ancient character and the want of refinement that rude times almost
invariably produce. A farmer all his life, he has been such a farmer as
would buy among a choice of fertile land that which was most picturesque ;
and who, in the midst of co-appreciative friends, would salute from his
hall door his glorious view bathed in a golden sunset, with a bumper of
good red wine in true poetic fashion. Such a farm is Thistlebottom that
it is not surprising that it should be so chosen, so drank to, so sung.

Mr. Hedley published his first volume of poems in 1885, and a political satire entitled "Four Years of Misrule," in 1886.

T. TINDALL WILDRIDGE.

THE BALACLAVA CHARGE.

Forth flew the dire command
   For Lucan to advance,
Forth dashed his gallant band,
   Swift as a meteor's glance.

Five hundred to each man,
   In horrent phalanx stood ;
And, from each flank and van,
   Death's bullets drank our blood.

In agony intense
   Whole armies watched the shock,
Till, through their columns dense,
   As lightning cleaves the rock,

Full flashed our gallant band,
Like deities on earth,
And scattered o'er the strand
These vultures of the North.

But quick the conflict thickens,
Outnumbered and enthralled;
Each pulse to madness quickens—
Girt, goaded, not appalled.

Hoarse roar the Russian cannon,
Fierce gleams the British blade,
As rank from rank is riven,
Each foeman prostrate laid.

White foams the jaded steed,
Red reeks the slippery sward,
As back to back they bleed,
Dash forward, smite, and guard.

Hurrah! shouts Cardigan,
As bloodier grows the fight,
Let horde on horde come on,
They may slay, but ne'er affright.

Heaped barriers of their dead
Shall be laid on every yard;
And our best blood stain the glade,
Ere one cry for quarter's heard.

THE SEA IN ITS FURY.

A Fragment Written at Tynemouth in 1879.

The revels of the winds and waves are over,
The shores are strewn with wrecks of dead men's homes;
Sick are the hearts of many a friend and lover
For creatures dear, now lost in watery tombs!

The roaring ocean, like a savage wild beast
  Who's gorged his bowels with prey of every kind,
Now sinks to rest, and with its froth and mild yeast
  Just laps the shore for peacefulness inclined.
The raging tiger of the wild and prairie,
  So smooths his rough face when destruction's done ;
And licks the blood gouts from his cheeks so hairy
  Ere other deeds of terror are begun.
O sea ! beatific in thy glassy mildness,
  Could'st thou but know the depths of suffering caused
By these, the last acts of thy lashing wildness,
  Amidst thy frightful fury thou would'st paused.
The peaceful shores lie strewn with rib and rafter,
  Huge massy plate, long beam, and iron bar,
Twisted and rent, amidst thy savage laughter
  And man's poor prayers, while sea-gods were at war.
Amidst the wreckage, white with spume and splinter,
  There lies thy stalwart son, a sailor bred ;
Headless, blanched, stark naked in mid winter—
  Thy foam his shroud, thy rocks his latest bed.
In yonder cove, upon the red-brown shingle,
  Behold a form look white as mountain snow ;
A woman tender, whose fair hair doth mingle
  With sand and shells, and weeds from ocean's flow.
Without the bar, beneath yon towering castle,
  A Titan form is swept with furious force ;
It grasps an oar, and in its long death wrestle
  Swims like a Viking, or a King of Norse !
Dash'd from wave to wave, through trough and current,
  Wrecked from his ship—that noble being fought
Ten hours 'gainst death, cold, cruel, and abhorrent ;
  Then lifeless sank close to the shore he sought.
Beside, around, on rocks and sandy beaches
  On lonely isle, in haven smooth and calm,
The storm-fiend's work is seen, and grimly teaches
  How all thy smiles, O ocean ! are a sham.

Perhaps far off some group half nude is starving,
  On barren rock where cormorants perch and prey ;
And nought is heard save they and billows carving
  Their grotesque caves where sea brutes swash and slay.
Where many months they've watched with aching eyeballs
  For some poor sail to beckon them in vain ;
And swept the waves each hour to where the sky falls
  To water line, but blankness doth remain.
Nor food, nor fuel, save what seas may yield them,
  In fish and wreckage on this frigid isle ;
Nor house, nor cave, save sodded huts to shield them
  From freezing winds, while suns refuse to smile.

DOWN AMONG THE YELLOW FIELDS.

Down among the yellow fields,
    Where buttercups and daisies grow,
And where the fragrant hawthorn yields
    Its sweetness in long lines of snow,
I met my love a-plucking May,
    Her hand far whiter than its flower :
She trembled as I bade her stay,
    And blushed, a rose in lilied bower.
The mavis sang his love-mate's charms
    From 'midst a copse of golden broom ;
The starling, free from love's alarms,
    Sat in her beech-bole nest of gloom ;
The eager kine, with odorous breath,
    In line lushed o'er the flowering sward ;
And from each sister vale and strath
    All sounds of peace and love were heard.
Nor song of bird nor sight of kine,
    Nor vernal breaths of life so gay,
Can ever half my joys define,
    With Marian sweet a-plucking May.

SONG.

Bard of the West, whose tender chords
   Through Taff and Rhymny echo still ;
Bard of the West, whose magic words .
   Could wake to love and bliss at will ;
Your votive incense still remains,
And breathes in Charlotte's mellowed strains.

Come weave a wreath of flowerets bright
   To bind my lady's raven hair—
Primroses yellow, daisies white,
   Camelias ever rich and rare ;
Still on your steeps the wild flower grows,
And in your valleys blooms the rose.

And pour your pure libations down,
   From towering crag to mead and sedge,
Where sleep the wild geese white and brown,
   Then cleave the ether like a wedge ;
The streams of Wales are nectar sweet
To those whose hearts in Hymen meet.

O, fair and true ! O, fair and true !
   Dear daughter of my native land ;
Sweet branch of Bard I fly to you,
   With Cambrian trophies in my hand ;
Old Cambria's harp must still be strung
While Charlotte lives and Love is young.

William Renton.

ILLIAM RENTON, son of the Rev. Alexander Renton, was born in Hull, February 6th, 1850. He was educated at the Edinburgh Academy, Kornthal, near Stuttgart, and the Edinburgh University. He is Scottish by descent. The family to which he owes his origin is that of the Rentons, of Renton, in Berwickshire; hence the strong current of Scottish sympathies which may be observed in his poems.

Mr. Renton has adopted the profession of letters, and now lives at Randapike, a lovely cottage in a delightful wood near Ambleside, in the Lake District. Prior to his settlement there, he resided for some years in the Highlands of Scotland, and divided his time betwixt the contemplation of Nature in her misty mountain solitudes, and the study of Art in Paris, Rome, and Florence.

His chief works are as follow :—" The Logic of Style," 1871 ; " Oils and Water-Colours," 1876 ; " Jesus," 1879 ; " Bishopspool," 1883 ; " The Analytic Theory of Logic," 1887.

The subjoined poems are extracted from that overflowing storehouse of colour, entitled " Oils and Water-Colours," which no painter should be without, but which is, I understand, unfortunately out of print: it will be found that they are chiefly characterised by vigorous artistic feeling. Mr. Renton is by no means a stranger to the palette, and it is quite clear that he sees Nature invariably with the artist's eye, revelling in colour, quaint conceits, and high individual expression. The originality of his genius is apparent in nearly all his poetical pieces ; his thoughts are not usually "cribbed, cabined, and confined " by the harsh exigencies of metre, but he allows his graceful fancy to run away with the pen into the cloistered, nectared by-ways of the Muses, and sets it spinning exquisite little tendrils of rhyme and haunting suggestions of mystical thought in unmeasured strands of wording ; dipping his brush into the ever-changing mountain glories of colour, to give us subtle sketches of that never-to-be-forgotten Poets' Paradise, Lakeland.

John Walkle.

THE GARDEN OF A DAY.

Our wood has tall and slender lines.
The stream runs steep beneath the pines.
By stump and stone it runs alone,
It will not own a helping hand,
But picks its way on either strand :
   And if a stone say " why,"
     It makes a pout

And gives him the go-by,
Stirring the butterwort about.
This stream, it is our running fence
For our sweet garden-innocence.
　The leaf is sweet
　And gently closes
　About the feet
Of the gold-moth rock-roses—
　That same gentle knight who poses,
　Read the scutcheon on his shield :
　Whiskers, on a golden field !
White-bugle gapes and scents afar
After all honeyed scents that are.
　Stellaria, star-gazing silver star,
Smiles through the chasm of the shrouds,
Coquetting with the silver clouds.
The speedwell true fronts the sky-blue ;
And there are plots and plots and plots—
　We know them as of old,
　　Forget-me-nots,
In lavender and grain of gold :
　The bubble birdsfoot, laid at rest,
　Dilates the saffron of its breast,
　The saffron of its morion-crest.
The spread-wing milkwort, and the cell
　Of the dim bell
That hangs the head and saith, " 'Tis well,"
　Are purple round the still
　Gold of the tormentil,
Three crosslets on a mound—but they
　Are gay as other flowers are gay,
　Where all are quiet round,
　And listen to the running sound,
　　The water's roundelay.
　It is enchanted ground,
　　This garden of a day !

TO THE FADING BEECH.

Fare on, dear Beech ! thy dead leaves tremble down,
   Thy hundred wounds are vivid in the sky ;
   The russet clustering fringes scarce belie
The furrows riven on thy giant crown.
The dead leaves drop : the very sod is brown
   With fallen umbrage shrivelled far and nigh.
   But when thy bravest shall be fain to die,
And thou swart-grey in grey—fret not nor frown ;
Thy fallen rally from the quick of hell ;
   They will be powers ere the year is gone !
Even as we pass, thou kindlest to the spell ;
   Thou wilt be crimson when we look anon.
We pass and know ; we only *say* farewell.
   Vast is thy heritage ! Brave Beech, fare on !

AFTERTHOUGHT.

Even so, dear Beech, we would be wise with thee,
   Who have our dead leaves beaten down by fate,
   Our living blown by many a dead man's gate.
We know the abasement of adversity,
   But not its patience ; in our apathy
Are only not enough dispassionate,
Who languish when we should be bravely great—
   Yet bluster when we should be silent. We
   Are maimed of shadows, wrought upon of straws,
Dealing our smiles by lot, our frowns in zeal
   Of dull mischance. Ah ! might we learn the laws
   Of just forgetfulness, the genial cause
Of timeous hope, we should be free to feel ;
   And live a life transcending woe or weal.

George Hull.

EORGE HULL was born on May 10th, 1863, at Blackburn. He did not "lisp in numbers," nor was he
at all aware that he possessed the gift of song until he
was in his late "teens;" but the perusal of Longfellow's
poems, and the charming prose romance of "Hyperion,"
settled the matter beyond doubt, for he set to work at
once, and poem after poem was despatched to different
magazines, the first of his productions being inserted in
Facts and Fancies some half-dozen years ago. Since then, Mr. Hull has
written for the *Lamp*, a Roman Catholic Magazine, a considerable quantity
of devotional poetry, in which the influence of Adelaide Procter and Longfellow may be clearly traced ; in addition, Mr. Hull contributed a series of
papers entitled, "Cracks bi th' Winter Fire," to *The Lancashire Evening
Post*, and these were followed by a series of sketches in the dialect which
appeared in the *Preston Guardian*. From one of the songs in the "Cracks"
the following verse will best indicate the nature of his dialect work :—

When the leet fades away
    At the closin' o' day,
An' toylin' an' scrapin' are done,
    It's merry an' sweet
    Wi' mi true mates to meet
For an heawr or two's Lancashire fun !

The following are examples of his poetry.

JOS. BARON.

THE WINTER'S COMIN' ON, MI LASS.

The winter's comin' on, mi lass ;
    The north wind's blowin' cowd :
Aw'm sure we've cooarted long enough,
    It's time cawr tale wer towd,
The brids 'at sung i' yonder tree
    Are flown aeross the brine,
An' aw've a cheery hooam for thee,
    Where love's breet sun can shine.

Tha doesn'a want to ged mo lost
   Among the moorland snow ;
Thi laugh belies tha when tha says
   Aw needn'd come at o.
When t' weather's wild, we cornd ged cawt
   A-walkin' hafe an heawr ;
There's awlus summat rough abeawt,
   A snowstorm or a sheawr.

An' when aw come an' stop i' th' heawse,
   Yore lads mek sich a din
That iv aw've bod two words to say
   Aw connod ged un in.
Thi fayther will toke politics,
   An' likes a reawnd wi' me ;
He thinks aw come a-campin' him
   An' nod a-cooartin' thee !

An' when there's nobry else i' th' place,
   Yore Molly ceawrs i' th' nook,
As quate an' wakken as a meawse,
   Wi' th' papper or a book.
Hoo reads a deeal ; an' one would think
   Her common sense would tell
'At cooarters sometimes like an heawr
   To whisper bi' their-sel' !

Thi fayther thinks when fooaks ged wed
   They should hev lots o' brass,
A mon should hev his fortune med
   Afoor he claims his lass.
Ay, well ! aw'm woth a field or two,
   A bonny cot an' o ;
An' when there's steady hands at th' plough
   Sich things are sure to grow.

The sweetest charm o' wedded life
  Is nod i' fortunes grand;
It's nobbut known to th' mon an' wife
  'Ats strivin' hand-in-hand.
The lark 'at builds her own wee nest
  Is merry wi' her mate,
While mony a soul can find no rest
  Inside a palace gate !

An' neau aw've welly done, mi lass,
  Mi stooary's getten towd;
An' winter's comin' on, mi lass,
  The north wind's blowin' cowd,
Come, show thi bonny e'en to me,
  Clasp thi two hands i' mine,
An' say tha'll claim wod waits for thee,
  An' mek yon sweet cot thine !

THE REBOUND.

Against a stately forest tree,
  That long through storms had held its own,
  When but a child, I flung a stone,
Which, bounding backwards, wounded me.

The tree bore not the slightest trace
  Of injury upon its bark;
  Yet I for months retained the mark
Left by that wound upon my face.

Long afterwards, a foolish dream
  Had half destroyed my sense of right;
  And dazzled by its visions bright,
I rowed against Fate's mighty stream !

I had a friend most fond and true,
  Who gently shewed me where I erred ;
  But, all by pride and anger stirred,
At him a word of scorn I threw.

He stood serenely, like the oak,
  Surrounded by the golden light
  Of conscious truth and sterling right,
And braved, unscathed, the maddening stroke !

But I—though years have passed away,
  And Friendship binds our souls again,
  Still feel the self-inflicted pain
Shoot through my weary heart to-day.

And often, when I hear him speak
  Words, noble, manly, sweet, and wise,
  With goodness beaming from his eyes,
There comes a blush upon my cheek :

While Conscience crushes all my frame,
  As when that cruel word of scorn
  Drove through my heart the double thorn
Of keen remorse and lowering shame !

Carey Williams Craven.

AREY WILLIAMS CRAVEN was born at Keighley, April 23rd, 1855, and received his education at the elementary schools of that town. Early in life he commenced contributing poems and descriptive sketches to the local press, and also took a very active interest in political questions, and despite the paucity of his years, soon became known to the public as an original thinker, and of bold and decided opinions on the current topics of the day, and also through the telling manner in which he wrote on matters of local interest. The refinement and tenderness of his poetical conceptions now became noticeable, but, although contributing largely to local journals, it was not until the year 1884 that he published a collection of his poems, under the title of a " Wreath of Flowers," which was the means of introducing him to the notice of many literary characters. In the same year he wrote the historical portion for Craven's Directory of Keighley, Bingley and Skipton, a work entailing a considerable amount of labour, Mr. Craven shewing a keen perception of the public requirements. About this time he became acquainted with H. J. Butterfield, Esq., of Cliffe Castle, who the following year, with characteristic generosity, furnished the means for an extended tour through France, Italy and Switzerland, a description of which was published by Mr. Craven in a work of 70 pp., entitled, " With Mr. Butterfield on the Continent." This pamphlet obtained a good sale and is now out of print. Mr Butterfield has continued to show his appreciation of Mr. Craven's varied talents, by the kindest encouragement and friendship. In 1885 he became the editor of the *Keighley and Airedale Tattler*, a journal which for about two years was exceedingly popular, and enjoyed a large circulation. In 1886 he commenced business on his own account as a printer and stationer, and published the Keighley series of poems, tales and sketches, and other publications. In 1887, the year of Jubilee, he on two occasions had the honour of having his compositions accepted by Her Majesty the Queen. From the press of Mr. E. Craven, Keighley, in 1889, appeared a volume entitled, " Poems," containing 127 pages, and including his best productions. The critical press in many quarters warmly praised the book, and has given Mr. C. W. Craven a more than local reputation. From the same publisher, in 1889, a smaller work was issued under the title of " The Eiffel Tower, and other Poems." He was elected in 1887, after severe contests (his outspokenness having caused him many enemies) as member of the Keighley School Board and Keighley Town Council, in which positions he has shown that although ardently devoted to poetry, he possesses a shrewd intellect, and is as capable to deal with the more arduous duties of a popular representative, in the interests of his townsmen, as he has proved himself to be in literary work, both in prose and poetry. As Mr. Craven possesses that which too many lack, viz., a resolute will, and a devotion and perseverance both in his duties as a public man, and in the lighter and more congenial pleasures of imagery, we may expect, as he has now altogether devoted himself to a public life, having given up business at the end of 1887, that his future career will be a successful continuation of his work to the present date.

THOMAS SPENCER LISTER.

THE BRONTES.

Amongst the hills with heather clad
   These strange and marvellous spirits grew ;
Admiring Nature in its strength,
   With it they formed a compact true.

The fragile forms, as hand in hand
   They lovingly the bleak path trod,
Might scarcely think how great a name
   Would follow from their trust in God.

Discouraged not by Fortune's frown,
   In hope they struggled bravely on,
Nor ceased to labour for their right
   Till Death proclaimed the victory won.

Save one, and he a genius born,
   In wild rebellion sunk to naught ;
O ! what a noble soul was here,
   Had he his sisters' faith but sought.

The good old father, upright, stern,
   In secret of his children proud,
He watched their efforts to be great,
   Yet spoke his praises not aloud.

The fearless Ellis, bending not,
   Whate'er her pathway might beset,
She fought with death up to the last,
   And bravely paid her human debt.

And Acton, gently good to all,
  Shrinking from jarring worldly strife,
She lived resigned, and passed away,
  Peace crowning her unerring life.

A little longer Currer stayed,
  The greatest of the magic three,
But ere she went the world bowed down
  And worshipped her ability.

The Summer's sun may radiant smile,
  Dark Winter's cold wind howl and blast,
But after these have ceased to be,
  The sisters' fame shall ever last.

Enshrined in Memory's dearest nook,
  Their works immortal have a rest;
Humbly I now this tribute pay
  To such as rank among the best.

A FADED ROSE.

Within a little fancy box,
  Safely secured by lock and key,
A sacred treasure I do keep—
  One that is ever dear to me.

It is a faded emblem now,
  Yet always fresh unto my sight,
Touching the chords of memory sweet,
  And o'er my pathway shedding light.

Though but the remnants of a rose,
  That fair, soft hands did once bestow,
How much it of the past reveals,
  None but myself may ever know.

"Take this, and keep it for my sake,"
  In smiles and tears, she softly said ;
How happy was I on that night—
  What dreams of joy around me spread.

But since a journey she has gone,
  To brighter climes and fairer skies ;
She was too frail a flower for here,
  And Heaven soon claimed her as its prize.

When looking on the withered gift,
  I seem to see her form again,
And wonder when we two shall meet :
  Her spirit answers low, "O when?"

WHAT THE LARK SANG.

Lonely, depressed, in body and in mind,
Seeking in vain to leave the past behind,
I sought a quiet, sheltered spot,
Where I might muse upon my troubled lot.

There was no chance to shirk what lay in store,
No going back on deeds which left their sore,
My will could not stamp out existence here,
Nor change the bearings of a sad career.

"Is life worth living?" questioned I at last,
While thinking of the miseries of the past ;
"It is not, if one never made a start—"
Thus came the answer from my bleeding heart.

But pitchforked here, even against one's will,
A coward's heart only would rebel still ;
And not afraid to realise my fate,
I then determined patiently to wait.

Silence now broke, and from the radiant sky
I heard the lark sing in sweet ecstacy,
And as it warbled upwards, loud and long,
Methought I felt the spirit of its song.

" Child of the earth ! O ! why dost thou repine,
When all the beauties of the world are thine ?
When, after earth, there also may be given,
The greater glories of a tranquil heaven.

" Thou canst not go backwards, therefore look on,
And think what the pilgrims of ages have won ;
'Tis better by far to do right than do wrong,
O ! listen to that which is good in my song ! "

I listened, and cheerfully took it as true,
And from that time forward saw all things as new ;
I learned then a lesson shall last me for long,
" 'Tis better by far to do right than do wrong."

Alfred Thomas Story.

TILL in the prime of life, Mr. Alfred T. Story has already a large record of literary labour. He has been a worker in many fields, but such is his versatility that he has gathered golden produce from them all. It is chiefly as a votary of the poetic muse, however, that we must view him. He is a native of North Cave, in the East Riding of Yorkshire, and must therefore be included in a work devoted to the North of England poets ; and as such he deserves to take very high rank amongst them. Possibly his success as a writer of prose exceeds even that which he has achieved as a poet. If he had never written epic, elegy, ballad, or song, his romances of " Only Half a Hero," and " Fifine," his briefer miscellaneous tales, his numerous magazine sketches of men and things, and his philosophic homilies—often cynical, but always on the humanitarian side—would have marked him out as a man of high talent, worthy of a lasting place in the literature of his country.

Before surnames came into use men were often named after their trade or occupation, or because of some personal peculiarity or cast of mind. Had the subject of our sketch lived under such conditions the patronymic he bears would have fitted into them. A teller of tales by nature, he is Alfred Story by name. With all his variety of gifts he has a special aptitude for narrative ; and this is shewn still more in his prose productions than in the poetical effusions that have come under our review.

Young Story received a fairly good education at school before entering into the profession of journalism, which he did at an early age ; and all his life since he has been undergoing a process of self-culture in the academy of experience, the lessons of which were sometimes to him bitter in the mouth, however profitable they might prove to be morally and intellectually. A few years ago, in company with another congenial spirit, he wrote " Wayside Thoughts " under the title of " Low Down "—showing a keen sympathy with the condition of the social waifs of our large cities, many of the character sketches having been drawn from life, and showing some of its shadiest aspects. As Mr. Story's career has had in it both ups and downs, he was all the more competent for the task of producing these ballad annals of the poor. Not that he ever became a Bohemian in the literary sense ; many though the difficulties were which he was fated to encounter, he was enabled to maintain his upward and onward career.

As a poet, Mr. Story is fond of dealing with out-of-the-way subjects. He has produced several sketches in which the grotesque and picturesque in rural life are graphically depicted. One of these has for its hero John Ambler, the village Icarus, who made wings for himself, hoping thereby " to get right up above the earth, and heaven's free breath to draw ; " but after a flight of nine or ten feet, fell in the mire amid the jeers of his matter-of-fact neighbours. Another recounts with grim humour how "Samwell's Mare Maggy" was the pride of her master, though she was never done playing him mischievous pranks, and at length kicked him so savagely that he died in consequence, but retained his love for the creature to the last; and how during Samwell's season of suffering, two of his friends, Abner, the barber, and Nathan, the wheelwright, plagued him with their advice, given in the style of Job's comforters. Now and again Mr. Story falls into a misanthropic mood as he contemplates the sufferings of the masses; and at other times he applies the satiric lash to the shoulders of their oppressors; or, rising into a serener atmosphere, heralds the good time coming with strains of hope and joy. We like him best of all, however, when he communes with Nature at large, or celebrates her floral pets or feathered favourites; making these his own in virtue of his poetic instincts and privileges; or when he meditates on the past as recalled to his fancy by the relics of castles and abbeys old and grey.

A provincial journal had the benefit of his first efforts in the newspaper line, and, these being deemed full of promise, off he hied to the great metropolis to occupy the sub-editorial chair of *Human Nature*, a monthly periodical, to which he contributed his first poetical effusions—one of them on children having had the honour of being extensively quoted by the American press. Subsequently, our adventurous journalist went to Germany, where he resided in the historical city of Frankfort-on-the-Maine. To him the Fatherland was as a new world, and he levied tithe on everything that was within his reach for the purpose of increasing his hoards of knowledge, and of being turned to account by him as a professional author. He saw much that was painful as well as pleasurable during the course of his sojourn abroad, witnessing horrors on horror's head accumulate on the battlefields of the Franco-German war, the pictures of which he reproduced in "Only Half a Hero." Two other years were spent by Mr. Story in the Land of Tell, he acting as a foreign sub-editor of the *Swiss Times*, published in Geneva. But, "England, with all thy faults, I love thee still." So saying or thinking, Mr. Story returned to his native country, joining the staff of the *Northampton Mercury*, to which he remained attached for several years. Whilst residing in the district he wrote "Historical Legends of Northamptonshire," a most readable volume; and taking to his "guid auld harp aince mair," made it ring with the legends of the locality in the style of a minstrel of the olden time.

Entering into connection with another Midland Counties paper, the promise which it held out proved deceptive, and he, being of the stuff that is not easily daunted, returned to the troublesome world of London journalism. There he has contributed, editorially or otherwise, to many newspapers and literary periodicals. A tale of his that attracted much favourable attention was recently published in the *Christian Million*, under the title of "The Lordly Fortune of Hiram Booth."

WILLIAM McDOWALL.

TO AN EARLY DAISY.

Thou constant, red-rimmed daisy,
I feel inclined to praise thee,
   Beyond each other flower;
For thou dost ever cheer me,
When winter cold and dreary,
   O'er all the land doth lour.

Thou, faithful flower and humble,
When coming tempests grumble,
   Dost only close thine eye;
And when they're overpast, thou
Dost raise again thy fair brow
   To th' fretful, wounded sky.

When fields are all forsaken
By bird and flower and brecken,
   And all is lone and wild,—
And man goes forth in sadness,
The only look of gladness
   Comes from thine eye so mild.

We may, perchance, neglect thee,
When o'er the proudly decked lea,
   So many a fair compeer
Is flaunting forth in beauty,
While thou, as is thy duty,
   All lowly dost appear.

But when all these have left us,
And we are quite bereft, us
   Thou cheerest with thy ray,
Like one true friend, when trouble
Hath driven from us the rabble
   That throng'd our prosperous way.

No parasite of fortune
Art thou, to aye importune
  Thy cheer in days of joy,
But e'en dost bless us meekly
When winter glooms so bleakly
  All other bliss destroy.

THE ROBIN'S SONG.

My bird sings not to day—my little bird
  That in these yellow autumn mornings sad
On a bare branch of linden shrill is heard
  Chirping his lay half sorrowful, half glad ;—

I watch in vain for his bright ruby throat,—
  Brighter than all the ruddy leaves that still
Cling to their parent twig or groundward float,
  And sadder feel to hear not his sweet trill.

The rain falls slant, the wind sighs through the trees,
  The star e'en hides him in his sooty home :
No song to-day of robin's shall there ease
  My heartache or bid gentle comfort come :

So I myself must sing to soothe my pain—
  Must sing to raise my spirit 'bove the dull
And chilling weather, 'till it joy again
  In the bright clime where earthly care is null.

RETURN OF SPRING.

When snowdrops white, with drooping head,
  And crocuses of varied hue,
Peep forth from out their wintry bed
  All dripping with the chilly dew ;

When robins hop on naked boughs
  And swell their ruby throats with song ;
When lab'rers trudge behind their ploughs
  And blithely whistle their teams along :
      Then sighs the heart with eased pain,
      Soon gladsome Spring will come again !

When glints of summer sunshine chase
  Dark shadows o'er the distant hills,
And scented tufts of pansies grace
  Moist grots that 'scape rude Borean chills ;
When skylarks fill the azure cope
  With intermittent bursts of praise,
And lambkins on the sheltered slope
  Their tiny, bleating voices raise :
      Then sings the heart in joyous vein,
      Now gladsome Spring doth come again !

When hedgerows burst with pouting buds,
  And weedling flowers the wayside throng ;
When soft winds, fresh from out the woods,
  Wake mem'ries that have slumbered long ;
When Day doth tarry as t'would fain
  Hold commune with his sister Night,
And woo the stars that in her train
  Make all the eastern gateway bright ;
      Then sings the heart the glad refrain,
      Now gladsome Spring is come again !

John Ramsden Tutin.

R. TUTIN was born at Fencote, near Bedale, January 21st, 1855. He resided at Halifax from 1872 to 1880, and in the following year commenced business as a bookseller and publisher in Hull. He is more widely known as a painstaking editor than a writer of poetry, although his verses are numerous and of considerable merit. Mr. Tutin compiled the " Wordsworth Birthday Book," issued by Hamilton, Adams & Co., in 1884; also the "Shelley Birthday Book and Calendar," published by Mr. Fisher Unwin in 1885. Both the works were warmly praised by the critical press. In 1887 he issued for private circulation the " Poems of Richard Crashaw," selected and arranged with notes. The merits of this book was recognised by *The Spectator* and other leading journals. He edited, in 1889, for Routledge's " Pocket Library," " Selections from Keats, " and the " Early Poems of Wordsworth." For John Morley's poetical works of Wordsworth, published by Macmillan and Co., in 1888, Mr. Tutin compiled the bibliography, which extends to sixteen closely-printed pages, and forms such an excellent feature of the book. He was an active member of the Wordsworth Society, and contributed notes to its Transactions. He has written an essay on " Wordsworth in Yorkshire." He cheerfully rendered important help to Professor Knight when he was editing the poetical works of Wordsworth, and his labour of love is gracefully acknowledged. Mr. Tutin has nearly ready an index of persons and places mentioned by Wordsworth. His private library contains nearly the whole of the original and early editions of Wordsworth's works, the chief lives of the poet, etc. His poems and sketches have appeared in several English and American magazines and papers.

WILLIAM ANDREWS.

INVOCATION TO SLEEP.

Come, heavenly Sleep, and steal into my brain ;
    I'm weary with the din and toil of day :
    Mine eyelids droop, and long for thy calm sway.
O come, dear Sleep, with all thy blessèd train—
Forgetfulness, sweet Dreamland, and the twain
    Good sisters, Peace and Balm ; O come and stay
    Until the Bard of dawn with his clear lay
Wakes up each songster to his morning strain.

Thou visit'st not the sick man's dreary bed ;
To childhood thou'rt an ever-ready friend ;
And on tired Labour dost thine influence shed.
Let this day's cares and weariness now end :
Thy soft and downy pinions o'er me spread ;
Thy Lethe let me drink.   O Sleep, descend !

TO A BLIND CHILD.

I saw thee 'mid the noise and stir
    Of street life, in thy mother's arms.
Thy sweet young face, I do aver,
    Was full of childhood's tenderest charms.
At first I knew not thou wert blind,
    Playing as any child might play
    With its small toy or flow'ret gay.
Oh ! never hath there to my mind
    A sadder, sweeter, picture shone,
    Than that of thee, when there, alone
I saw thy pretty childish ways,
And wept to know that all thy days
    Since thy first breath on this bleak scene,
Had been a desolate blank to thee :
    The soft blue sky, the fields in green,
And everything that's fair and free,
Thou never saw'st ; and there may be
For thee in store a darksome life.
Sad thought ! yet, for the coming strife
Of living, may thy mind be strong,
And ne'er despair, though 'mid the throng
    Thou tread'st the dark world all alone.
        Then still hope on
        Thou sightless one.
But once I saw thee.   It may be
That not again thy face I'll see ;
Yet, little one, I'll pray for thee.

LINES.

O little book ! thou hast to me
Brought visions of the fair and free.
In youth I read thy pages bright,
Which shewed to me sweet Nature's light.
In manhood still I own thy power
To gladden many a lonesome hour.
If 'mid the din of towns, I turn
To thee, I in thy pages learn
Of January's frost and snow ;
Of cheerless February's thaw ;
Of wild, cold March, when Winter dies ;
Of April's tear-drops in her skies ;
Of May with all her buds and flowers,
And sweet songs sung in leafy bowers ;
Of June's sunsets, and balmy nights,
In which the quiet soul delights ;
Of hot July, when Sol's bright beams
Gild mountains, plains, and placid streams ;
Of August and her sheaves of corn,
And dewy fields at early morn ;
Of still September, and its clear,
Bright, and harmonious atmosphere ;
Of fickle October's shortening days,
When on the woodland slopes we gaze
On beauty hastening to decay ;
Of dark November's cheerless sway ;
Of Nature's stern and wintry face
When bleak December runs his race.
All these, and more, I see again
As when I roamed through woods, on plain,
By brooklet's side, on mountain height,
And my heart beat with full delight.

And, Howitt ! now the book is mine
   Which once was thine, O Nature's friend !
And in it writ the name that's thine ;
   And with thy hand that name is penned !

Fred Holmes.

RED HOLMES was born at Northallerton, the county town of the North-Riding of Yorkshire, on the 13th February, 1865; was educated at the Grammar School there, under the Rev. W. E. Scott, B.A., where he showed great inclination for learning, gaining a Durham University Certificate during his tuition. He was apprenticed to the printing trade in his native place in the year 1880, where he still remains. His life, so far, has been uneventful, living in the midst of a rural district. Being ever fond of the gentle and graceful language set forth in poetry, he has given much of his spare time to studying it. His first poem, "Christmas Bells," appeared in the year 1884. This was followed in 1886 by a small volume entitled "Two Christmas Eves, and other poems," and is the only collection from his pen which has yet come before the public. These appeared in several local newspapers, and were well received; and, in a review, the *Richmond and Ripon Chronicle* stated of his publication:—"It deserves a word of welcome which we are happy to give. The poems are agreeably varied—not all grave, nor all gay; but alternating from one to the other, with pieces of description or historical reminiscence between."

This poet is a young man of genial character, and of no mean musical ability; and his ever-ready wit and kindly disposition have won for him many friends.

C. PEACOCK.

CHRISTMAS TIME.

The years pass on with changes fraught,
   Rewards bestrewing as they go;
And one is ending which has brought
   To many joy, to others woe;
Yet may all feel the joy to say,
   In blithest morn or darkest night,
"Thrice welcome, gladdest, holiest day!
   Hail, festive time, December's light!"

We keep the feasts of earthly kings,
    Of temporal monarchs (as they are),—
Each loyal breast with rapture rings,
    And praise is sung from near and far.
Much more, then, should we honour One,
    Whose kingdom ne'er shall pass away;
Let honour due to Him be done,
    For Jesus Christ is born to-day.

Old Christmas lends his powerful aid
    The dearest friends to re-unite;
He comes, the miser's store t' invade;
    To make hearts glad, and faces bright.
Gay mistletoe and holly berry
    The cottage and the hall adorn;
Our host invites us to be merry—
    We all rejoice, for Christ is born.

The crackling yule-log blazes higher,
    And steam proclaims the feasting-time;
The carolling waits are drawing nigher—
    The bells ring out a jovial chime.
Though streams outside are cold and still,
    Which in the summer briskly ran,
Yet frost and snow can never chill
    The heart of a true Englishman.

We know each Christmas of our life
    But nearer brings the time to part;
Then may all hatred, greed, and strife,
    Be banished from each evil heart.
" A happy Christmas, bright and fair,
    A season free from want and woes,"
Oh! let this be our heartfelt prayer,
    Our Christmas wish, our Christmas rose.

EVENING.

Sweetly sinks the sun to rest,
O'er the verdant mountain crest,
Gilding beauteously the west.

Winds of night are gently blowing,
Sounds arise of cattle lowing;
Sons of toil are homeward going.

Birds their tiny homes have found;
Tinted flowers have closed around;
Brooks flow on with murmuring sound.

Fragrant scents pervade the air;
Bats now venture from their lair;
Night dews o'er the earth repair.

Curfew's notes have died away;
In God's dwelling, old and grey,
Saints alternate praise and pray.

Some still work, for as I stand,
I see reapers o'er the land,
Stepping, staying not their hand.

Soon the rural sounds shall cease;
Soon the darkness will increase;
Soon will night be rob'd in peace.

When I reach life's solemn night,
Day scenes waning from my sight,
Saviour, be my guiding light.

A FAREWELL.

My soul is sad, for we must part,
　　And with a sigh
I take thy hand, oh! dearest heart,
　　And say " Good-bye."
Full many a long and dreary week
Must pass before I hear thee speak,
Or gently kiss thy dainty cheek,
　　And feel thee nigh.

Full oft my mind doth doubt the love
　　Thou bearest me;
But constant as the stars above,
　　Oh! may'st thou be.
If amity thy heart doth fill
To one who says he loves thee, still
Forget me not, I ever will
　　Remember thee.

In silence I have lov'd thee long,
　　And 'twill not die,
For now 'tis grown than death more strong,
　　So deep! so high!
Then farewell, dearest; think of me;
Where'er thou art in mind I'll be—
I'll long for thee, I'll sigh for thee—
　　" Good night! Good-bye."

John Sewart.

HIS rural and legendary poet, who has been locally called "The Lunesdale Minstrel," was born at the lovely village of Casterton, in Westmoreland, January 24th, 1810. He was the fourth child of John and Phœbe Shaw Sewart, a family that has produced some famous champion wrestlers, in which old English sport our hero also shewed good prowess. He received his early education at the schools founded by the late Rev. Wm. Carus-Wilson, well known as a philanthropist. John's father died when he was six years old, and his mother, who was left with a family of six, was given by the benevolent Carus-Wilsons—who held much land in the district—a cottage to live in, at Whittington, a neighbouring village. John, in his young days became a great reader, and an uncle, who took much interest in the lad, fired his love for the natural beauty and historic lore of his native county, of which he afterwards sung. At the age of eleven John became monitor in the Whittington School, and thus early determined to make teaching his profession. In 1854 he was appointed pupil teacher at St. Ann's National Schools, Aigburth, near Liverpool. While there his mother and also a brother and two sisters died, under circumstances which made a great impression on the lad. On the conclusion of his term as pupil teacher, in order to return to his native county, he applied for and obtained the appointment of time keeper and stone measurer on the Lune Valley (Ingleton and Lowgill) Railway, then being constructed. Thereafter, Sewart, who had a strong desire to visit the historic scenes of his native country which had filled his imagination, seems to have lived a roving sort of life for years. He traversed the island on foot from John O'Groat's house to Land's End, and also visited Ireland. In the course of his nomad life he met with some strange adventures and narrow escapes, being more than once nearly drowned, owing to his proclivity for solitary wandering along unknown paths, over flood and fell, by night as well as day. In a somewhat exhausted state he eventually rambled back to Westmoreland, and for a time settled there. During the period of his wanderings he contributed to the *Lancaster Observer* and other newspapers stirring narratives of his adventures, and legendary ballads respecting spots he had visited.

In 1867 he obtained the mastership of Raseh School, Dent, in his native county, and in January, 1869, married Isabella Mason, daughter of Robert Mason, of Baxengill Farm, Dent, by whom he has had eight children, three of whom are dead. In 1869 he published a volume of "Poems in Westmoreland Dialect," which had a very fair sale. He also published "Legends of Lunesdale," and contributed prose and verse to a number of journals in the North of England. Most of his poems are of a legendary character, couched in nervous but somewhat illiptical English, and they deal largely with the wonderful and supernatural. Of one of these legends, "Lonsdale Bridge," a local critic wrote, "Mr. Sewart had built his name into the stones of the bridge at Kirby-Lonsdale."

Subsequently to 1869 Sewart was for a time one of the masters in Penrith High School. A year or two after the passing of the Education Act, he entered a Welsh College, and obtained the new Government master's certificate, enabling him to take charge of any public elementary school. He continued at the work of organising village schools, and visited several parts of the kingdom for that purpose. In 1882 he had a slight stroke, and has since been in delicate health.

In 1885 he opened a private school at Kendal, but it did not succeed. He next went to Scotland to organise a new Episcopal School in Argyleshire, under the direction of the Lord Bishop of Argyle and the Isles. His work there was finished in 1887, and since then Sewart's health has entirely broken down, his eyesight having failed him, and a weak heart preventing his engaging in any laborious occupation. Save an unsuccessful attempt to carry on a private school at Lower Ince, near Wigan, which had soon to be given up, he has not recently had any regular means of livelihood. He is now living in extreme poverty at Little Harwood, a suburb of Blackburn, where, in addition to the burden of his own ill-health, he has a sickly family dependent upon him. When this notice was written, Sewart was endeavouring to obtain subscribers for a new volume of poems, entitled "Legends of Loyne," with the author's romantic autobiography appended. Though an eccentric versifier, his productions display much originality, true pathos, and dramatic power.

JESSE QUAIL.

A NEW YEAR'S ODE.

1889.

Hark! for the joyous bells
Through Merrie England's dells
    Are happy sounding!
The Old Year's care,
    Careworn,
Fasts in his lair,
    Care shorn;
Hearts feast this blessed morn
    On hope abounding!

Hark! how the greeting thrills
O'er Bonnie Scotland's hills,
    With happy sounding!

The Old Year's grief,
          Grief torn,
Lies on his fief,
          Grief lorn;
Hearts' joy this promise-morn
          In hope abounding!

Hark! now no longer sad,
Green Erin's harp, right glad,
          Is happy sounding!
The Old Year's woe,
          Woe cast,
Buries all show,
          Woe past;
Hearts sing this morn—at last—
          With hope abounding.

Hark! filling Christendom,
The nations pæans come—
          O, happy sounding!
Lo! Old Year's time,
          Time lent,
Circles sublime,
          Time spent;
Earth, like my rhyme, content—
          All hope abounding!

THE PETITION OF THE POOR.
Tempus—A.D., 1878-9.

Our Father which in Heaven art,
     Our load is long a lightening!
Reach low Thine Hand to lift our heart,
     Smile! Set our faces brightening!
Strike pride tyrannic impotent,
     Thy Truth and Justice ratify,
With speed avenge the innocent,
     And trampled patience gratify!

O

We've villas, mansions, castles built,
    Halls, churches, forts and palaces,
To prove that holiness is guilt,
    Nobilities are fallacies ;
Array'd in fur they wade the snow,
    When moonbeams chill are shimmering,
To pry if cotters' fire grates glow ;—
    'Tis bliss if not a glimmering !

War ! is their cry ; our brethren die
    To glut crowned heads' malevolence ;
Wives, children gasp starvation's sigh,—
    Our rulers' kind benevolence ;
O music in their gentle ears,
    That voice of anguish harrowing ;
O joy to note their paupers' biers
    In *weight* and *measure narrowing* !

Our sweat the merchant prince has made
    In deadly mines and factories ;
The glebe has fatten'd to our spade
    Where flaunt the broad phylactaries.
We've cushion'd soft the Upper Ten
    In broughams, in drags, in chariots,
And of a dozen of these men
    Eleven are Iscariots !

Where are the fruits of vale and plain
    So late our vision gladdening ?—
Our wan babes plead in famine pain,—
    O God, their looks are maddening !
We bow before Thee in the dust,
    Submitting to Thy chastening ;
Despair succumbs to steadfast trust,—
    Proclaim Salvation hastening !

We sow hard times with faithful prayer,
 We water with humility,
We leave the harvest to Thy care,
 Undaunted by sterility.
Thou hast not left us quite alone
 And friendless in extremity ;
True hearts yet throb, which like Thine, own
 Sweet Mercy's bless'd supremacy !

Cheer ! Messmates all, who with me sup
 This cup of winter sorrowing ;
Our pangful meeting shall break up,—
 We'll rise upon the morrowing
To quaff the wine of laughing day,
 More sparkling for the lingering,
And hymn our hearts' triumphant lay
 As blithe as morn's glad singer in ! *

* Skylark.

ON HUMAN FREEDOM.

As river rolls from mount to sea
 Eternal and invincible,
So flows the human principle
 From birth hill to eternity ;
The river will have channel free
 He brooks no counter flood, nor rock,—
These aye in vain invite the shock,—
 His ever is the victory.
He grinds the rock, the flood must blend.
 And shall the torrent from I AM
 Halt for your artificial dam ?
No, no, ye fools ! its wrath will rend
 You, with your bank of selfish Might.
 God's order'd race makes good its Right.

INDEX.

	PAGE.
ABDAY, REV. RICHARD	79
Templum Veneris (Claude)	80
The Dying Naturalist	81
Advice	82
ABBOT, RICHARD	66
The Song of Ingleton Bells	66
O, turn aside thy loving eyes	68
Fading Beauty	69
BARKER, JOHN THOMAS	134
Bramla' Band	134
Bubbles	137
The Newspaper	138
BARON, JOHN THOMAS	167
Johnny's Clogs	167
A Comfortable Smook	169
The Mountain—Nightfall	171
BATIGAN, BERNARD	172
Reconciled ; or, Not in the Play	172
Not all a Dream	176
Immortality	176
BILLINGTON, WILLIAM	71
The Singer	72
Fraud : the Evil of the Age	74
Capital and Labour	75
BUCKLE, Anthony	190
Sister Dora	190
Kirkstall Abbey	191
O Crucified !	191
York Minster	192
Home	192
BURNS, THOMAS	83
Come, sing a song to me, my love	83
The Human Mind	85
CARLISLE, THE EARL OF	186
The Abolition of Slavery in 1834	187
Niagara Falls	189

	PAGE
COTTERELL, GEORGE	53
England and Greece	53
In the Twilight	55
A Child's Thought	57
CRAVEN, CAREY WILLIAMS	206
The Brontës	207
A Faded Rose	208
What the Lark Sang	209
DIXON, CANON	47
Ionua (from " Mano ")	48
Humanity	49
The Holy Mother at the Cross	50
EMMET, JOHN	146
Golden Stairs	147
A Litany	149
Love and Beauty	151
After the Rain	152
GADD, REV. JAMES	92
Welcome Rest	94
Recollection	94
Spring Breezes	95
To-morrow	96
Light in Darkness	96
HALL, REV. ARTHUR VINE	42
From " To an Eagle "	43
After the Wreck	44
From " Night "	45
On a Picture	45
Mont Blanc	46
HARBOTTLE, JOHN	33
The Tyne	34
The Coquet	39
The Dawn of Morning	40
The Fisher's Courtship	40
HEDLEY, GEORGE ROBERTS	193
The Balaclava Charge	194
The Sea in its Fury	195
Down among the Yellow Fields	197
Song (" Bard of the West ")	198

	PAGE
HOLLAND, JOHN	6
The Rainbow	7
To a Primrose	9
Native Scenery	11
Summer Evening	12
Solitude	13
The Swallow	13
HOLMES, FRED	219
Christmas Time	219
Evening	221
A Farewell	222
HUGHES, ALLISON	28
Joys of Life	29
The Grandmother	31
Silences	32
HULL, GEORGE	202
The Winter's Comin' on, mi' Lass	202
The Rebound	204
INCHBOLD, JOHN WILLIAM	25
Art	26
Stratford-on-Avon	26
One Dead	27
KAYE, REV. J. W.	119
Live to a Purpose	119
The Blue Forget-me-not	121
Makkin' it up ageean	123
Me dear Owd Woafe an' Me	124
LE GALLIENNE, RICHARD	128
A Bookman's Confessio Amantis	129
Matthew Arnold	129
The Song of the Morning Wind	131
LITTLE, THOMAS W.	114
Bamborough Castle	115
I thought of thee	115
Cousin Lillie	116
As soothing as the Zephyr's Roll	117
A Patterdale Leaf	118

	PAGE
LISHMAN, ALFRED	59
Glencoe	60
Ye Labourers of England	63
Integrity	64
LONGSTAFF, WILLIAM	87
The Wild Helm Wind	88
When the Swallows come again	90
MC. GOVERN, REV. JOHN BERNARD (J.B.S.)	101
Keats (1796-1820)	102
The Tomb of Scott	102
Our Wedding Day	103
Ierne	103
NICHOL, H. ERNEST	125
The Artist of the Sunset	125
A Rondel ("Let us go home")	126
Mendelssohn's "Gondola Song"	126
The Snowflake	127
PRATT, FRED	109
The Broken Column	110
The Little Folk	111
The Avalanche	112
PRESTON, BENJAMIN	178
Aw nivir can call her my wife	179
T'Weyvver's Deeath	181
The Mariners' Church	183
READMAN, JOSEPH	76
Sharow Bells	76
Awakened Memories	77
RENTON, WILLIAM	199
The Garden of a Day	199
To the Fading Beech	201
To the Fading Beech— After-thought	201
ROBINSON, JOHN RYLEY	14
Kirkstall Abbey	15
Gordale	18
Flamborough Lighthouse	20

	PAGE
ROBSON, JOSEPH PHILIP	141
The Auld Wife's Plaint	143
The Wail o' the Fallen	144
The Tyne Exile's Return	145
SEWART, JOHN	223
A New Year's Ode, 1889	224
The Petition of the Poor	225
On Human Freedom	227
STANSFIELD, ABRAHAM	104
'Ere March arrive	105
Amor Redivivus	105
On a Book-worm (F.S.)	106
The Shepherd	107
Journey by Night	108
STORY, ALFRED THOMAS	211
To an Early Daisy	213
The Robin's Song	214
Return of Spring	214
TONKIN, MRS.	153
Wimberry Ripe	154
Cornwall	156
Only Two Little Shoes	157
Growing Old	158

	PAGE
TUTIN, JOHN RAMSDEN	216
Invocation to Sleep	216
To a Blind Child	217
Lines (written in Howitt's "Book of the Seasons")	218
WALKER, JOHN	160
Even Tryst	161
The Housing of the Hay	162
Young Love	165
WATSON, ROBERT SPENCE	21
Pygmalion and Galatea	21
Love only lives	23
Spring	23
WHITWORTH, MRS. LAURA A.	1
The Deserted Mansion	2
A Little Grave	3
A Sunny Picture	3
St. Botolph's Bells (Boston)	4
By the Ocean	4
Cradle Song	5
WIGHT, GEORGE OSWALD	98
Blindness coming on in youth	98
The Sea	100

INDEX OF POEMS.

PAGE

A Bookman's Confessio Aman-
tis 129
A Child's Thought 57
A Comfortable Smook............ 169
Advice 82
A Faded Rose........ 208
A Farewell 222
After the Rain 152
After the Wreck..... 44
Afterthought (To the Fading
Beech) 201
A Litany............ 149
A Little Grave 3
Amor Redivivus 105
A New Year's Ode (1889) 224
A Patterdale Leaf................. 118
A Rondel (" Let us go Home ") 126
Art 26
As Soothing as the Zephyr's
Roll 117
A Sunny Picture 3
Awakened Memories... 77
Aw nivir can call her my Wife 179
Bamborough Castle 115
Blindness Coming on in Youth 98
Bramla' Band 134
Bubbles 137
By the Ocean...................... 4
Capital and Labour 75
Christmas Time 219
Come, sing a Song to me, my
Love 83
Cornwall 156
Cousin Lillie 116
Cradle Song 5
Down among the Yellow Fields 197
England and Greece... 53
'Ere March arrive...... 105
Evening 221

PAGE

Even Tryst........................... 161
Fading Beauty 69
Flamborough Lighthouse 20
Fraud : the Evil of the Age ... 74
From " Night " 45
From " To an Eagle " 43
Glencoe 60
Golden Stairs...................... 147
Gordale 18
Growing Old 158
Home 192
Humanity 49
Ierne... 103
Immortality 176
Integrity 64
In the Twilight......... 55
Invocation to Sleep 216
Ionna 48
I Thought of Thee 115
Johnny's Clogs 167
Journey by Night................. 108
Joys of Life 29
Keats 102
Kirkstall Abbey............. 15
Kirkstall Abbey......... 191
Light in Darkness................. 96
Lines (written in Howitt's
" Book of the Seasons ") ... 218
Live to a Purpose 119
Love and Beauty 151
Love only Lives............ 23
Makkin' it up ageean 123
Matthew Arnold 129
Me dear owd Woafe an' me...... 124
Mendelssohn's "Gondola Song" 126
Mont Blanc......... 46
Native Scenery 11
Niagara Falls 189
Not all a Dream.................... 176

	PAGE		PAGE
O Crucified!	191	The Holy Mother at the Cross	50
On a Book-worm	106	The Housing of the Hay	162
On a Picture	45	The Human Mind	85
One Dead	27	The Little Folk	111
On Human Freedom	227	The Mariners' Church	183
Only two little Shoes	157	The Mountain—Nightfall	171
O, turn aside thy loving eyes	68	The Newspaper Boy	138
Our Wedding Day	103	The Petition of the Poor	225
Pygmalion and Galatea	21	The Rainbow	7
Recollection	94	The Rebound	204
Reconciled; or, Not in the Play	172	The Robin's Song	214
Return of Spring	214	The Sea	100
Sharow Bells	76	The Sea in its Fury	195
Silences	32	The Shepherd	107
Sister Dora	190	The Singer	72
Solitude	13	The Snowflake	127
Song ("Bard of the West")	193	The Song of Ingleton Bells	66
Spring	23	The Song of the Morning Wind	130
Spring Breezes	95	The Swallow	13
Stratford-on-Avon	26	The Tomb of Scott	102
St. Botolph's Bells (Boston)	4	The Tyne	34
Summer Evening	12	The Tyne Exile's Return	145
Templum Veneris	80	The Wail o' the Fallen	144
The Abolition of Slavery in 1834	187	The Wild Helm Wind	88
		The Winter's comin' on, mi lass	202
The Artist of the Sunset	125	To a Blind Child	217
The Auld Wife's Plaint	143	To an Early Daisy	213
The Avalanche	112	To a Primrose	9
The Balaclava Charge	194	To-morrow	96
The Blue Forget-me-not	121	To the Fading Beech	201
The Broken Column	110	T'Weyvvr's Deeath	181
The Brontës	207	Welcome Rest	94
The Coquet	39	What the Lark Sang	209
The Dawn of Morning	40	When the Swallows come again	90
The Deserted Mansion	2	Wimberry Ripe	154
The Dying Naturalist	81	Ye Labourers of England	63
The Fisher's Courtship	40	York Minster	192
The Garden of a Day	199	Young Love	165
The Grandmother	31		

INDEX OF FIRST LINES.

	PAGE
A boat is sleeping underneath the moon	126
Across the sea, across the sea	116
A deep grave dug by Time holds all	161
After the rain and the swirl	152
Against a stately forest tree	204
Ah love, if love had willed that I should ne'er	23
Ah! Sally lass, it's trew enough	124
Air made sweeter by her breath	105
A lovely boy of child-like grace	137
A man of middle size, and middle age	106
Amongst the hills with heather clad	207
And I am growing slowly blind, and feel	98
As on yon bank I calmly lay	115
As river rolls from mount to sea	227
A singer there dwelt in a city of yore	72
As soothing as the zephyr's roll	117
Aw Mary, me heart's dlad an fain	181
Aw'm a weyver ya knaw, an awf deead	179
Aw'm bothered nooan wi' acres broad	169
Banks of the Mersey! afar and on high	183
Bard of the West, whose tender chords	198
"Behold," said Fancy, pointing to the sun	125
Behold these hallowed walls; these ruined towers	15
Beyond the hill I watched the bright-haired sun	94
Bird of strange instinct and untiring wing	13
Blest word, thou dost recall the dearest place	192
Blow, winds, blow	95
Born where the Sheaf and Don unite their streams	11
Brightly from the beacon streaming	20
By the window there they stand	111
Circled the sea-mews o'er the fishers' haven	110
Come, heavenly sleep, and steal into my brain	216
Come listen, ye people, the song from the steeple	66
Come, sing a song to me, my love	83
Cornwall, my country! the home of my childhood	156
Deal gently, Time, with all these reliques grand	191
Dirty and ragged, with matted hair	138
Down among the yellow fields	197

PAGE

Dread monarch! mountain king! well may we gaze 46
Drear is the heart, no pleasant past recalls........................ 35
'Ere March arrive, must roll another moon—... 105
Even so, dear Beech, we would be wise with thee 201
Fading beauty, bending o'er thee 69
Fair was Ionna ever, I avise 48
Fare on, dear Beech! thy dead leaves tremble down 201
Far off? Not far away 55
Forth flew the dire command........... 194
From the farthest shores of the farthest sea 165
From wandering in a distant land, an exile had return'd 145
Gan yam, gan yam, ma bonnie lass 82
Growing old! growing old 158
Hail! lordly castle on this rocky steep 115
Hark! for the joyous bells 224
Hast thou against grim poverty........ 64
He loved her as they love who early throw 45
Heroic soul, with tenderest woman's heart! 190
Howd on, theer! Dunnot use 'em rough........................ 167
How facile and free is the mind... 85
I canno' come to thee, mither........... 144
I care not for splendours that man can achieve......... 81
I cull'd this leaf by the silver lake 118
I had a dream. The breath of beauteous Spring 176
I hae naebody now; for my bairns are a' gane 143
I heard the voices of children......... 4
I lie awake in my bed 57
I saw thee 'mid the noise and stir 217
I sing of a charm which to music is wedded 77
Is it deep sleep, or is it rather death? 27
I sometimes sing a weak and broken song 94
Into the gloomy land I ride 108
Its chambers are deserted now 2
Just as of old sweet Avon winds its way...... 26
Just to lie at early morning 29
Let us go home, my love, the sun is low 126
Lonely, depressed, in body and in mind 209
Lord, leave us not to wander lonely 149
Love makes love where'er it be 151
Majestic pile! O glorious house Divine! 192
Meek little flower, retired and shy...... 9
'Mid scenes like this how sinks the human mind 18

PAGE

'Mid Nature's beauties and fane's decay 102
My bird sings not to-day—my little bird 214
My own, my bonnie native hills... 88
My soul is sad, for we must part 222
Mysterious force, as beautiful as strange... 26
'Neath chancel arch we stood ; without, a sea 103
No surer guide than perfect analogue 176
Not Britain, but the land the Tiber laves 102
O Crucified, with arms outstretched so wide ! 191
Of Mary's pains may now learn whose will 50
Oh changeful mirror of the skies, how dull thy look ! 100
Oh, for the touch of that deft hand which drew... 80
Oh ! sweet St. Botolph's bells 4
Oh ! rouse you from slumber 119
Oh, what a glorious harvest-field of thought 12
O little book ! thou hast to me 218
O loveliness sublime ! 45
On bright to-morrow much we love to dwell 96
Once Capital and Labour pulled... 75
Only a little grassy mound, no headstone marks the spot 8
Only two little shoes 157
O Snowflake, whirling and dancing 127
O, turn aside thy loving eyes 68
Our Father which in Heaven art 225
Our wood has tall and slender lines 199
Proudly on Cressy's tented wold 187
Queen, O Queen of the Sea ! 53
Sae blithe owre the hills when the spring breezes blaw 40
She was not woman ! No—too doubting wife 21
Sleep, baby, sleep 5
Sweetest time of all the year 23
Sweetly sinks the sun to rest... 221
The day's turmoil is ended 76
The evening was glorious, and light, through the trees 7
"The gloaming shadows gather 162
The man who, when with toil or care distraught 13
The morning wind came whispering by 130
There is a cottage by the stream 147
There is a soul above the soul of each 49
There's nothing great or bright, though glorious Fall 189
The revels of the winds and waves are over 195
The silences that float 32

PAGE

The Sun forsakes the valley 163
The Sun had set, and dark'ning shadows crept 112
The wind blaws saftly frae the west, the dew hings on the lea... .. 39
The winter's comin' on, mi lass 202
The years pass on with changes fraught 219
The youthful shepherd, tall and fair... 107
Thou constant, red-rimmed daisy 213
Thou, Niobe of Nations, sad Ierne.. 103
Through the wide open window the westering sun 31
Time flies, and from his waving wing 96
'Tis said that once upon a time 121
Upon a couch of dreams the morning lay 40
We stood amidst the golden corn 3
We took her away 41
When do I love you most, sweet books of mine? 129
When snowdrops white, with drooping head 214
When the swallows come again 90
Who hesn't heerd o't' Bramla' Band 134
What though thou seem'st but a speck in the blue 43
Whoay, Sally lass, what's happen'd thee? 123
" Wimb'ry ripe ! Wimb'ry ripe ! " " Well done, old man !......... 154
With eye undimmed and stalwart form 60
Within a little fancy box... 208
Within that wood where thine own scholar strays 129
With what unutterable shame and scorn.................................... 74
Ye labourers of England !... 63
Yon kingly mountain, like a wearied knight 171
You've heard, I dare say, of Ben Rivers, and the scene he enacted
    one night 172

www.ingramcontent.com/pod-product-compliance
Lightning Source LLC
Chambersburg PA
CBHW020105030726
47498CB00006B/1960